THE ANGEL OF AN ASTRONOMER

LINDA RAE SANDE

Twisted Teacup
PUBLISHING

AN EPIPHANY IN THE PARK

Hyde Park, early October, 1838

On such a brisk and bleak day as this, George Grandby, Viscount Hexham, might have forgone the afternoon ride in the park. The one that usually took place every spring day at five o'clock in the afternoon and featured a parade of aristocrats either riding on the backs of their favorite mounts, riding in their showiest of equipage, or simply walking.

In the autumn months, far fewer participated, and on days such as this, he was sure the park would be abandoned.

But his twin sister, Angelica, insisted they go. "This will be one of the last opportunities to see everyone before they leave town," she argued.

Tempted to tell her that "everyone" would rather be at home close to a fireplace or in their clubs, George instead held his tongue for a moment. Sometimes it was easier to simply let his twin sister have her way.

Usually, in fact.

Parliament was due to end its sessions within a week, and then all the aristocrats who had country estates or mansions in other parts of England would depart the capital, including the two of them and their parents, the Earl and Countess of Torrington.

They wouldn't return to London until the spring, so perhaps it would be a last chance to at least see those who dared to brave the weather in favor of a ride in the park.

"I am quite sure it's going to rain," George said as he inhaled, sure he smelled it in the air around them.

Angelica, about to allow a Worthington House groom to assist her onto her horse, glanced up to find blue skies above. However, a bank of ugly gray clouds to the west threatened to overtake the blue. "Then we shan't ride long," she reasoned, stepping onto the mounting block next to her bay stallion, Hermes. She placed a foot into the side saddle's stirrup and was soon seated, the hem of her hunter green riding habit artfully displayed in an arc along the side of the horse. Her dark green kid gloves weren't especially warm, but she could always tuck her fingers beneath the hem of her velvet jacket should they get cold.

Her brother had already directed his black Irish walker toward Stanhope Gate, and Angelica and her mount were soon abreast of him. "Race you to Rotten Row," she challenged, and then before he could respond, she had Hermes galloping to the gate.

"Angel!" he scolded. But his walker, Ares, was anxious to rejoin his stable mate, so George allowed him the rein. They passed dozens of bare elms and maples, the trees having shed their leaves the week before, when the chill autumn evenings had grown colder than usual.

By the time they were on the crushed granite path that led past the east bank of the Serpentine, George had caught up to Angelica.

"What's your hurry?" he asked, his voice raised so he could be heard over the sound of the horses' hooves.

"I hope to see Lady Anne," Angelica replied as she gently slowed her mount.

George followed suit. "Who?"

Angelica laughed. "Lord Trenton's daughter, of course. She is leaving for Staffordshire in the morning, and I won't see her again until the spring."

Allowing a sound of disappointment at learning why they were heading to Rotten Row, George gave a shake of his head. "What is she? Twelve years old?" he asked. "How is it you even know her?"

Angelica regarded her brother with a look of surprise. "Lady Anne is nearly eighteen years old and will finally be making her come-out in the spring," she explained. "And I know her because she was friends with one of my classmates at Warwick's," she added. "I think we got on so well because our fathers are both earls, and because we both have brothers intent on making our lives miserable."

Warwick's referred to Warwick's Grammar and

Finishing School in Glasshouse Street. Although it was popular with daughters of bankers and rich tradesmen, a few daughters of aristocrats attended as well. Their burly footmen would stand outside the classrooms, guarding the entrances and riding with them in the carriages that took them to and from the venerable school.

Those who attended Warwick's agreed it was far more enjoyable than the schooling they received from no-nonsense nuns at seminaries. Angelica had managed only one year at a seminary and then begged her father to allow her to attend Warwick's.

He, of course, allowed her whatever she wanted.

To a point.

She had learned long ago just how far she could get with her requests. *I can spoil you rotten until you have everything you want, and then you'll run out of things to want and have to be satisfied with what you have*, he had said when she was but ten years of age.

She hadn't understood his comment then, but over time, she slowly came to realize he spoke the truth.

There was no use *wanting* something only to discover the *having* wasn't nearly as satisfying.

These days, she only asked for what she *really* wanted. He obliged her, but she knew it was only because he could afford to do so. Had he become impoverished as so many lower aristocrats had with this past year's devastating crop failures, he would have denied her.

Ignoring the comment about making her life miserable, George said, "I cannot believe Lady Anne is nearly eighteen."

Her brother's comment brought Angelica out of her reverie. "And I cannot believe Gabe the Younger has not introduced you to her," she countered, referring to Anne's oldest brother.

"As a matter of fact, he did, but it was... years ago. Probably when she was twelve," he murmured. His recollection of the girl included his surprise at how tall she was and the fact that she looked rather angelic— curly blonde hair surrounding a porcelain complexion highlighted by bright blue eyes and bow lips.

The twins had made it to the edge of Rotten Row, and Angelica allowed a sigh of disappointment. Apparently the impending rain and chill in the air had most of the *ton* ensconced in their homes, for only a dozen or so carriages lumbered along in a haphazard line. "Well, just a quick ride then," she said as they slowed their mounts to a walk.

Waving or speaking briefly to those who passed going the other direction, the twins quickly made it to the end of the line of carriages and horses. Turning their mounts to complete the circuit, George surveyed the equipage that had been behind them.

His gaze fell on the nearest curricle, and his heart seemed to stop.

The air around him crackled.

The hair on his head felt as if it wished to stand on end, as did the hairs on his forearms.

Time slowed to a stop.

He held his breath.

The most beautiful girl he had ever seen was staring at him, an expression of delight displayed beneath her dainty blue hat and halo of blonde curls.

Angelica had already directed her horse to walk alongside the young lady's curricle, and she was speaking to her as if they were long-lost friends.

George struggled to take a breath.

"Hexham," his sister called out, in a voice suggesting she was scolding him. She waited for him to join her before continuing. "May I have the pleasure of introducing you to Lady Anne?" She turned her attention back to the curricle and the two who occupied it. "Lady Anne, this is my brother, George Grandby, Viscount Hexham," she said as she held out a gloved hand in his direction.

George didn't even notice that one of his acquaintances, Gabe Wellingham, oldest son of the Earl of Trenton, was driving the curricle. "It's very g...good to meet you, my lady," he managed to get out, wondering why it was he stuttered.

"And you as well," Anne replied with a nod. "As I recall, we were introduced many years ago. May I call you Hexham?"

George stared at her, the sound of her voice positively angelic. The voice had sounded through lips the color of summer berries. Her cheeks nearly matched, their blush heightened by the chill in the air.

But it was her eyes that had him mesmerized. They

were blue. The shade of blue found in cornflowers. "Of course, my lady," he replied, about to add that she could call him anything she wanted to.

He would come running.

Kneel before her.

Do her bidding.

He could only imagine what his reward might be.

Perhaps she would allow him to kiss her. The thought of capturing the berry-colored lips with his own had him imagining far more he could do with the comely blonde. Especially after he removed all the clothes from her body and from his.

George suddenly wanted nothing more than to spend the rest of his days in a bed with Anne Wellingham. Spend them pleasuring her in every conceivable manner, making love to her morning and night. Coaxing her to come at the very moment his body could hold back no more and he allowed his own release.

As if his thoughts had been overheard and deemed inappropriate by Zeus, a bolt of lightning lit the darkening sky. The scent of ozone filled George's nostrils. Thunder rolled above him.

And then the ugly gray clouds, pregnant with rain, gave birth.

"Hexham! I'll see you at White's!" Gabe called out as he slapped the ribbons over the backs of the matched grays that pulled his curricle. The equipage jerked into motion and sped off.

Despite the downpour that had water streaming from the brim of his top hat, George managed to keep his eyes locked onto Lady Anne's until she was well past him.

Reluctantly, he turned his attention onto his sister, who regarded him with a smirk that suggested she had enjoyed his moment of fascination with the gorgeous Lady Anne.

"*That* was the Lady Anne you were speaking of earlier?" he asked, ignoring the rain that poured down around them.

"Indeed," Angelica replied, her gaze taking in the quick exits of the other riders and vehicles that raced to the main gate. "We should be going," she added, when George still didn't make a move.

His horse took matters into its own hooves, and began a quick trot back the way they had come.

Angelica allowed her stallion to follow, and then urged it to move faster.

There would no doubt be mud splattered along her habit's hem and on her back, but she knew she would be drenched to the skin if she didn't get to cover soon.

Meanwhile, George seemed lost in thought as she passed him at a gallop.

She didn't look back as Hermes flew over the crushed granite and out to Park Lane through Stanhope Gate. A few minutes later, and she was allowing the groom to help her down from her mount.

A quick glance in the direction of the park had her

shaking her head, drops of cold water dribbling down her cheeks and neck.

George hadn't picked up the pace one bit, his horse merely trotting along.

Fool, she thought. And then she allowed a brilliant smile.

A fool in love.

CHAPTER 1
A FATHER PLOTS

*M*id-November, 1838, Torrington Park near Hexham

"There you are," Adele, Countess of Torrington, remarked once she'd found her husband in his study. She leaned against the door jamb, her arms crossed beneath her generous bosom. "I thought you might want a spot of tea. Or some coffee."

Milton looked up from his desk and gave her a grin. "I haven't exactly been hiding, my love," he replied. He held a quill in one hand and was regarding a note he'd just written. "Just finishing up a letter."

"Correspondence about the earldom?" she guessed, an eyebrow arching up with her query. At eight-and-fifty, her blonde hair was streaked with gray, but her elegant features remained youthful.

"About the Wadsworth earldom, actually," he replied. Nearing seven-and-sixty, Milton Grandby, Earl of Torrington, was still handsome despite the white hair that had replaced his dark waves just the year before. A pair of wire-rimmed spectacles were perched on the end of his nose.

Adele angled her head to one side. "Anything amiss?"

He took a deep breath. "At the moment, yes. Four daughters, all about to have their come-outs in the next few years," he replied with a smirk. "I am happy we had just the one."

"Oh, poor Sylvia," Adele replied with a shake of her head, referring to the countess and the mother of the four girls he mentioned. She knew the countess preferred living at the Wadsworth estate in Suffolk, so the family was rarely in London.

"You mean, poor Wadsworth," her husband countered. "Entire wardrobes *and* dowries for *four* daughters? His earldom is barely solvent as it is." He didn't add that there wasn't yet a single son to inherit the earldom, which meant it would probably go to Wadsworth's younger brother.

"Oh, dear. What will he do?" Adele knew what Wadsworth's father had done, and she surely didn't want Sylvia to have to endure what the Dowager Countess of Wadsworth—the current Viscountess Lancaster—had to suffer when she had been married to the late earl.

Tempted to tell her the plan, Milton instead inhaled slowly. "I think Wadsworth and I have worked out a solution that will benefit us both," he said, as he signed his name to the letter. "In the meantime, I'm thinking I'd like you all to myself for Christmas this year."

Adele's eyes widened. She was used to hearing similar comments from her horny husband when they were home at Worthington House in Mayfair, but never this time of the year. Not when they were at Torrington Park in Northumberland. Not when there was a foot of snow and the possibility of family sleigh rides to Hexham every day. Not when Christmas was still over a month away. They'd only just made the trip from London five weeks ago. "But, what do you intend to do with our children?"

"Our twenty-one-year-old twins can go back to London. 'Bout time we kicked them out of the nest, don't you think?"

Blinking, Adele looked as if she was about to faint. "Milton!"

"George needs to meet with the solicitor and prepare for Parliament in March. Angel needs to learn how to run a household," he said as he stood up to join her. He wrapped his arms around her shoulders and pulled her into a hug. "They can live at the house in Mayfair," he said just before he nibbled on her ear and then sprinkled kisses along her jawline. "And we may or may not join them in the spring."

His lips covered hers, and he thrilled when she moaned and one of her hands moved to his head, her fingers spearing his silken hair. Meanwhile, his hands had moved down to cup the globes of her bottom, pulling her firmly against the front of his tightening breeches.

When he finally ended the kiss and straightened, he

added, "George can act as chaperone for Angel. What say you?"

Her eyes darting to one side, Adele blinked a couple of times. "Who are George and Angel?" she whispered, although a grin teased the edge of her lips.

Milton shut the door to the study and kissed her again, rather glad there was a comfortable sofa only a few feet away.

It was another hour before they rang for tea.

CHAPTER 2

TWINS ON A TRAIN

Late November, 1838, somewhere in Yorkshire

The gentle sway and measured clacks she felt beneath her half-booted feet would usually send Lady Angelica into a state of blissful sleep. Only the occasional sound of a steam whistle or the abrupt stop of the train car might jolt her from her nap.

On the latter occasions, she could count on her twin brother, George, to catch her should she be dislodged from the leather-covered seat and sent pitching forward.

She rather doubted he could be counted on for such a chivalrous act on this day, though. From the time they had boarded the train in Northumberland, George's attention had been directed out the window to his right. Seated across from him, Angelica sensed he wished to say something of importance but couldn't seem to muster the courage.

Or perhaps just the words.

"You have kept me on pins and needles for at least an hour—"

"We only left the station a few minutes ago," George interrupted, a clear indication he wasn't wool-gathering as he was staring out the window. "Besides, I thought you would be asleep by now."

"I'm not yet bored," she replied. "Are you nervous?"

George furrowed a brow. "About what?"

Angelica gave him a quelling glance. "Parliament, of course." She knew part of the reason they were making their way back to London was so that he could accept a writ of acceleration and take a seat in the House of Lords in the spring. When their father, Milton Grandby, Earl of Torrington, announced that at the age of six-and-sixty he no longer needed to attend sessions of Parliament, George hinted it was because the Whigs had won the general election the year before.

My work is done, Angelica could imagine Father saying.

Angelica had resisted the urge to remind the earl he was really seven-and-sixty. She was his favorite daughter —his only daughter, really—and she wanted to remain in his good graces.

"I am not nervous," George stated. "But I wish to be prepared. Besides, I have to meet with the solicitor and..." He sighed, "See to another matter."

The mention of the solicitor had Angelica's thoughts going to their fortunes.

Her fortune, for she had recently reached the age her father had deemed appropriate for her to claim her inheritance. She hadn't yet done so, mostly because she hadn't yet decided what she wanted to do with it.

Her mother, Adele Slater Worthington Torrington, had a fortune because of her first husband's involvement with the early steamships.

Her father's fortune was because the earldom always did well financially, but also because Milton's cousin, Gregory, was a master at making money. The man seemed to know exactly which ventures to invest his funds in, or he helped create what he knew should exist.

In fact, part of the money that had been used to build the very train and tracks on which they now traveled had been from Gregory's investment. There were other new railways that also benefitted, including the Great Western Railway, the Newcastle and Carlisle Railway, and the London and Birmingham Railway, which had all opened earlier that year.

Claiming his children would share equally in his good fortune meant Gregory's estate would be split eleven ways, but even so, every one of Angelica's ten first cousins, once removed, and their mother, Christiana, would one day be rich.

Angelica would be rich, too, but mostly because she and her twin brother were the only children of Milton and Adele.

Although the bulk of the Torrington family fortune would end up with George, Angelica didn't begrudge him his right. He was the one who was going to have to take over the Torrington earldom, after all. See to the business of running it—he already was, to some extent

—and acting for all intents and purposes as if he were already the earl and not just an honorary viscount.

Since the current Countess of Torrington had no intention of leaving her husband to go back to London for the Season—despite being married for two-and-twenty years, her parents were still hopelessly and embarrassingly in love with one another—Angelica had agreed she would take on the duties of hostess for her brother while they were in the capital.

Given the Season wasn't going to start for several months, she was stunned when George announced just two nights ago and during the dessert course that she and he were leaving the Torrington ancestral home near Hexham to spend a few months in the capital before the rest of the aristocracy descended on London.

"But... why?" she had asked, incredulous. They had spent every Christmas Day at Torrington Park for their entire lives.

"I will explain it all on the way," George replied, uncharacteristically silent for the rest of the meal. Then he and their father had disappeared into the billiard room to enjoy their port and a game or two before bed.

"What is this about?" she had asked her mother.

Adele had replied with a slight shrug. "A surprise of sorts. I wasn't let in on it, though, but your father has obviously been scheming with your brother."

"And you let them?" She remembered her alarm at hearing her brother and father had planned something together—the two weren't particularly close.

Dimpling, her mother had leaned forward and said, "Any time those two are together is a good thing."

Which was true. Angelica had always been her father's favorite, because he had wanted a daughter before an heir. Having twins meant he got what he wanted and what he needed all at once.

Afraid her husband would ignore George, Adele had seen to providing extra attention to her only son. She often wondered if Milton didn't know how to behave with a son because his own father hadn't spent much time with him before he died. Milton had inherited the Torrington earldom when he was but sixteen years old.

Then Adele had leaned over and added, "Especially since they're working on a *surprise*."

Angelica had relaxed at hearing those words, if only because her father's surprises were always the best.

*A*ngelica had been patient. She hadn't asked but that one question of her brother since his announcement. But now that nearly every gown, slipper and frippery she owned was packed into trunks and they were on the train to London, she wanted answers.

"What's this early trip to London all about?"

CHAPTER 3

A HOMECOMING OVER TEA

*M*eanwhile, in Mayfair

Sarah Wellingham, Countess of Trenton, stared out the front window of the richly-appointed Trenton House in Curzon Street and sighed. Just outside, two footmen were seeing to unloading several trunks from a traveling coach, and behind her, a maid had just set down a tea tray.

Her daughter, Anne, would see to pouring, eager to practice the steps so that she would be ready to host callers when she had a household of her own.

The moment Anne's older brother, Gabe, entered the front parlor, Sarah turned and her gloomy disposition dissipated. She allowed a brilliant smile. "I am *so* happy to see you," she said as Gabe quickly approached and kissed her on the cheek. She in turn pulled him close and hugged him hard.

Taken aback by her greeting, Gabe's blue eyes darted to one side. "You as well, Mother," he replied as he pulled away. "It's only been… a few *weeks* since I last saw you," he added.

Although she never looked as if she aged, he noted a few gray strands in the honey blonde hair that was rolled into an elegant bun atop her head. A gold filigree bracelet dotted with sapphires encircled the wrist at the base of her right hand. His father had given it to her as a means to remind her she was a countess when they wed, and now it was worn from years of wear.

"I did not expect to miss you as much as I did," she replied, another sigh escaping as she studied her oldest son.

At three-and-twenty, Gabe had matured into a younger version of his father, complete with the blond curls and blue eyes that had Sarah remembering when the young man had been conceived.

She had almost felt ashamed of herself that evening, but the sovereigns she had accepted from the new Earl of Trenton for a tumble and a few minutes of conversation were much needed at the time.

She often wondered what life would have been like if Gabriel Wellingham had not returned to The Spread Eagle Inn to seek her help in his pursuit of a wife. What life would have been like if he hadn't discovered he had fathered a bastard son during their first encounter.

She would no doubt still be managing the coaching inn, much as she had continued to oversee its operation well after she agreed to wed the earl.

Helping Gabriel Wellingham run the Trenton earldom proved much the same as running a business, which she continued to do between the births of two more babies.

Legitimate children.

Gabe's younger brother, William, was away at university and would one day inherit the earldom. His sister would finally be making her come-out during the upcoming Season.

Anne was already scheduled to be presented before Queen Victoria, the reason the family had returned to London earlier than they would have otherwise. A court gown had to be created by a modiste, and reports from other mothers of young ladies had Sarah realizing the project might take more than a month to accomplish.

If only the gown could be worn to a ball or two after the court presentation! Unfortunately, the queen required a court gown that would have been suitable to wear to a ball in the century prior, which meant the gown they would be ordering later that week would be worn once and then packed away in a trunk and stored in the attic.

Perhaps it might make an appearance as a costume during a house party or a masquerade ball.

Such a waste!

"If you remember, I was not pleased about leaving you behind when we left for Trenton Manor," Sarah said as she stepped back and regarded Gabe. "You hadn't been home from university for very long when we returned to Wolverhampton."

Gabe had finished his Ancient Greek studies at Cambridge and then, because he refused to live a life of leisure, he had accepted a position at the British Museum as an archivist, cataloguing artifacts that were shipped from the Continent on a daily basis. As a result, he was only in residence at Trenton House for breakfasts and dinners and to sleep.

"I would have been home sooner today, but a *kyathos* arrived from Vulci today. Part of the same purchase that brought us an exquisite black-figured hydria last week. I had to unpack and catalogue it, which I was honored to do, of course," he explained. "I am the first to see it before it goes on display."

Sarah noted the excitement in his eyes as he talked about his work, happy he had found a calling suitable for a man in his situation. "Remind me again what a kyathos is?"

Gabe dipped his head and then formed his hands into a bowl shape. "A red-figured pottery."

"Oh," Sarah acknowledged with a nod. "Did you get enough to eat?" she asked, continuing her perusal of her oldest son.

He stifled the urge to laugh. "Yes, Mother. In fact, I think the cook continued to make meals as if you were all still here," he complained as he patted his mid-section. Despite his words, he still displayed the physique of an active young man. "I have been forced to ride in the park at least once a day, and I've taken up fencing at Angelo's Academy in St. James Street," he added with a grin.

The family had been in town for the Little Season,

and all but Gabe had returned to Wolverhampton when sessions of Parliament ended in early November.

Intending to stay in Trenton Manor near Bilston until Parliament resumed in the spring, Sarah's husband, Gabriel, surprised them all when he announced he wished to spend Christmas in London. "We may as well, given Anne's appointment with the queen. William can join us when his term is finished," he had said when they were discussing where to celebrate Christmas.

"Besides, this may be our last opportunity to spend the holiday together."

When Sarah questioned his comment, he reminded her that one or more of their children might be married before the following Christmas.

"London is not as quiet as one would expect in the winter," Gabe said as he led Sarah to her usual seat—a floral upholstered chair facing the brick fireplace. He waited for her to be seated before he took a chair across from his sister.

"There are entertainments?" Anne asked as she handed a cup of tea to her mother.

Gabe nodded. "The theatre, of course. The old Royal Sussex is now The Marleybone, and the Haymarket Theatre Royal is now featuring comedies exclusively."

Anne handed Gabe a cup of tea. "Where might one find marriage-minded men during the winter months?" she asked, her manner serious despite the glint in her eye.

Blinking, Gabe let out a guffaw, nearly spilling his tea. "Is there such a thing as a marriage-minded man?"

"Gabe!" Sarah scolded, although she might have at one time given the same response. She couldn't help but grin.

At that moment, Gabriel Wellingham, Earl of Trenton, strode into the parlor and then halted next to the chair in which Sarah was seated. "Rotten Row in the afternoons if it's not too chilly. Shopping in Jermyn Street, a soirée or two," he stated, in answer to his daughter's query. "The National Gallery in Trafalgar Square is open now, and Almack's will open again in late January," he added, before he bent and kissed Sarah on the cheek. "Excuse my tardiness," he whispered.

Sarah couldn't help the frisson that darted through her when his lips touched her ear. "You can make it up to me later," she replied, a dimple appearing in one cheek.

"Oh, I intend to," he countered with a grin. In a louder voice, he said, "I have managed to read all my correspondence, but only found invitations for two winter balls and a *musicale*. I expect we'll receive more once word makes its way down Park Lane that we have returned to London."

Despite his seven-and-forty years, Trenton's once cherubic face still appeared youthful, and his blond curls barely showed a hint of gray. Although he had napped in the traveling coach most of the morning with Sarah's head tucked into the small of his shoulder as his cheek rested atop her blonde coiffure, the overcast skies had him feeling more tired than usual.

"Would you like tea, Father?"

Trenton took the chair opposite of Sarah and said, "I would, indeed. And that Dutch biscuit, too." He glanced at the three who sat around the low table, well aware they were as affected by the gray skies as he was. "As for marriage-minded men, we might discover one or two in the park. I know we're all weary from travel, but when we are finished here, would you agree to a ride?"

"Won't it be dark soon?" Anne asked as she held out a cup for him, dimpling when she realized he had over-heard her query.

Trenton dared a glance out the front window and then to the mantle clock. "Well, not for a couple of hours. Perhaps just a quick tour down Park Lane and back? Maybe stop up the street and pay a call at Lily's house?" he suggested. "Let her know we're back in town?"

His illegitimate sister, Lily, was married to William Overby, a broker from Wellingham Imports. They lived in a townhouse not far from Trenton House with their five children.

"Oh, yes. I'd love to see my newest nephew," Anne said with some excitement. "And a drive down Park Lane would be invigorating if we rode in the barouche."

Trenton allowed a grin, remembering how both of Lily's daughters looked as if they could be Anne's younger twins. Despite William Overby's darker hair, all of the couple's children were blonde and blue-eyed like their mother.

"Gabe tells me there's been more work done at Bradford Hall," Anne said, her comment directed to her father.

"There's definitely a tall structure there," Gabe offered, "As if there's been a turret added onto the house. But since I don't pass by there on my way to the museum, it's been some time since I last saw it. Not sure if it was finished at the time, nor do I know if anyone has moved into the house."

"You three should go," Sarah said as she helped herself to a lemon biscuit. "I still have to read my correspondence," she added, not wanting to admit she was avoiding the cold. Despite having worn boots in the traveling coach, her feet still felt chilled.

"It would be good to see who might be in residence," Anne agreed. "For paying calls."

"And to discover if there are any marriage-minded men living there," Gabe teased.

"That, too," Anne replied, not the least bit embarrassed by her brother's comment.

This would be her first Season, but she was determined it would be her last.

CHAPTER 4

A PLAN IS REVEALED

*M*eanwhile, back on the train

George angled his head to one side and inhaled slowly. "This will be your last Season. You've already reached your majority," he stated, his gaze going from the window to Angelica.

The comment was made in a manner suggesting he didn't agree with his father on the matter of her majority. He thought she should be five-and-twenty while their father had insisted she could lay claim to her fortune when she was but one-and-twenty. Although she could do so—she and George had just had their twenty-first birthdays in September—Angelica had decided to wait until the end of this next Season.

Angelica arched a brow, not liking how his statement made it sound—as if there wouldn't be any more Seasons after this one. "And?" she prompted.

"You haven't a single marriage prospect."

Her mouth dropping open in a most unladylike

manner, Angelica was about to wallop him with her reticule. Given everything she had stuffed into it that morning, she was quite sure she could knock him out cold with a single, well-placed swing. "What of it?" she hissed. Her eyes widened when she considered what her father's surprise might be.

A husband.

She blinked and struggled to breathe. "Oh, don't you dare," she whispered hoarsely. "I cannot believe you would do this," she added as a gloved hand went to her chest, as if she might need to hold herself up.

She couldn't believe her father would do this. She couldn't believe George would be a party to an arranged marriage!

George furrowed his brows together. "Angel," he scolded. "Whatever has you looking as if you're about to faint? And don't you dare—"

"I will faint if that's what it takes to abuse you of the idea of—"

"Angel!" he repeated as he leaned forward. If she fainted, she would require a vinaigrette, and he was quite sure she didn't have one in her overstuffed reticule. There wouldn't have been room for it.

He knew her lady's maid was in the next compartment, sitting across from his valet.

Or perhaps sitting *on* his valet.

The two had married the week before and were still enjoying the bloom of early matrimonial bliss.

Mary Banks was the first-born daughter of his mother's lady's maid, Alice, and their father's valet,

Alonyius Banks. Mary had met John Fitzhugh, the born-and-London bred son of one of his uncle's servants, when the family had gathered at Slater House for a huge dinner. That was the night before the Torringtons departed for Northumberland and Torrington Park.

George was sure he felt sparks in the air that night. A sort of electric *thrum* that had several family members ceasing their conversations to watch in wonder as two people who were destined to be together regarded one another for the very first time.

The women gathered in the Great Hall of Slater House in Mayfair immediately knew something momentous was happening. The men were a bit obtuse, if only because several were anxious to make their way to the study to begin an afternoon of imbibing Uncle Donald's scotch.

Not particularly interested in drinking scotch so early in the day, George had hung back and watched the proceedings in a state of curiosity. The memory of the *thrum* that had permeated the air had stuck with George ever since.

He *wanted* that same sort of reaction to occur when he spotted his intended for the very first time. He wanted to *desire* his future wife.

He wanted the sparks. The air charged as if a thunderstorm was about to loose its power. A sort of assurance that the woman who caused such a stir in the air might do the same for him for the rest of his life.

Perhaps it had, he thought as he remembered a day in the park the month prior.

The memory had him considering that his sister might want the same. To desire the man she would eventually marry.

Would she desire the man Father had in mind for her?

There was only one way to find out, but since she hadn't yet met the man—and neither had he—George was trying to decide how he might arrange an introduction when it became apparent he was about to be walloped by his twin sister's reticule.

And he knew he would suffer a terrible blow should her aim be spot-on. The damn thing may as well have been a hammer, given how much was stuffed into it and its weight.

Having taken a direct hit from Angelica's reticule in the past—she could only take so much teasing before she took action—George managed to duck at exactly the right moment.

Angelica's reticule sailed within inches of his perfectly coifed Brutus-styled hair and hit the wall of the compartment with a resounding *thunk.*

"Father only wishes you to *meet* the man," George said quickly. "There is absolutely no requirement in place that you accept a..." George ducked as the reticule once again passed within inches of him, this time about to break a nose of which he was rather proud. No bump and no hook meant he might actually remain handsome until he reached his forties. "... A proposal," he finished at the same moment Angelica let out a growl of frustration.

"Some duke's whelp, I suppose?" she ground out.

George blinked, shocked at how ornery his sister could sound when given the chance. She would never behave like this in public.

He hoped.

"No," he replied with a shake of his head. His brows furrowed when he considered the young man's lineage. "Although he might be distantly related to one."

He caught the reticule in both hands before it impacted his cheek. Had it hit him, he was sure he would have a shiner. George considered how long he might have had to wait for the bruise to abate before he could make an appearance at White's. It was that or take up bare-knuckle fighting at Jackson's Boxing Saloon. Then he would have a good excuse for sporting a black eye.

"Really, Angel. There are times I think our father should have named you 'Kate'," he murmured under his breath, thinking she was acting like the Bard's perfect shrew.

Then he saw how tears streamed down her cheeks.

"Angel," he whispered in alarm, setting aside the reticule so he could move to her side of the compartment and gather her into his arms. "You're taking this far too seriously," he murmured once Angelica had her cheek resting in the small of his shoulder. "Father merely wanted you to consider this knight—"

"A knight?" Angelica repeated as she lifted her head from his shoulder.

"I know. It was a surprise to me as well, but... Father wants you to be *happy*. He doesn't care if you marry beneath your station if it means you end up with a man worthy of you."

Angelica wiped the tears from one cheek with a gloved hand and sniffled. "Do you know this knight?"

George's eyes darted toward the window. "I know *of* him. I haven't yet met him."

Angelica blinked, sensing evasion in his answer. "How much do you know?"

Her brother shrugged one shoulder. "The earldom has properties in Suffolk. A well-respected family. Excellent lineage."

Frowning, Angelica straightened. "You make him sound like a contender for the Derby," she murmured.

"I believe his brother has one of those, too," George replied. "He had a nag last year that won a couple of the races."

Angelica punched him in the arm, which had George letting out an 'ouch' before he slid sideways on the leather squabs.

"Where is this meeting to take place?" Angelica asked as she straightened and dabbed her hanky beneath her eyes.

Deciding he was safe from her reticule—it was still on the seat opposite—George straightened in the squabs and said, "I was thinking of hosting a dinner party at Worthington House. Invite a few of my fellow lords and him so that we can ruminate on the upcoming session."

Angelica furrowed a brow. "With their wives in attendance, surely."

George held his breath a moment. "Well, we could," he hedged, "except that none of my... well, that is to say, I am not acquainted well enough with those who are old enough to have taken a wife to invite them," he stammered. "And besides, all the married aristocrats are spending the holiday at their estates in the country."

Blinking, Angelica dared a glance out the window and decided the sudden dreariness beyond the glass matched her mood just then. It had been snowing when they left Hexham. "Not a single wife? No other person of my sex will be there?" she queried in disbelief.

Goodness. Was this to be her lot in London? Hosting entertainments at her childhood home that would only be attended by men?

On the one hand, she would be the talk of the town! Other hostesses would either display their jealousy with whispered murmurs in Mayfair parlors or beg to know her secret. Having only one brother who wasn't yet married was the trick, of course.

At that thought, Angelica reconsidered the situation. Would it really be so bad to be the only woman at the table? Why, if one of the gentlemen grew bored with talk of politics, surely he would turn his attention on her and ask her opinion of something.

What did she think of the London and Greenwich

Railway, for example? She made a mental note to ask George to take her on it one day.

Or what was her opinion of the recent marriage act that established civil marriage? She wasn't sure what she thought of a wedding taking place anywhere but in a church, but the thought of marrying in a folly had a slight grin appearing at the edge of her lips.

Wouldn't a wedding within the columns of a folly surrounded by pink and white rhododendrons be ever so beautiful? The air sweet with the scent of their blooms and birdsong providing the music?

Angelica gave a shake of her head.

Father would insist she marry in St. George's, she was sure. Which meant she could end up marrying at any time of the year.

Christmas, she thought with a sigh. With snow falling, and the scents of fresh-cut evergreens and a yule log burning in the large fireplace. Her bouquet of flowers could include holly and their bright red berries.

Cold winter nights wouldn't seem so cold if she was nestled in the arms of an attentive husband.

That's the way her parents slept.

She knew this only because she had sneaked into her father's bedchamber several times as a child during thunderstorms and discovered them together. Given the lack of space on the bed, she had simply curled up into a chair and then woke up when her father was carrying her back to the nursery in the morning.

The memory from her youth had her giving a start.

She loved being carried like that, the familiar scent

of her father's cologne surrounding her as she buried her head in the warmth of his robe.

Whomever she married probably wouldn't carry her like that. Well, perhaps he would carry her over the threshold when they entered his home for the first time after the wedding.

A finger snapped in front of her and she gave a start. "What is it?"

George rolled his eyes. "I said you should invite some of *your* friends," he said, obviously perturbed she hadn't been paying attention. "Cousin Emily is still in Chiswick. The Norwick twins should still be in town. Even out the numbers. It's what Mother would do."

"I suppose," she murmured.

"We make it clear that this is just an evening to share a meal and mayhap to play cards. Maybe have some music? I'm quite sure the new butler has seen to keeping the piano-forté tuned."

Winslow, the former under-butler, had replaced Bernard earlier that year, and although he was thorough in his duties, Winslow was freer in sharing the gossip he learned from the other servants.

The thought of a dining room full of young, unmarried aristocrats had Angelica wondering where all the chaperones would be expected to sit. Worthington House's dining room could easily accommodate four-and-twenty guests, but would the maids be expected to sit in chairs lined up against the long wall? "How many gentlemen are you considering?" she asked.

"Six. Eight at the most," George replied. He was

about to name them off when he noticed how Angelica was staring at him. "What is it?"

"Is that all?" she asked. "You had me thinking the dining room would be *full*," she accused. "Eight gentlemen is reasonable, although I rather doubt I can find eight friends still in London this time of the year. Most have gone home for Christmastide and won't be back in town until the Season starts."

"Well, we don't *require* an even number," George murmured. "But I would hope you weren't the only one of your sex at the table."

Angelica allowed a shrug. "How is it you will find eight gentlemen who are still in London?"

George displayed a smirk. "Bachelors, all," he replied. "I think most have rooms at The Albany or own townhouses in Green Street," he went on, and then added, "Where they prefer to stay over the holiday because the alternative would be to spend it in the company of an elderly aunt or cousin in some snowbound manor house far from any entertainments."

"George!" Angelica said in a scolding voice. Her brows suddenly furrowed. "Is that what you think of our parents? That they're... *elderly?*"

"They are," he replied with a shrug. At her look of alarm, he added, "They are a half-generation older than the parents of our contemporaries."

Angelica sighed, knowing he spoke the truth. Their mother had been eight-and-thirty when she gave birth to them. "This... knight. Does he have a name?"

she asked, deciding she may as well learn what she must of the man her father thought a suitable husband for her.

George sighed. "Sir Benjamin. His ancestral home is in Suffolk, but he has recently taken up residence in London."

Blinking, Angelica mentally reviewed the names of the men she remembered from her dance cards. She didn't recognize the name Benjamin. "Why haven't I met him?"

His eyes darting to one side, George shrugged and said, "Hasn't spent time in London. Been living in Cambridge, I think. His father was an earl, and when he died, this man's older brother inherited."

Angelica furrowed a brow. "How did the second son of an earl become a knight?" she asked, almost to herself, imagining that some derring-do in a war might have been involved. As to which war, she could only think of the war where Greece gained its independence. Or perhaps Sir Benjamin had fought in the Anglo-Burmese War.

"He did something to impress the king, I should think."

"How old do you suppose he is?"

"Five-and-thirty," he guessed.

"You're joking," she replied, her eyes wide. "He's practically old enough to be..." She stopped her complaint, noting how one of George's brows had arched up.

Was he daring her to continue the comment?

At least this Sir Benjamin was half their father's age. "He was born in this century, at least," she conceded.

George gave a one-shouldered shrug. "True, and he's apparently very intelligent. Completely opposite of his father, if what our father said is true."

Angelica furrowed a brow. "Oh?"

Once again allowing a shrug, George replied, "I cannot put voice to the reason, for I would be subjecting you to inappropriate words and images."

Her eyes widening before a grin touched the edge of her lips, Angelica guessed, "His father was an ass?"

George's eyes rolled and he cleared his throat, deciding he couldn't admonish her for her unladylike guess. "Exactly."

Edmund, Sixth Earl of Wadsworth, had been far worse than an ass, practically abandoning his family in favor of spending time with his mistresses.

"Is his brother—the current earl—is he of similar disposition?"

"The exact opposite. Responsible to a fault, except when it comes to the most important duty."

Frowning, Angelica straightened in the squabs. "He doesn't attend Parliament?" she guessed.

George shook his head. "He hasn't yet produced an heir."

Blinking, Angelica angled her head to one side. "Then... why does Father want me to meet this man's *brother* when the *earl* is obviously the one in need of a wife?"

Wincing, George took a moment to decide how to

respond. "Oh, he has a wife," he finally said. "And four *daughters.*"

Angelica hissed, immediately feeling sorry for the man's wife. She would no doubt be the one blamed for a nursery empty of any heirs. "Would I have met the countess?" she asked.

"Doubtful," her brother responded. "She and the four daughters prefer to spend the majority of the year in Suffolk. Meanwhile, the earl has managed to restore his earldom to its former glory, but now he will have to come up with dowries. Given that the past two springs have been some of the coldest on record and crop yields were so poor, he may have trouble in that regard."

Her eyes widened in sudden understanding. "Our Father must think he won't sire an heir, and that the earldom will then go to Sir Benjamin should the earl die first."

George nodded. "Which means *you* would eventually become a countess."

Angelica blinked, awed by her father's plan. She regarded her brother a moment, trying to decide if she wanted to be married to a man who *might* one day inherit an earldom. Her mother had made being a countess look easy, but she'd had years of practice. Adele was the daughter of a marquess. The sister of a marquess. She had been the wife of a wealthy man prior to her marriage to the Earl of Torrington. Playing hostess and acting as a helpmate—and bedmate—was easy for Adele Torrington.

Will I find it as easy? Angelica wondered.

"Whether you do or you don't become the countess, your son will be the next earl," George stated.

Angelica straightened, now fully understanding just how important her role would be in such a union.

When she caught George regarding her, as if he was expecting more questions, she obliged him. "Oxford or Cambridge?" At his advanced age, the knight would have already finished his education.

George screwed up his face. "I've no idea," he replied, a look of surprise appearing. "I'm obviously too young to have attended school with him, and I neglected to ask Father what he knew of his education." He furrowed a brow. "But I suspect Cambridge, since that's where he was apparently living before moving to London."

Angelica remembered how she missed George when he attended Oxford. She had been attending finishing school at a seminary for one of those years, and then begged her father to allow her to attend Warwick's Grammar and Finishing School in London just so she could continue to live at Worthington House in Mayfair.

Of course the Earl of Torrington agreed—he gave her everything she wanted and more.

The only daughter of an earl at the finishing school, Angelica enjoyed the company of other young women her age without having to live within the strict confines of a school run by nuns. And since she attended at the same time as a viscount's daughter and a baron's daughter, their protection was supplied by a burly bodyguard who stood watch whilst they attended classes. Then he escorted them to their waiting carriages when classes ended each day.

Oh, how she missed those days!

The daughter of a viscount was now betrothed to an earl's son, and the baron's daughter was married to a wealthy tradesman—one of Angelica and George's cousins, in fact—and was already expecting her second child!

"What if during this dinner party I happen to find one of your other friends more appealing than the knight?"

George blinked, not having thought of that possibility. He had assumed Angelica would simply do as Father wished. "Well, I suppose it will all depend on if they find *you* appealing," he countered, which also applied to the knight, now that he gave it more thought.

He quickly slid sideways on the seat, but still wasn't far enough away to avoid her right-hand punch into his upper arm. "Ouch!" he complained, his opposite hand coming up to rub the spot. "Dammit, Angel. Father should have named you after the devil's daughter," he complained, not bothering to apologize for his use of the word 'devil'. Or 'dammit'.

"Have you already disabused your friends of the idea of marriage to me?" she asked, obviously annoyed.

George furrowed a brow, obviously offended. "I have not," he replied. "You may find this a surprise, dear Sister, but you are not the center of all that is London, nor my life, for that matter."

"And yet, you will have your say as to whom I shall marry," Angelica countered.

"I will," he agreed with a nod. "But not to the degree Father has. Or did." He stared at her a moment. "There are times I wish we weren't cousins to the Grandby brood," he added, referring to the ten children of Gregory and Christiana Grandby. "Or I would have you marrying Thomas."

Angelica considered her cousin Thomas for a moment, understanding why George would say such a thing. At three-and-thirty, Thomas was most like his father in terms of his business sense. He would no doubt carry on managing Gregory's investments and take on clients of his own, which meant he could afford to keep a wife in the very best of houses, clothes, and company. He already owned one of the largest estate homes west of London. "He will be a catch for any woman," Angelica agreed with a nod. "And he is handsome."

George blinked, letting out a sound of disgust. "I did not need to hear that," he responded.

"He looks just like you," she argued, and then let out a giggle.

"His hair is not nearly so light as mine," George argued, but he glanced away when a flush colored his face bright red. "You think me handsome?" he asked in a whisper.

Continuing her giggling, Angelica finally allowed a long sigh. "It matters not what *I* think, but rather what Lady Anne thinks, I expect," she countered.

His eyes rounding, George regarded his sister with alarm. "Anne Wellingham? Trenton's daughter? Whatever has you thinking—?"

"I saw how you looked at her the last time we were in Hyde Park. Do not deny it. And if you don't make a move to court her soon, you will lose her to some rich tradesman in Wolverhampton. Or Alistair Comber's oldest. Or the heir to the Everly earldom."

For a moment, hope filled George Grandby's chest. And then reason returned to squelch the sensation. "Nonsense," he replied, his manner rather surly. "She's probably been betrothed since the day she was born." His stern expression slowly softened, as if he were reconsidering his words.

He remembered that day in Hyde Park. When he and Angelica were on horseback, and Lady Anne was riding with her older brother, Gabe, in a curricle led by a pair of gray horses.

George had never been caught staring at a curly blonde young lady before—there were so many in the Beau Monde—but there was something about Lady Anne's cornflower blue eyes and quick smile that had him doing so.

There had also been that sudden tightening in his loins, the crackling air around them, a flash of lightning, and the boom of thunder above that suggested he had best get his mount moving more quickly lest he get soaked by the storm that threatened. And yet, he had remained in place, as if Ares' hooves had been rooted into the road.

"She's the daughter of an earl. Cousin to our cousins," Angelica reminded him, remembering how the blue-eyed, curly-blonde-haired young lady had captured her brother's eye that day in the park. "She isn't betrothed to anyone, but she is finally making her come-out this Season."

Angelica was sure she had felt a change in the air around them that day in the park, a sort of charged atmosphere that had her hair lifting from their roots in an attempt to escape the elaborate coiffure Mary had created earlier that morning. She had expected fireworks to appear in the sky above them at any moment. Angels to begin singing.

Instead, a bolt of lightning flashed and thunder rolled over the park, suggesting the angels were playing ninepin and wouldn't be singing anytime soon. The impending shower had most scattering to their respective homes. A moment later, and the downpour had everyone else heading for home as fast as possible.

Her own eyes widened. "She is probably back in London by now. She wrote last week that they were returning so she could be fitted for a presentation gown." Her face screwed up in mock pain. "Poor thing has to go before the queen in January," she murmured, remembering her own presentation for Queen Adelaide.

Her gown wasn't as hideous as some since she had simply borrowed her mother's court gown. The gold netting over sky blue satin was perfectly elegant, but then a stomacher and dozens of blue bows and a series of furbelows along the hem had set it back another century. To make matters worse, the neckline had to be heightened considerably. Queen Adelaide had been a bit of a prude and eschewed broad expanses of décolletage —for herself as well as those in her court.

"Lady Anne is probably at Trenton House in Curzon Street right now. I can invite her—"

"Would you do that?" George asked, with perhaps too much enthusiasm.

Angelica blinked, rather shocked to see the quick change in her brother's demeanor. "Yes, of course," she whispered. "You should invite Alexander, too, just to provide a solid contrast," she suggested, her teasing voice hiding the fact that she thought the heir to the Everly earldom might be someone *she* should be considering as a husband.

Alexander's mother was a duke's daughter and half-Greek. Given his father's dark hair and sapphire eyes, Alexander had no choice but to be incredibly gorgeous. Even if he spent the morning meal espousing the qualities of some rare plant or animal, Angelica thought just staring at him while she ate her coddled eggs and toast would make for a good beginning to any day.

Why, she might even learn something important.

Besides that, all their children would be handsome. And probably clever, too. Which meant she might be the least intelligent member of the household.

Perhaps she shouldn't consider Alexander.

George shook his head. "I have no intention of giving anyone else any sort of edge when it comes to Lady Anne," he stated, the words at odds with his earlier assertion that she was probably already betrothed. "But if he is in town, I will invite Alex."

Angelica blinked. "So… you are quite serious about her," she accused. She stared at her brother a moment. He hadn't said a word about the young lady during their six weeks at Torrington Park. "Have you told Father?"

George dipped his head. "I spoke with Mother."

"Mother?" Angelica straightened in her seat, her gaze darting to the window as she contemplated just how serious her brother must have been about Lady Anne.

"Yes, of course," he replied, ignoring her look of disbelief. "I know it's hard to believe, but Father isn't a godfather to *every* young lady in the *ton*," he argued, a reference to the number of young women Milton Grandby, Earl of Torrington, had taken on as goddaughters before he and Angelica were born. "And Mother happens to know Lady Anne's mother."

Angelica was about to say something else, but her brows furrowed. "She does?"

Until about five years ago, the Countess of Trenton was rarely in London, agreeing to join her husband for only a few weeks each Season in favor of staying at their earldom's seat near Wolverhampton with their three children.

Sarah Cumberbatch had been a commoner when Gabriel Wellingham married her, but she was never given the cut direct whilst in London.

Had she been, it would have been due to jealousy,

for the woman was most adept at managing the same coaching inn where she and the earl had originally met.

The Spread Eagle Inn in Stretton, purchased by the earl when the original owner wished to retire, hosted a steady clientele and was renown for its cleanliness, pot pies, and the number of ales it kept on tap.

There were those in the *ton* who claimed Gabriel Wellingham, Earl of Trenton, was a better man as a result of his marriage to Sarah. Apparently life with a commoner—and children—had humbled the once proud peacock-of-an-earl.

As for their offspring, Lady Trenton and the earl had an illegitimate son who was even more gorgeous than the Everly heir. Gabe the Younger, the moniker made popular by those in London, would be enjoying an income in excess of ten-thousand pounds a year once he reached his majority in just two years.

With a mother as pretty as the Countess of Trenton, was it any wonder his blond hair and blue eyes made him the epitome of his father at the same age? At least in appearance?

Legitimacy be damned.

Gabe the Younger had a parade of aristocrats' daughters vying for his hand in marriage, and he was, as one mother described him, "a truly nice young man."

George was fairly sure Gabe's agreeable manner was due to his mother and not because of any influence his father might have had over him.

Which is why Lady Anne was so intriguing.

She was... *nice*. Pleasant. Ever so polite. Not the

least bit proud. He knew this because his mother had sung the girl's praises when he mentioned he was considering Lady Anne for courtship. Anne was beautiful, too, for she possessed those same blue eyes and curly blonde hair her father and Gabe displayed.

Their children would be...

George blinked.

What the hell?

Angelica giggled, which had George giving her a quelling glance. "Wot?" he asked in dismay.

"Your children with Lady Anne," she replied. "They will all be blonde, blue-eyed cherubs. They'll look just like the statue of Cupid in Lord Weatherstone's garden," she accused. "And they will all be delightful, happy little babes. Not a colicky one in the bunch." Then she suddenly sobered. "And I'll be their old, spinster aunt, charged with spoiling them rotten."

George allowed a guffaw. "You, my sister, shall never be a spinster aunt, and much needs to transpire before you can ever *become* an aunt," he reminded her. He took a breath and let it out. "But I do so enjoy the image you have conjured for my children," he murmured, his mind's eye displaying a series of beatific cherubs, dimples in their cheeks and knees. "Yours would be the same if you ended up with Gabe as your husband."

He knew Gabe had at one time had a crush on his sister, although since attending university, he no longer seemed enthralled by her. The recent graduate of Cambridge had instead focused his attentions on Ancient Greek artifacts and was employing his newly-acquired knowledge cataloging Greek acquisitions at the British Museum.

Angelica blinked. "But, Gabe doesn't have a title. He can never inherit," she reminded him, wondering why George would even make such a suggestion. Father would never approve a match to someone who wasn't titled, let alone an illegitimate son.

Would he?

"True," George agreed. "But in the event our knight is not to your liking, perhaps Gabe the Younger is."

"I hardly know Gabe Wellingham," she argued. "Although, we have been introduced," she added in a quieter voice. That had happened at a ball the year before, when Gabe was between terms at Cambridge. Although they hadn't danced, she remembered him complimenting her gown. He had been... *nice.* Far nicer than most of the young bucks, although she had no real reason to expect he would be anything else.

Sometimes bastards grew up with a chip on their shoulder, though. Because the eldest son had been born before his parents were wed meant he wasn't entitled to a title—or to inherit. As a result, some bastards were bitter. Gabe wasn't.

A generous inheritance helped to alleviate some of the bitterness, of course, and Gabe would have a much larger allowance in just a couple of years. When his father died, he was due to inherit a princely sum.

No wonder he was nice.

Angelica blinked.

With her dowry and his inheritance, they could be one of the wealthiest couples in all of London!

"The pound signs are reflecting in your eyes," George accused, a smirk causing a dimple to appear at the base of one cheek.

About to wallop her brother with another fist to his shoulder, Angelica pulled it back when a knock sounded at the door to their compartment.

George slid the pocket door aside and gave a nod to the conductor.

"Tickets, please."

George pulled four tickets from his top coat pocket and handed them to the portly man. "For us and for our servants in the compartment across the aisle," he said in a low voice.

The conductor arched a brow and jerked his head in the direction of the opposite compartment. "Newly-weds, I suspect?"

Blinking, George dared a glance back at his sister before he allowed a nod. "Is it that obvious?"

Rolling his eyes, the conductor handed the tickets back to George. "If this train jumps the tracks, we'll know why," he replied in a manner so deadpan, it took George a moment to catch the man's meaning.

When he slid the pocket door closed, George turned to find his sister struggling to keep a straight face.

"Angel!" he scolded.

"I cannot help it," she whispered as she dabbed at new tears, these due to mirth at hearing the conductor's comment. She finally let out a loud giggle and fell sideways on the bench.

"It's not that funny," George said, although he struggled to keep a grin from lighting his face.

Sniffling, Angelica finally returned to sitting up straight and regarded her brother with a wan smile. "It's funny and endearing and ever so…"

New tears fell, and Angelica allowed an audible sigh. "I am so jealous of my lady's maid," she whispered.

George frowned, rather dismayed by his sister's behavior. Angelica wasn't usually like this. All weepy and easily amused and bothered all at the same time. "I am of the same mind as it applies to my valet," he agreed somberly. "Which means we really need to find spouses as soon as possible."

Angelica furrowed a brow as she regarded her twin brother. "Agreed," she replied. Then she sniffled and said, "Wait. You would marry this young?"

Dipping his head, George considered his options. He could remain unmarried for another six or more years. Sow his wild oats and behave as others his age were wont to do. But he yearned for the sort of relationship his parents had. They were so in love, it was almost enough to make him sick to his stomach.

Now that his valet had married a woman he claimed to love, George had no desire to seek companionship with a mistress or with a prostitute at a brothel. He wanted a woman of his own.

A wife.

A lover.

The distant sound of the train's whistle had them both glancing out the window. The few buildings that made up the outskirts of northern London passed by their view.

"Do you suppose we should warn your valet?"

George shook his head. "I will not."

"But... but what if they don't come out, and end up—?"

"Euston is the last stop on the line," George reminded her. "Everyone has to get off."

Angelica inhaled and then allowed a sigh. "Well, let us hope they don't appear too disheveled when they do," she replied, suppressing another grin.

*T*en minutes later, the four that made up George's party stepped down from the Midlands train. Although the servants appeared as if they had dressed in a hurry, they both displayed happy countenances and color in their cheeks.

The same could not be said of the twins.

Lost in thought and contemplating the next few weeks in London, the two boarded a hackney, followed by their servants, valises, and trunks, and made the trip to Worthington House in relative silence.

CHAPTER 5

A KNIGHT SPIES A LADY

Meanwhile, back in the Euston station Sir Benjamin Fulton stood transfixed as he watched an elegant young woman step down from the train.

The lady's maid who followed her appeared most cheerful, while the mistress seemed...

Heartbroken?

Sad?

Contemplative?

Or perhaps her eyes were bothered by the coal smoke that hung in the chilly air.

She looked as if she'd been crying.

A woman as beautiful as this one shouldn't have a need to cry, he considered. From her smart ensemble—a bright navy carriage gown and matching redingote—he knew she was a woman of some substance. The color of her hair—honey blonde—was evident given it was toppcd with a petite hat worn at a rakish angle and adorned with a short feather.

Was she traveling alone? If so, she seemed quite at ease despite the new mode of travel.

Confident, even.

He liked that in a young woman.

Not because he liked being kowtowed by a woman, of course, but because he'd had quite enough of helpless females.

Having a brother with four girls—all being brought up by a governess to believe they would never survive without the help of a husband—Ben wasn't about to seek out the same sort of woman for himself.

He wanted someone educated enough to carry on a conversation about topics other than French fashions or gossip overheard in a Mayfair parlor. Someone who would be interested in what he found interesting.

A tall order, he supposed, given his interest in the heavens above.

Until the week before, he hadn't even been thinking of young women. Of marriage and what might—or rather what would—occur should his older brother die without having sired an heir.

I might become an earl.

Then two missives had arrived from the north, and ever since, he found he could think of almost nothing else.

Well, he could, and at the moment, he should. He had a reason for being at the Euston train station, and it wasn't to admire lovely young ladies or pontificate on the possibility of becoming an earl.

His latest acquisition should have arrived on this afternoon's train.

A telescope. A reflecting telescope. The same sort of instrument Sir Isaac Newton had used the century before to study the heavens above. One with a large lens at one end and a small one at the other, housed in a broad steel tube mounted into a rotating metal fork.

Once installed on the base he'd had constructed in his back garden observatory, the scope would allow him to see well beyond the limits of his naked eye.

When last summer had finally paid a call on an impatient London—winter had been especially harsh with cold—he had commissioned an observatory to be built behind his mansion in Mayfair. Located well away from the soot-stained skies of London, his garden was a perfect place from which to stargaze. Although he would have preferred a property out in Richmond or Chiswick, his brother, Benedict, Earl of Wadsworth, insisted he live in the house the earldom had recently acquired. "I need a place I can go besides White's should my visiting daughters threaten my sanity," Benedict had said last spring, when he explained how he had acquired the property.

Ben rolled his eyes at remembering the incident.

The Wadsworth earldom already provided him with a modest allowance every month. Given his brother hadn't yet sired an heir, though, there was still a chance

Ben would end up inheriting the earldom at some point.

Given his lack of interest in government and politics, he really hoped a boy would appear soon. His brother was eight-and-thirty, and although his wife, Sylvia, was younger, they didn't behave the same as they had when they were first married.

Ben feared his brother would follow in their father's footsteps—abandon his wife and take a mistress or two.

That's why they had a half-sister. Marguerite was doing fine in her marriage, having borne four boys with the tradesman she had wed when she was but two-and-twenty. Ben's nephews, all younger than his nieces by Benedict, were treated with equal love and devotion. He may have spent more time in his nephews' company, if only because they showed more interest in his avocation than his nieces did.

Astronomy.

Upon Ben's discovery of a comet the year before, the Prime Minister had taken note and recommended an honor be bestowed on him. With the King's agreement came word that Ben would be knighted. The ceremony, painless despite the huge sword that had tapped his shoulders, was over in a moment. A few days later, the king died.

Ben often wondered if the sword had been too heavy for the aged man.

Thank the gods his new title didn't require him to take a seat in Parliament. That meant he could spend his nights perusing the heavens and recording his findings in his very own back garden.

After only a few weeks of late autumn construction, the brick and steel observatory was complete. Benjamin owned an exceptional pair of opera glasses to use as a finder scope, although he had ordered a finder scope be made so that he could mount it on the new telescope.

Once the instrument was installed this afternoon, he could spend his evenings staring at stars. Communing with comets. Peeking at planets. Making moon eyes at the moon.

His skills at sketching would assist in documenting his discoveries. He had an easel, pencils, and pens with a variety of nibs that would allow him to perfectly replicate what he saw in the telescope lens.

He was determined to discover something new about which he could speak at a Royal Society meeting.

The man in the moon? Or craters on the moon?

Or the moons around Jupiter? Surely there were more than just the four.

Or what of Saturn's rings? And why did Saturn have rings while none of the other known planets could claim such a trait?

And just why was Mars red?

Ben was contemplating this and more when he suddenly blinked.

The beautiful blonde had just been joined on the platform by another blond. But this one was a young man, well-dressed and sporting a top hat of good quality.

Damnation!

A servant, probably his valet, followed the young man out of the train car and offered his arm to the lady's maid. Meanwhile, the young man offered his arm to the woman of Ben's dreams, and the four made their way toward the station.

Double damnation!

She was already spoken for!

Married, no doubt, although how was it she had managed to land a husband who could have been her twin brother? The two looked alike in a manner that was most unnerving.

Ben blinked.

After further study of the young man, he thought he recognized him. A fellow aristocrat's son, but one who held his title as a courtesy, because he was due to inherit...

Ben struggled to remember just which earldom the young man would one day inherit. Although he couldn't come up with a name, the thought that the beautiful blonde might *not* be married had his heart skipping a beat.

Something that rarely happened.

When he sneezed, of course, for he knew it was a well-documented side effect of a sneeze. But other than that, when had his heart ever stopped?

Well, there was that one time when he had paid witness to a total solar eclipse. But did that really count? The other three gentlemen in his company had all clutched their chests in awe as they stared at the ring of fire that perfectly surrounded the black moon.

They would probably be blind before they reached their fifties, but he had decided paying witness to such a spectacle was well worth the consequences.

Given his current view of the young lady, he was glad blindness hadn't yet taken his sight.

"Sir, are you here to collect that crate?" a uniformed man asked as he pointed toward a wooden box mounted on a two-wheeled cart. He held a manifest in one hand, the perfect penmanship displaying his name in black ink. "Benjamin Fulton?"

Pulled from his reverie, Ben dared a quick glance around. He was now the only other person on the plat-form besides the rather portly porter. "I am," he acknowledged. "Is it heavy?"

"Nothing I can't manage, although you'll want assistance to get it off of your carriage," the porter replied. He saw to grabbing the handles of the luggage cart and then gave the knight a salute.

Once he was sure the short man was dutifully following him, Ben made his way to an ancient town coach parked in front of the train station—just in time to watch as the beautiful blonde stepped up and into a hackney. Ben hadn't intended to allow his attention to wander, but the sight of the young woman must have had him making some sort of noise, for the porter was regarding him with an arched brow.

And a look of amusement.

"Lady Angelica," the short man said in a hoarse whisper.

Ben arched a brow, immediately recognizing the name.

Unless there was more than one.

"Daughter of...?"

"Torrington, of course," the porter replied, his look of amusement quickly replaced by a display of his contempt for the knight, as if ignorance of the Torrington family was beyond the pale.

"*That* is Torrington's daughter?" Ben half-asked in disbelief, acting as if he knew exactly to whom the man referred. He knew *of* her, of course. She had been the subject of the two letters he had received the week before.

Which meant she *definitely* wasn't married.

Thank the gods.

Good God! What am I thinking?

At the porter's continued expression of disappointment, Ben sighed. "I have only been living in London a couple of months. I haven't had the pleasure of an introduction, but I shall see to one once the entertainments begin in the spring," he added, hoping the porter wouldn't leave him—as some sort of punishment for his ignorance—before seeing to it the heavy crate was loaded onto the back of his town coach.

The equipage had definitely seen better days. At one time, it had belonged to his father and probably his grandfather before that. The gold paint that had long ago displayed the crest of the Wadsworth earldom had peeled off or been painted over with a glossy black lacquer that was no longer glossy. The axels were still good, though, as were the wheels, and besides, the town coach was his only means of getting the crate to Bradford Hall.

"Sort of a surprise to see them here this time of the year," the porter murmured.

"Them?" Ben repeated. He still wondered about the identity of the lady's escort. Her brother, perhaps?

"It ain't yet been Christmas. Usually don't see the earl's family in London until well after January."

Ben inhaled, the letters now making more sense. *Earl's family.* The porter referred to Milton Grandby, Earl of Torrington. The young man who had followed Lady Angelica was definitely George Grandby, Viscount Hexham, which meant Lady Angelica was his sister.

Ben ignored the thrill he felt just then at sorting she was most definitely the subject of the missives.

His short-lived euphoria abated. "I didn't see the earl," Ben commented, hoping to draw out more information from the short man.

The porter loaded the crate onto the back of the town coach with the help of another porter. "Neither did I, nor the countess," he agreed, pausing in his effort to secure the crate with leather luggage straps. His brows waggled, and he seemed about to say something before he suddenly sobered and quickly finished his task.

Pulling a coin from his waistcoat pocket, Ben offered it to the porter. "Perhaps they'll come on a later train?" he half-asked. He pulled yet another coin from his waistcoat pocket and held it out to the porter.

Taking the proffered coins, the porter tipped his hat. "Much obliged, guv'nor." He paused before adding, "Doubt the earl will be in town 'afore Parliament starts in the spring."

Ben considered the comment. The thought of Lady Angelica without more than her brother as protector had him wondering if he might gain an audience with the young woman before the first ball of the Season.

And then he rolled his eyes.

Whatever was he thinking? He would never have enough courage to approach Lady Angelica, despite the information contained in the letter he had received from the Earl of Torrington. And given that his hobby —astronomy—kept him up late at night and abed until past noon most days, it was unlikely he would ever see her again.

Well, in his dreams, of course. For he was quite sure he would have a hard time forgetting the young woman.

CHAPTER 6

HOME AT WORTHINGTON HOUSE

early two hours later George nudged the napping Angelica with a poke to her shoulder. "We're home," he murmured.

Angelica opened her eyes and dared a glance out the hackney window. "Finally," she sighed. The train stop was well north of the city, and the last leg of their trip, taken in a hackney that was cleaner than most, was the least comfortable portion of what had seemed the longest day of Angelica's life.

She almost yearned for the days when they did the Hexham to London trip by coach-and-four over a period of four days.

Almost.

Their servants, likewise napping on the bench opposite, stirred to life and straightened.

"I'll have the butler see to new quarters for you,"

George commented, knowing the newlyweds would prefer a shared room as opposed to the separate quarters they had been occupying prior to their departure from Torrington Park.

"Much obliged, my lord," Mr. Fitzhugh replied, his hand moving to cover his new wife's hand.

Angelica caught the simple gesture, and she felt a wave of jealousy pass through her. She didn't envy her lady's maid for the man she had married, but rather for her blissful state as a result of her wedding. Never one to complain about anything or say an unkind word about anyone, Mary Banks seemed ever so happy. So pleasant to have in her company.

"Do you suppose Cook might make us some dinner?" Angelica asked of her brother. "I am starving."

George gave her a quelling glance. "Well, we are expected," he replied, heartened when two footmen hurried from the front door of Worthington House.

As servants saw to unloading trunks and opening the doors, the travelers unfolded themselves from the cramped quarters of the hackney and made their way to the front door.

Angelica paused to shake out her carriage gown. She gazed up at the Georgian-era mansion before her, relieved to see it hadn't changed since the last time she had lived there.

Only six weeks ago.

Her time at Torrington Park had seemed far longer. Given its distance from Hexham, she had felt cut off from all civilization. Not a day went by that she didn't miss Hyde Park or the pleasures of window shopping in Jermyn Street, or New Bond Street, or at one of the new shopping arcades.

At least the library was well stocked, although after having spent every Christmas holiday at Torrington Park since she was born, she had read all the tomes that interested her. She would have had to start reading the books on modern farming techniques and husbandry for racing horses had she remained another day longer.

How did her mother abide the quiet after a busy London life of entertaining?

The sound of a coach-and-four had her turning her attention back to Park Lane. The equipage had just pulled up to the curb in front of the adjacent house. Seemingly empty when they had departed for Northumberland, Bradford Hall had been owned by Baron Bradford. Excessive gambling had left the baron in dire straights. He had taken his leave of London under a cloud of scandal—and unpaid vowels—and no one seemed to know where he had gone.

Angelica briefly wondered if the baron had returned, but before she could ask, George offered his arm.

Winston stood aside as they entered, greeting them as they stepped over the threshold. He was joined by their Olde English sheepdog, whose rear end moved back and forth much like a tail would have done if he'd had one.

"Correspondence?" George asked before they had even finished removing their coats. He gave the dog, Muffin MacDuff Paddlepaws, a quick scratch behind the ears.

"In the study, sir," the butler replied.

"Dinner?"

"Five o'clock." Winston's expression indicated he didn't agree with such an early meal time, but George had sent word ahead that an early dinner would be warranted after a long day of travel.

"Anything I need to see to right away?"

Winston shook his head. "Nothing, sir," although his gaze darted to the valet and lady's maid.

"Ah. Larger quarters for my valet. He and Miss Banks have recently wed in Hexham." George secretly thrilled at seeing how the news had Winston's eyes nearly popping out of their sockets. Their former butler wouldn't have batted an eye, let alone given away his reaction to such an announcement.

"Oh, course. I will see to it the housekeeper has a room ready later this afternoon."

George allowed a grin and gave his sister a nod. "I'll collect you at five," he said, and then disappeared into the study off the main hall.

Angelica allowed a sigh and was about to say something to Winston when he turned and said, "I'll have a tea tray delivered to your rooms in just a moment."

"Bless you." She paused and watched as her lady's maid and the valet made their way out of the vestibule and toward the back of the house. "Tell me, Winston. Has Baron Bradford returned?" she asked in a low voice. At the butler's furrowed brow, she added, "A town coach just parked in front of Bradford Hall."

"Ah. That would be the new occupant," he replied, his face having returned to its normally stoic countenance.

Her eyes widening, Angelica regarded the servant a moment before she was forced to ask, "Does he have a name?"

Winston's appearance took on one of discomfort, as if he were experiencing a gastric disturbance. "I am most sure he does, but it is unknown to me."

Angelica blinked. "How can that be?" Servants were always the first to know the gossip.

Winston allowed a shrug before he leaned towards her. "Our servants have yet to make the acquaintance of his servants," he whispered. "All are new, you see, since the prior staff all left the employ of Baron Bradford well before the house was sold. That is, all but the butler, Peters."

"When did that happen?" she asked. Angelica knew of Peters, although she had never actually met the man.

"A month ago, at least. Nearly two. The workmen just left yesterday."

Workmen? Goodness, had the baron left the house in such poor shape that it had to be renovated to accommodate its new occupants?

"I left your correspondence in your salon, my lady," Winston said then, interrupting her reverie.

"Thank you. I'll take my tea there."

With that, Angelica made her way up to the first floor and the letters that awaited her.

A RIDE IN PARK LANE

A bit earlier, in Curzon Street
    "The barouche has been brought around and is ready, my lord," Barclay, the Trenton House butler, said from the parlor threshold. "May I suggest to the driver that he raise the hood?"

Trenton regarded first his daughter and then Gabe. "What say you two?"

"Leave it down," Gabe said on a sigh. "Anne wishes to be seen, and it will make it easier to see out."

"Barclay, you may not," Trenton called over to the butler. He set down his teacup and moved to kiss Sarah on the cheek again. "We won't be long. Have a maid put a hot brick in your bed and try to warm up your feet," he murmured. "I will do my best to see to the rest when I return."

His eyebrows danced while he said the last, and Sarah allowed a demure smile. "You will have to do it quickly if we're to have dinner at seven," she replied in a whisper.

"Or we can have our dinner delivered to your bedchamber," he countered with a grin.

"When you two are finished flirting with one another, I will be ready and waiting at the front door," Anne announced as she stood up. She made her way out of the parlor.

Gabe rolled his eyes and gave his parents an apologetic glance. "I do not believe I have ever known a young lady so desperate to marry," he complained. "But then I see you two together and realize you have raised us so that we will have the very highest of expectations when it comes to our marriages."

"Does that frighten you?" Sarah asked, understanding her oldest son's comment. She desperately hoped he might one day find a wife who would love him despite his lack of a title, and not because he was worth a fortune.

"Truth be told, you have set standards for a happy marriage quite high, Mother," he replied. "But I also know that if I do not find love with the daughter of an aristocrat, I may very well do so with a commoner, so I thank you for that."

Trenton moved to place a hand on his son's shoulder. "I will give you my blessing no matter your wife's birth," he said, and then quickly added, "Well, except if she's a serving wench—"

"Gabriel!" Sarah exclaimed as she gave him a quelling glance. "I cannot believe you said that!"

But her husband was displaying a huge grin. "And especially if she runs a coaching inn." With that, he hurried out of the parlor before Sarah could scold him some more.

few minutes later

Bundled into a redingote, fur hat, and muff, Anne allowed Gabe to help her up and into the barouche. When her father stepped up, he took the seat next to her, riding in the direction of travel, while Gabe took the seat opposite.

"We can make room for you on this side," Anne suggested as the driver set the horses in motion.

"I don't mind riding like this," Gabe replied with a shake of his head. "It's a nice change from how I travel to Bloomsbury." He usually drove his father's phaeton to the museum, but on days it rained, he opted for a hackney.

They passed by rows of four-story townhouses on their way to Park Lane, some obviously shuttered for the winter while others were lit from within. After the turn onto Park Lane, traffic increased despite the gray skies.

"It smells as if it will snow," Gabe remarked, his gaze going to the park.

"All I can smell is coal smoke," Anne replied, her attention on a hackney just ahead of them. From the trunks loaded on the back, it looked as if its occupants had just come from a coaching inn or the train station.

When it pulled over and halted in front of Worthington House, she inhaled sharply. "Have the Torringtons returned?" she asked.

Her father's attention went to the front door of the mansion, where a butler was standing. "It would seem so," he replied. "I've never known Torrington to be in London for the holiday, though. He's usually in Northumberland."

"There's that building I told you about," Gabe said, angling his head in the direction of a tall, cylindrical-shaped structure that stood off to one side and behind Bradford Hall, right next door to Worthington House. "It was built of brick," he remarked. "I suppose it will eventually be covered with a layer of stucco to match the house. And there's a dome atop it now," he said in wonder.

"Ah. The new owner must be an astronomer," Trenton commented as he stared at the building.

When Anne didn't say anything, he turned to find her staring at the hackney that had pulled up in front of Worthington House. Several people were climbing out, and he immediately recognized George Grandby, Viscount Hexham, as the first to set foot on the pavement. "It appears our newest addition to Parliament has come home for Christmas," he murmured. "With his twin sister and... their servants." When no one else emerged from the equipage, he made a sound in his throat that indicated he was surprised.

"Perhaps Torrington is coming in a different coach," Gabe suggested, his attention going from Bradford Hall to the four people making their way up to Worthington House. He had to angle his head over his shoulder to see them, but he quickly turned around when he thought one of them might have seen him gawking. "What do you mean by 'newest addition to Parliament?' Did Torrington... die?" he asked, *sotto voce*.

His father shook his head. "Hexham has accepted a writ of acceleration. With the Chartist movement, word is Torrington may not attend sessions of Parliament any longer. This gives his son a chance to learn the ropes before he inherits," Trenton explained. After a moment, he added, "I rather wish I'd had the same opportunity."

"Oh?"

"Made a damned fool of myself during my first sessions," his father replied. "Took the wrong side on several issues. Dressed like a peacock. I was not well-received."

Gabe frowned, trying to imagine his father in the manner he was describing. Then he noted how Anne continued to stare in the direction of Worthington House. He waved a hand in front of her face, and she let out a sound of complaint before she turned her gaze on him. "It's just Hexham and Lady Angelica. I recognize her lady's maid, so I believe the other young man must be... oh!"

The exclamation had Gabe once again turning around to see that the other young man had offered his arm to the lady's maid, and she had not only taken it, but was bussing him on the cheek as she did so. "Oh," he said, just before his face lit up with a huge smile. "It seems Lady Angelica's maid has made a match," he said in a quiet voice, as if he feared being overheard. "I guess that means she won't be marrying me," he added in jest.

His words trailed off, though, when he noticed a coach-and-four pulling up to Bradford Hall.

Trenton allowed a grin. "I wonder if her husband knows he has married into the family that owns Banks Textiles?"

Although Mary Banks' father, Alonyius, could have had a role in the family business in Darlington, he had instead opted to work in service as a valet to the Earl of Torrington. He had married Lady Torrington's lady's maid, Alice, one Christmas, and Mary, their daughter, was now Lady Angelica's lady's maid. He only knew all this because Sarah had regaled him with the story after she spent an afternoon in Lady Torrington's parlor.

Isn't it romantic? Sarah had asked when she finished telling him the tale.

He remembered wondering if she thought so because the couple had grown close as a result of being stranded at a coaching inn due to snow.

He certainly understood how it was possible. If it hadn't been for The Spread Eagle Inn, he never would have met Sarah Cumberbatch. He wouldn't have fathered Gabe, or later married Sarah, and she wouldn't have given birth to their other two children.

The oddest sense of wonder gripped Trenton just then, followed by a thought of how different his life would be if he had never stepped foot in the coaching inn.

Would he still be as arrogant and self-obsessed as he was back then? Still dressing like a peacock? Employing not one, but *three* mistresses?

He shuddered at the thought. He suddenly wanted nothing more than to hurry home to Sarah, to kiss her as she had taught him how to kiss and to hold her as tightly as possible.

Trenton was pulled from his reverie when the objects of their attention disappeared into Worthington House and Anne allowed a long sigh. "Do you suppose Hexham will wait until he's in his forties before he marries?"

Gabe and his father exchanged glances filled with amusement. "Is he one of the men you would *like* to be marriage-minded?" Gabe teased, even as his attention went back to the coach-and-four in front of Bradford Hall. "And I wonder who that man is that just went up to Bradford Hall," he added, not expecting his sister to answer.

Although he had heard Bradford Hall was now a property of the Wadsworth earldom—the baron's vowels had apparently been purchased by Benedict, Earl of Wadsworth—Gabe was sure the man who disappeared into the house was not the Earl of Wadsworth.

At hearing her brother's teasing query, Anne stared at him. Didn't he remember that day, not long ago in Hyde Park? When she had spotted Viscount Hexham atop a majestic horse while she rode in their father's curricle? Lady Angelica had been there, too, although

Anne could hardly tear her eyes from George Grandby as they conversed.

She hadn't even noticed the thunder, thinking it was the sound of her beating heart. The air had seemed charged with anticipation. Excitement crackled. The roots of her hair seemed to lift from her head, threatening to dislodge the dainty hat she had chosen to wear at a jaunty angle. Deep down, something tickled. Her breasts tightened. She felt damp and only then noticed it had begun to rain.

Both Hexham and his twin sister had held their horses steady as she and Gabe had said their farewells. Anne remembered watching as the twins rode away, urging their horses in the direction of Worthington House. She watched in wonder as she slowly deployed her parasol, knowing the accessory would do little to keep the rain off of her.

She found she didn't care.

Even now, the memory of seeing George Grandby mounted as he was had her body responding as it had that day.

"So... that's a yes then," Gabe said in response to his own query as to whether or not she wished Hexham were one of the marriage-minded men. He was well aware his sister's attentions were on her mind's eye.

Gabe dared a glance at his father, and found him staring at Anne before his gaze went heavenward. Following suit, Gabe's face screwed into confusion. "What is it, Father?" he asked.

"You were right," Trenton said before he sniffed. "It

smells like snow." But his mind wasn't on the impending snowfall. He had paid witness to how Anne stared at George Grandby, and he wondered about the young viscount.

A few flakes of snow danced around their heads before he gave the driver instructions to head to Lily's house.

CHAPTER 8

A BACK GARDEN BECKONS

few minutes later, at Bradford Hall

"Do be careful," Ben pleaded, watching as the footmen undid the leather straps holding his crated telescope to the back of the ancient town coach.

"Where would you like it, sir?" one of the footmen asked. The two had the crate suspended between them as a groom saw to the coach.

"In the observatory. On the top floor," he replied, hoping they would be able to negotiate the curved staircase that lined the interior of the building while carrying the crated scope.

He had thought to simply have a one-story dome built, but adding the height of a second and third story meant his telescope would be level with the tops of most of the nearby houses. The fewer obstacles around it, the more sky his telescope would be able to see.

Engineering the rotating dome had been left to the welder. He claimed he could build a track atop the building's round wall in which several wheels, attached to the inside of the dome, could ride.

As for how the dome would move? "You will have to provide the manpower, sir," the welder replied, adding that he would see to installing several handles to help in the matter as well as a grease that would make the wheels turn more easily.

Giving the dome an open window through which his scope could see had been the last challenge. The craftsman who built the dome cut out the necessary slice of metal, but the portion he removed was then too small to use as a covering when the scope wasn't in use.

He had planned to meet with another member of the Royal Society to determine how that gentleman had addressed the issue in the observatory behind his estate in Richmond. The next meeting wasn't for another fortnight, however.

Tempted to pay a call on Elias Pershing, Ben instead penned a letter to the earl, asking if he might take a tour of his observatory. He later learned, when the footmen who had been tasked with delivering the letter returned to Bradford Hall, that the gentleman was on the Continent and would not return to London until Easter.

Not to be deterred, Ben had paid a call at the estate in Richmond just the week before and asked the butler if he might be allowed access to Pershing's observatory.

He should have known from the butler's look of surprise that the observatory was by no means a proper example of a scientific workplace. The interior looked as if it hadn't seen the services of a maid since the day it was built. "Mr. Pershing doesn't allow any servants to enter," the butler said as Ben swept a cobweb from in front of the stairs.

Once he reached the level upon which an ancient telescope was precariously mounted between two vertical iron fences—Ben was sure they were the same as any of the green fences that fronted most modern homes—Ben determined the observatory probably hadn't been used in over a decade.

"How can this be?" he asked, not intending for the butler to overhear him.

"Because he can no longer climb the stairs, my lord," came the simple answer. "That, and loss of interest. He has taken an interest in other... other natural sciences."

"Oh?" Ben had queried in response, thinking Elias Pershing had turned his attentions to geology or chemistry.

The butler appeared for a moment to experience gastric distress before he murmured, "One involving milky white globes." When the knight continued to stare at him, the butler added, "For the first time in his life, Mr. Pershing has taken a mistress. As a result, he has lost interest in everything but her."

Ben's eyes darted to the left and then to the right. Was the butler implying Mr. Pershing had never bedded a woman before he employed said mistress?

Before he could ask, the butler gave a nod. "He is new to the experience of spending time in a woman's company. When his mistress insisted on a trip to the Kingdom of the Two Sicilies, he did not argue."

Thinking he probably wouldn't argue if he'd had a mistress who likewise insisted on such a trip—Ben had never been to the Kingdom of the Two Sicilies, but thought it an excursion he might take if he ever took a wife—Ben gave an understanding nod.

At least he'd had an opportunity to review how the observatory was constructed. Learned immediately that, although the dome did not easily rotate, there was a sort of sliding square that traveled along a track to reveal a very small portion of the night sky. And even more cobwebs as well as a hornets' nest that came to life quite suddenly when the door was opened.

Ben shut the door before any of the buzzing insects could make their way into the observatory.

Not bothering to disturb the thick layer of dust that had settled on the telescope, Ben had simply taken his leave of the observatory and returned to Bradford Hall knowing he had a much better arrangement than Elias Pershing.

Well, except for the mistress. And maybe the door over the hole in the dome.

Ben's door was a sliding curved rectangle, secured below and above in tracks welded to the dome. A long pole allowed him to snag the door's handle so he could open and close it without having to climb a ladder. Which was rather fortuitous, since there was simply no room for a ladder on the floor that housed his telescope mount, a chair, an old desk, and a small cot.

Once his footmen had the crate up the spiral stairs and had removed the crate's lid, Ben began unpacking his treasure. To his relief, a metal cover had protected the large lens. Smaller pieces—various lenses and tools—were tucked inside a smaller pasteboard box in one corner of the crate.

A footman helped him lift the telescope from its bed of packing and place the mount atop the stand he'd had the carpenters construct. A metal plate provided the base for the forked array in which the tube of the telescope was mounted. A bit of finagling, and soon he had the base of the mount lined up with the metal plate.

He was in the process of threading large screws through the matching holes of both when he noticed how the footman watched his every move.

"What is it?" he asked, sure the servant was frowning.

"Begging your pardon, sir," the footman whispered. "But what's to keep the whole thing from falling over?"

Ben's attention went to the floor, where wooden braces had been installed on all four sides of the base. He tested the strength of the assembly with an attempt at jiggling the base, relieved when it gave no quarter. "Lots of wood and screws," he replied with relief.

The footman nodded. "Ah, well, that's good, since I wouldn't want this to fall off and roll down all them stairs."

The very thought of such a catastrophe befalling his new instrument had him visibly shaking. "Me, neither." He glanced down at the packing materials and the wooden crate littering the floor. "Perhaps you can see to removing all this?"

"Right away, sir," the servant answered, giving him a bow.

"And let Peters know I'll be taking my dinner up here this evening. I have every intention of putting this to use once it's dark enough."

"Even if it snows, sir?"

Ben blinked. "Snow?" he repeated.

The footman allowed a shrug. "Might not be now, but it smells like it will."

Not having given the weather a thought since his return from the train station, Ben had only noticed the skies were fairly clear for his telescope's maiden night. "Then I have much to do before it does."

As for the weather inside the dome, it was chilly, but not yet cold enough to warrant wearing a great coat and leather gloves.

"Very good, sir." Not exactly sure what the contraption might be used for, the footman went about collecting the refuse before he made his way down the long, spiral staircase.

Ben regarded his new instrument with a sigh of satisfaction and got to work.

CHAPTER 9

A WEARY MIND WANDERS

An hour later, in the study at Worthington House
Propping his chin in his hand, George finished reading the last of the correspondence that had collected on a silver salver on his father's mahogany desk. Nothing required immediate attention, although there was a curious newspaper clipping included in a letter from his cousin, Thomas Grandby.

He read the accompanying note and frowned.

Hexham,

Thought you should see this in the event this issue of The Times *didn't make it up to Northumberland. Seems you may have new neighbors. When you are back in Town, do join me for a drink at White's. Town is so dull when everyone has left for the country.*

Thomas

George turned to the clipping and arched a brow as he read the newsprint.

Those who have been following the ever growing debacle that is Baron Bradford's life of late claim he has made a break for the Continent. His unentailed house, used as collateral in a game of chance in the East End, has been snagged by a member of the ton, *although it is doubtful the gentleman will move in anytime soon. Word is Bradford Hall is in as much trouble as its former owner. That can be the only explanation for all the workmen we have seen coming and going from the premises. Let us hope the new owner can afford all the necessary repairs.*

Frowning, George set aside the clipping and the note. Whatever had been done to Bradford Hall had been done on the inside. The house appeared the same on the outside, at least from what he remembered when they had returned earlier that afternoon.

As for a new neighbor, he figured he would discover the man's identity from one of the servants. They all seemed to know the neighborhood gossip well before it made it into Mayfair parlors.

His eyes darted sideways, thinking he hadn't even looked in the direction of Bradford Hall when the hackney had parked in front of Worthington House.

Upon his departure from the hackney, George might have paid more attention to Bradford Hall except he had become aware of a barouche passing by as he and Angelica were making their way up to the front door of Worthington House. On a chilly winter day such as this, only those intending to see and be seen would ride in such a conveyance.

His quick glance in their direction had him noting there were just three passengers, but for that fraction of a second, only one of them caught his eye. If he dared to stare longer, he would have been caught gawking.

He was sure the young lady in the fur hat was Lady Anne. Sure because his entire body had reacted much as it had done that day in Hyde Park.

The man next to her was no doubt her father, but the third occupant?

A streak of jealousy shot through him when he remembered it was a man. He hadn't seen his face, so he had no idea of his age, and his top hat had hid most of his hair.

What if Lady Anne was being courted? From what Angelica had said on the train, he was sure she hadn't yet made her come-out. That she would do so in the spring, during the Season. Surely he would receive an invitation to her come-out ball, if the Trentons planned to host one at their townhouse in Curzon Street. He made a mental note to ask his sister.

Now that he knew Trenton and the Wellinghams were in town, he would have Angelica invite Lady Anne to their dinner party.

The thought of dinner had him checking his Breguet. Noting the late hour, he realized he had little time to dress for dinner.

Making his way to his bedchamber, George found his thoughts returning to his earlier conversation with his sister on the train.

Specifically, the part of the conversation having to do with Lady Anne.

Was it possible she wasn't yet betrothed as his sister claimed? As his mother had inferred when she talked about the young lady and her artistic talent when it came to painting, drawing, and needlework?

If not, was Anne being courted by the gentleman in the barouche?

Thomas Grandby would know. He seemed to know the whereabouts of everyone, even those who made it a point to hide.

And by now, he might know more about what had happened next door.

"Fitzhugh, I'll be going to my club after dinner this evening," he announced when he stepped into his bedchamber.

"Very good, sir," the valet replied as he pulled a dark red waistcoat from the bed and disappeared into the dressing room. He returned carrying a more ornate version, this red one embroidered with brightly colored birds.

"Has the housekeeper finished preparing your new bedchamber?" George asked, allowing Fitzhugh to undo the buttons of his top coat and waistcoat.

"Indeed. Mrs. Fitzhugh and I are very grateful, sir."

For a moment, George felt a stab of jealousy. His

valet was only a few years older than he was, and yet Fitzhugh had found a wife without even looking.

Well, at least not far, given Mrs. Fitzhugh was his sister's lady's maid.

"So... being leg-shackled is not so bad?"

Fitzhugh shook his head. "Not with Mary... Miss Banks, I mean, sir. She's all sweetness, and she never complains."

"Never?" George repeated in disbelief. A memory of something his father had shared with him years ago came to mind. Something about Mrs. Banks—his mother's lady's maid—and the earl's valet, before they were married.

Fitzhugh shook his head. "Probably because she shares her parents' disposition. I have ever known Mr. Banks to complain, although I've heard Mrs. Banks used to back before she married him."

So Mrs. Banks hadn't always been happy.

George had heard this bit of gossip, although he had been a young boy at the time. Eavesdropping on the housemaids whilst they cleaned the upstairs parlor—he would be hiding under a settee or in a cupboard—allowed him to learn all sorts of things about those who worked at Worthington House.

Apparently Alice Simpkins, his mother's lady's maid, had developed a dislike for his father's valet, Alonyius Banks, when his parents first wed. Or perhaps she had felt threatened, for life in Worthington House was far different when it was occupied by just Adele Slater Worthington and her servants.

Once his mother married Milton Grandby, Earl of Torrington, the number of servants increased. The addition of another senior servant would have meant Miss Simpkins' rank in the house wasn't quite as high.

Or perhaps she had come to that point in her life when she started to ask questions. Questions like, "Is this all there is?" Or "What do I have to look forward to day after day?"

Questions much like what George had been struggling with lately—at least, until his father informed him he should accept a writ of acceleration and simply get on with his life as an aristocrat. Attend Parliament and start to learn how the country was run.

You're one-and-twenty going on thirty, his father had said. *May as well live as if you are.*

Alice Simpkins' discontent had changed when she and Alonyius Banks were stranded in a coaching inn, their traveling coach and his parents' trunks snowbound in Darlington whilst on the way to Torrington Park. He often wondered just what Banks had done to thaw the lady's maid's chilly disposition. Whatever it was, the two had ended up married shortly after their arrival at Torrington Park

George thought of how he might arrange for Lady Anne and him to be stranded in a coaching inn. He would ask for two rooms, of course, only to be told there was just one available. And then he would inform Anne that she could have the bed and he would sleep in a chair. Before the clock struck midnight, she would invite him to join her in the bed, if only to help keep her warm.

He would oblige her, of course, because what else could a gentleman do? Pull her into his arms and settle her back against his front as his knees tucked into the back of hers. Wrap a protective arm around her middle so that his hand just barely grazed her breast through the fabric of her very chaste night rail. Struggle to keep his cock under control, for holding her so close would have him thinking carnal thoughts. Thoughts of what he might to do her once they were formally betrothed. Thoughts of undressing her until she was nearly naked, her long limbs draped with nothing more than a linen, much like the statue of Venus in ...

"Sir?"

George blinked, his image of a naked Lady Anne slowly replaced with the visage of his valet. "What?"

"I asked if you wanted to wear the buckled shoes?" Fitzhugh held up a pair of black leather pumps adorned with an enormous silver buckle. "Or the more sedate pair?" The first pair dropped to Fitzhugh's side as he raised a pair with a much smaller gold buckle.

"The sedate pair," George murmured, deciding he needed to let go of the image of a naked Lady Anne that his mind's eye was trying hard to hold onto. His hardening cock would be noticed by his valet if he didn't put a stop to the Venus fantasy. "Tell me, Fitzhugh. When you saw your wife the very first time, did you... *know*? That she would be the one you would marry, I mean?"

His valet's eyes widened before they darted to one side. "I suppose I did, sir."

George made a motion for him to continue.

"You will think me daft, sir."

"I won't," George assured him, his head shaking from side to side.

The valet took a deep breath and then said in a lowered voice, "I was sure I heard angels singing, sir. The air was suddenly very still, and everything went quiet. And there was this light from above that showed just on her. Like the good Lord was trying to tell me she was the one."

George blinked. "Was it like that for her?"

Fitzhugh blinked. "Can't rightly say, my lord, as I never asked her. But she was staring at me like I was the only man in the entire house." His brows furrowed then. "Or perhaps because I was staring at her." He dipped his head. "I couldn't help myself, sir."

Thinking back to the day in Hyde Park when Lady Anne had been riding with her brother, Gabe, George tried to recall how she had looked at him. He didn't remember her expression as that of one who was besotted. In fact, after he initially spotted her, she had stared at him for only a moment or so before she turned her happy gaze onto Angelica. The two were obviously friends of a sort. As much as two young ladies could be when they lived so far apart most of the year.

But then she had stared at him as the curricle passed him, her gaze not wavering until the downpour hid him from her.

And her from him.

Damned rain.

"I suppose that was the sign you needed to know you could approach Banks about courting," George replied.

Fitzhugh shook his head. "Oh no, sir. I got that when she kissed me in the fourth story hall later that night. Just came right up to me, stood on tiptoes, and..." He allowed the sentence to trail off, probably because his master was staring at him as if he'd grown another head.

"She *kissed* you?"

His eyes darting to one side, Fitzhugh nodded. "I didn't mind. Not one bit. Saved me from having to sort how I was going to do it."

George's eyes rounded. "You must have thought her *fast*." What woman would simply walk up to a man and kiss him on the lips? When they hadn't even been courting?

Had they even been introduced?

Fitzhugh shook his head. "I didn't. I took it as another sign, like those angels singing, and I proposed marriage. She accepted right then and there."

George's mouth dropped open for a moment before he managed to get it closed. "No courting? No... walks in the park? No trysts in the library?"

His eyes darting to one side, Fitzhugh shook his head again. "No, sir."

"No regrets?"

Fitzhugh's eyes darted to the other side. "None, sir."

For a brief moment, George imagined Lady Anne approaching him from the first story parlor, stopping before him and raising up onto tiptoes to kiss him. He imagined proposing marriage and then grinning as her eyes widened and her face displayed one of its most brilliant smiles.

He was just about to hear her words of acceptance when the dinner bell chimed.

George shook himself from his reverie and slipped on the gold-buckled shoes. "You are an inspiration, Fitzhugh," he said, just before he took his leave of his bedchamber.

CHAPTER 10

A DISCOVERY OUT THE WINDOW

An hour earlier, in the upstairs salon Angelica reread her correspondence one more time before carefully folding the missives into their original envelope shapes. Draining the last of her tea, she furrowed a brow when she realized she had eaten both cakes and all the biscuits that had been delivered with the teapot the hour before.

Well, she *had* been hungry. Was *still* hungry. Dinner could not be served soon enough.

The reminder of the evening meal had her rising and shaking out her skirts. The sun had nearly set, although the sky was still light in the west. The dusting of snow that had settled since their arrival glistened in the waning light, at least in the places where it hadn't turned gray due to soot.

Making her way up to her bedchamber to dress for dinner, Angelica was soon joined by Mary.

The lady's maid had changed out of her traveling

clothes and into a simple, drab gown, but her cheeks still displayed a rosy hue. *No doubt from her afternoon delight in the train,* Angelica thought as she allowed a wan smile.

She turned so Mary could undo the buttons up the back of her carriage gown and then quickly whirled around to face the lady's maid. "What...!?"

Mary furrowed a brow before she slowly angled her entire body so that she might look beyond her mistress to see whatever it was that had the earl's daughter turning a ghastly shade of white. Her gaze shifted to the bedchamber's second window and the view beyond.

Or rather, the lack of it.

Mary's eyes widened. "Oh!" she let out, stepping backwards as her hands went to cover her mouth. "What is *that?*"

Angelica shook her head. "I've absolutely no idea," she whispered. She glanced over her shoulder and finally moved toward the window, her hands coming up to cup her temples so she could peer out without seeing any reflections in the glass. "It's a building of some sort," she murmured. "A round building."

At first, she thought it might be a very tall greenhouse—they had become all the rage in recent years—but it wasn't covered in oil cloth. At least, not all of it. The roof, in fact, appeared to be rounded and made of something solid.

"With a round top," Mary said. "Sort of like Winston's head." She was standing in the window on the other side of the dressing table, her eyes similarly shielded by her hands as she gazed at the building that had been erected during the time they had been at Torrington Park. "Or one of those churches where the Greek people worship."

Angelica straightened at hearing the last comment, wondering how her lady's maid would know such a thing. Then she remembered that despite being a valet, the girl's father was an educated man. Alonyius Banks had probably even been to Greece. "I don't see a cross anywhere," Angelica murmured.

"Is it allowed?" Mary queried.

About to ask what she meant by the question, Angelica suddenly understood. Someone had built a rather atrocious building right behind their house. Was such a back garden structure allowed here in Mayfair?

"I'll speak with my brother about it during dinner," Angelica said with a huff.

Whatever it was and whatever its use, the monstrosity was an eyesore.

Surely it would have to be taken down.

CHAPTER 11

A YOUNG LADY PONDERS HER FUTURE

eanwhile, back at Trenton House Lady Anne stared at her reflection in the dressing table mirror as her lady's maid began styling her hair. "You needn't do much with my hair, this evening," she said to Bradley, her lady's maid. "We paid a call at my Aunt Lily's before returning home, and I spent far too much time in the nursery," she murmured. "But I just loved holding little Todd."

Her aunt Lily had explained that the new baby was named for another broker at Wellingham Imports, one that her husband, William, had worked for when he was a child. "I can hardly wait to be married and to have a baby of my own."

Bradley blinked. "But... but you're only seventeen," she argued.

"I'll be eighteen soon," Anne countered, deciding now would be the perfect opportunity to learn what her maid might know about Viscount Hexham.

Bradley stayed at Trenton House year-round, taking on the duties of a housemaid when Anne wasn't in residence. She was apt to hear gossip. Anne was sure the entire household staff reveled in it. "Pray tell, have you heard anything about the Torringtons returning to town?"

Bradley angled her head to one side as she regarded the mass of curls she had quickly arranged atop Anne's head. "One of the Worthington House maids mentioned the twins would be in town early. Apparently the younger lordship is going into Parliament 'afore his father is even dead. But I can't say as to when they will come to town." She placed a few more pins into Anne's hair. "I suppose you're expectin' to renew your acquaintance with Lady Angelica?"

Anne allowed a prim grin. "Yes, of course. I adore her," she replied. "Father says Hexham has accepted a writ of acceleration," she added, "which is why he will be attending sessions of Parliament when they resume in the spring."

But before then? Why was he back in London? Would the Torringtons be joining him and their daughter?

Lady Angelica would know, and Anne thought of calling on her in a day or so.

She noticed the butler's reflection in the mirror and turned around. He was standing just beyond the open door of her bedchamber. "What is it, Barclay?" she asked.

"Dinner is served, my lady."

"I'll be right down," she replied. Turning her attention to her lady's maid, she asked, "Have you finished?"

Bradley nodded and stepped aside. "Will you be needing me later?"

"Thank you, but no. I can manage." She took her leave of her bedchamber and was joined by Gabe near the top of the stairs. "Eighteen, did I hear you say?" he asked as he offered his arm. Although he had only changed his waistcoat to one featuring more elaborate embroidery, he looked every bit as handsome as any other young buck in the *ton*.

"Indeed," Anne replied, giving him a quelling glance when she realized he had been eavesdropping on her conversation with her maid. "And I meant what I said earlier. I really do wish to be married as soon as possible."

Pausing on the first floor landing, which forced Anne to stop alongside him, Gabe regarded her a moment. "Is there a *reason* for your desire to wed so quickly," he asked, suspicion evident in his voice.

Anne shook her head, but said, "I really wish to have a baby. A husband and a house of my own." And then realized why he asked. "No, I am not with child," she whispered. "I haven't a secret lover, and I've not been ruined, if that's what you're thinking."

She knew as a bastard he had every right to suspect such a thing, but it bothered her that he would jump to such a conclusion given her wish to wed. "But I really do want a husband and a baby. My own house to oversee," she reiterated.

"And not just because of our visit to Aunt Lily's house?" he asked, still curious as to her motives. Although he had gone into the nursery with both Anne and their father to see his newest nephew, he hadn't been as overcome as Anne had been. She had nearly wept with joy as she held the babe, and would probably still be holding it now if their father hadn't pried the bundle from her arms and given it back to a beaming Aunt Lily.

Gabe had been glad to see Lily so happy, though. Of all the family members, he identified most with her simply because she, too, was illegitimate.

Lily's mother, Beatrice, had at one time been a housemaid at Trenton House. When her affair with Graydon Wellingham, the late Earl of Trenton, was discovered and her pregnancy became apparent, Charity Fitzsimmons Wellingham, Countess of Trenton, took immediate action in an effort to deter gossip. She terminated Beatrice's employment at the townhouse and then arranged for her to work for Charity's brother, Matthew, Viscount Chamberlain, at his manor house.

Fitzsimmons Manor had been Lily's home from the time she was born until Gabriel, the current Earl of Trenton, found her and claimed her as his sister.

Anne angled her head. "I have wanted to be married since that day in Hyde Park, when you were driving Father's curricle, and it started to storm," she said in a quiet voice.

Gabe furrowed a brow. "When we met Lord Hexham and Lady Angelica?" he guessed. At her nod, his eyes darted to one side. "Then you have set your cap on Lord Hexham?"

She took a deep breath. "I have," she replied, hoping he wouldn't tease her or claim it was simply a crush. "How could I not? He's gorgeous."

Dipping his head as he cleared his throat, Gabe wondered what to say. "Is his being *gorgeous* the only reason you wish to marry him?"

Anne rolled her eyes. "Of course not! His sister has told me much about him, both good and bad," she replied. "He's responsible to a fault. Anxious to do his duty. He'll be an earl some day, and he will inherit Worthington House. I could not ask for a better match, especially of those who are of an age to marry."

Gabe rolled his eyes. "Are you forgetting Everly's heir?"

"Too clever," she replied.

"You're educated," Gabe argued.

"Not in the natural sciences," she countered. "I would have to be satisfied with simply staring at him over my coddled eggs and toast in the morning, which might be enough for most women, because he is the most handsome man in all of London, but... not me."

Gabe cleared his throat, not having heard such an assessment of one of his best friends. "It's the Greek in him, I suppose," he murmured, wondering if he should see to having a marble statue commissioned of Alexander Tennison. It could be displayed in his wing of the British Museum as an example of the perfect Greek male. "What about one of the Bostwick heirs?" he suggested.

"David is sweet on one of the Grandby girls, and Daniel is younger than me."

Furrowing a brow, Gabe was about to suggest one of the Grandby boys, but Anne was quick with her response. "Thomas is too old and Father would never allow me to marry a commoner."

"Viscount Breckinridge's eldest," Gabe offered.

"Claims he will not wed until he is at least eight-and-twenty," Anne countered. "And then only to a young lady he discovers on the corner of Jermyn and St. James Streets," she added.

Gabe furrowed a brow. "Near White's?"

She nodded. "It's where his parents met. His father kissed his mother there in broad daylight," she explained.

Blinking, Gabe was about to ask for more details. Kissing a woman in broad daylight was certainly one way to ensure a betrothal. But then he noticed his parents had passed them on their way down the stairs and would be waiting for them outside the dining room.

"Please say you'll help me."

Startled by her response, Gabe boggled. "Help you? How? I barely know Hexham. He was several years behind me at Eton," he argued.

She pushed out her lower lip. "Oh," she sighed. Then she brightened as if his news had been good after all. "Are *you* looking for a wife?"

Gabe resumed his descent down the stairs. "Not as yet. I have my position at the museum, and I've only been a member at White's for a few months. I think it best I wait until after you and William are settled before I consider marriage."

Nodding her understanding, Anne followed her parents into the dining room. Just before she moved to sit down, though, she turned and asked, "When will you next go to White's?"

Curious as to why she might ask such a question, Gabe said, "Tonight, actually." He had to delay the rest of his answer when the first course of dinner was served. "Pray tell, why do you ask?"

Anne allowed a shrug. "No reason."

Gabe couldn't help but notice his sister's happy countenance throughout the entire meal.

And his parents' good moods, too. He knew the reason for their happy dispositions—upon their return from Lily's house, his father had hugged his mother so hard, she squeaked. Then he had kissed her in front of them, the butler, and two footmen before he lifted her into his arms and carried her up the stairs.

But Gabe was left wondering about his sister's happy disposition.

Just what was she up to?

CHAPTER 12

DISCUSSING A DOME OVER DINNER

half-hour later

"Are you quite sure?" George asked, his expression indicating disbelief. "It's dark. How could you even see such a thing?"

Angelica gave him a quelling glance and set her fork down on her plate. "It wasn't *dark* when I noticed it," she argued. "It has a domed roof, and it's... it's *round*."

"Most domes are," George remarked.

If she hadn't been dressed in one of her very best dinner gowns, and if she hadn't been a lady, Angelica would have picked up one of the boiled potatoes from her plate and hurled it at her brother. "The *building* is round," she said from between clenched teeth.

That seemed to get George's attention. "Like a ball?"

He didn't duck quickly enough, for a boiled potato sailed directly into his cravat. "Angel!" he scolded as he moved to capture the offending food between a thumb and forefinger and pluck it from the silk. He held it up before tossing it to Muffin McDuff Paddlepaws. Despite his apparent lack of eyes, the Olde English sheepdog caught the root vegetable in his mouth and swallowed it whole.

"You shouldn't have done that," Angelica remarked.

"Oh, *I* shouldn't have done that?" George half-questioned.

"Now you'll have to let him sleep in your room."

George frowned. "Whatever are you talking about?"

"He'll be windy all night," she whispered hoarsely. "So I don't want him in my bedchamber." Usually she welcomed having the huge dog sleep at the end of her bed, if only because he kept her feet warm on cold winter nights.

Rolling his eyes, George turned his attention back to his plate, his fork stabbing a boiled potato. He had half a mind to throw it at his sister, but she was wearing one of her very best dinner gowns, and her lady's maid would be forced to clean the silk. The newlywed probably wouldn't mind, but it wouldn't be fair to her. "Is the dome blue?"

Angelica angled her head to one side. "I don't think so. Why do you ask?"

Her brother shrugged. "Our new neighbors could be Greek Orthodox and simply built their own church on the grounds of their house. It's very common in Greece."

Remembering her lady's maid's comment along those very lines, Angelica sighed. "But wouldn't there be a... a cross on top?"

George seemed to think on the query for a moment before he allowed a nod. "Yes." When he didn't elaborate, Angelica drained her glass of wine, frustrated by his lack of alarm. A footman was quick to refill the glass.

"Considering this building has only been constructed since we were last in London, it stands to reason it's not yet finished," he murmured. "It could be a greenhouse, or a guest house, or—"

"An observatory."

Angelica and George turned to stare at Winston. The butler had apparently been in the butler's pantry and overheard their conversation. Although Worthington House's former butler, Bernard, never would have spoken unless asked a question, Winston wasn't nearly as rigid when it came to the rules.

"Ah," George said with a nod before continuing to eat.

"For looking at stars?" Angelica asked, her interest piqued. She had used a telescope before—there were refracting telescopes in her father's study here at Worthington House as well as at Torrington Park—but she had only ever used them to look at birds.

The butler nodded. "And planets and comets and such," he added.

Angelica allowed a sigh. "Well, as long as he doesn't use it to peer into my bedchamber, then I suppose I have no complaints," she murmured. How often did she look out her window, after all? Another few weeks, and she wouldn't even notice its presence.

George frowned. "I rather doubt it's so high up that the telescope can be aimed in the direction of your bedchamber," he reasoned.

About to counter that it was indeed as high as her window, Angelica was prevented from saying so when Muffin suddenly lifted himself from the dining room floor and barked.

The potato at the end of George's fork was suddenly propelled toward the ceiling and Angelica's knife clattered to the floor. Unflappable, Winston merely furrowed his brows.

"What the...?" George started to yell, and then stopped when he remembered his sister was present.

Muffin quickly scarfed up the boiled potato and then angled his head at his master's look of alarm.

"He never barks," Angelica remarked, giving a footman a nod when he surreptitiously placed a new knife at her place setting.

"Unless something is amiss," George countered, his gaze going to Winston.

"I'll check the doors, my lord," the butler said, before taking his leave of the dining room.

Angelica stared at Muffin. "What is it?" she asked as the dog lumbered over to sit next to her chair. A slight whine was the creature's only response. "He must have heard something," she murmured.

"Perhaps," George agreed, before returning to his dinner.

When Winston reappeared claiming there was no one at either the front or back door, the twins regarded the dog with curious glances but resumed eating in relative silence.

"I'll be heading to White's this evening," George remarked once he finished his dessert. "I had a note from Cousin Thomas that he wished to see me this evening."

Angelica thought of writing letters, but the combination of the long day of travel and the huge dinner had her eyelids drooping. "Give him my love," she murmured. "I'm off to bed," she added, rising from the table when a footman helped with her chair. "Good night."

George watched her go, rather surprised Muffin didn't follow in her footsteps. Instead, the beast settled at his feet as George drank his port.

Noting the time, he called for the town coach.

CHAPTER 13

A NIGHT WITH VENUS

ifteen minutes later

"Should I be calling you Fitzhugh now?" Angelica asked as she sat at her dressing table, watching Mary's reflection as the lady's maid brushed her hair. Angelica had already shed her dinner gown in favor of her night rail and robe, and her warmest bedtime slippers adorned her feet.

Mary paused in her task and regarded Angelica's reflection in the looking glass. A smile lit her face. "You can, of course. But I will still answer to Banks." She was about to lift the brush when a movement caught her eye. Turning to her right, she gave a start. "Oh!" she let out, nearly dropping the hairbrush.

Angelica followed her lady's maid's gaze and quickly stood up. "Oh, indeed," she breathed. She rushed to the southeast facing window. Although it was dark beyond the partially-frosted glass, a light had appeared where one had never been before—a red glow in the shape of a slightly distorted rectangle. "What is that?" she asked before she turned around. "Turn down the lamps as far as they will go," she instructed.

Frowning at the odd request, Mary hurried to do as she was told, and soon the bedchamber's only light came from the flames in the fireplace.

Angelica placed her hands around her face and stared out the window again, her breath fogging the cold glass. She could make out movement beyond the rectangle and inhaled sharply when she realized what she was seeing—a round glass silhouetted in the dim red, and beyond that, a man's face.

The face disappeared a moment, something changed, and Angelica quickly stepped away from the window. "The nerve!" she breathed.

"What is it, my lady?" Mary asked in alarm.

"The dome now has an opening," she remarked. "That's a ... that's a telescope, and it's aimed directly at this window," she claimed. "At me!"

Mary hurried over and quickly closed the sheers and then the drapes. "You think the new neighbor a Peeping Tom?" she asked in a whisper.

Angelica blinked. How much of her could have been seen before the drapes were closed? She glanced back to the corner, to her dressing screen. Given its location, she wasn't in danger of being seen by the lens of the telescope whilst dressing, but she was whilst sitting at her dressing table.

Her dinner gown had been far more revealing than the chaste night rail and dressing robe she now wore—a thick winter robe—but the idea she was being spied on by the new neighbor had her incensed.

"Fitzhugh, I think it's time you join your new husband this evening," Angelica said with a curt nod.

It was Mary's turn to blink. "But I have twenty strokes to go on your hair," she argued.

"We'll do twenty extra in the morning," Angelica countered.

"Yes, my lady," Mary replied before giving a curtsy.

Once her lady's maid was gone, Angelica parted the drapes and stared over at the dome.

Perhaps the angle at which the telescope was aimed wouldn't have allowed it to see her at her dressing table exactly, but surely it could see her when she was standing. It could see her right now, in fact.

She studied just how the building was positioned in the neighbor's back garden, the free-standing structure showed no visible means of access from this angle. *There must be a door on the other side*, she reasoned.

With a huff, Angelica marched out of her bedchamber, hurried down the two flights of stairs to the ground floor, and then to the back of the house. In her growing anger, she ignored the blast of cold that greeted her as she made her way out of the house, across the frost-covered garden and to the back gate. A few steps later, she found the neighbor's back gate and opened it without a thought about trespassing.

There was a decided chill in the air, but she ignored the white clouds that puffed around her face with every breath she took.

Angelica halted once the gate was shut behind her.

Even in the dark, she could make out the looming brick building before her—it took up nearly all of what had been a garden only the spring before—and her gaze went up. From this angle, she couldn't see the opening in the dome, but there was a recently paved path that led around the base of the structure. She followed it until she found the door.

Wrapping her robe more tightly around her body, she paused before pushing down on the handle. The door opened easily. Stepping through, she halted after quickly closing the door, unaware someone else was approaching the same door from a different direction. Although the strange building was warmer inside than out, it was by no means comfortable.

She gazed upward and realized the red light was merely a lantern with red glass, where clear glass would usually surround the flame. Hanging near the top of a set of spiral stairs that lined the interior, the lamp made the opening to the floor above evident. It also provided enough light for her to see her way to the steps.

She quickly made her way up, her padded footfalls quiet while her pulse pounded in her ears.

"Ah, Peters. I was beginning to wonder if you had forgotten about me," a tenor voice called out from above.

Angelica stopped on the stairs. *Peters?* She rolled her eyes when she remembered Bradford Hall was run by a butler named Peters. He had obviously stayed with the property when it was sold to the new owner.

The Peeping Tom, Angelica reminded herself, once again climbing the stairs with some haste.

Once she reached the top and stood within the domed space, ready to scold the owner of the voice, she instead inhaled and simply stared.

Bathed in the dim red light from the lantern, the telescope sat mounted in a most unusual contraption and was aimed at something beyond the rectangular opening in the dome. A gentleman, dressed in a black greatcoat, was seated before it, his attention on an eyepiece. An easel directly to the right of the man's chair held a blank sheet of paper.

"You can just put it on the desk over there," he murmured, one gloved hand waving to a small escritoire.

Angelica's gaze went to where he indicated. Scattered with papers and an ink pot, the desk was one of only three pieces of furniture. The others were the chair in which the man was seated and a long cot. A neatly folded blanket lay atop the cot. Given that the opening from the stairs took up nearly a quarter of the round floorspace, there wasn't room for anything else.

"She looks amazing," the man murmured in appreciation. "What a golden beauty. A bit blurry, but that's to be expect..."

Angelica boggled. "How *dare* you spy on me," she scolded, newly incensed that he had apparently moved his telescope to gaze into another young woman's bedchamber.

The startled man whirled around as he struggled to

come to his feet, his chair toppling over backwards as a result.

"Good God! You nearly frightened me to death," he said as he regarded his intruder.

Angelica raised her chin in defiance as her hands fisted and settled on her hips. "A suitable punishment, I should think," she replied. "I should have you arrested for being a Peeping Tom," she added, her bravura slowly ebbing as she regarded her neighbor.

She wasn't sure what she had expected. Or rather, whom. Certainly not a man as handsome as this one. He was younger than she expected a Peeping Tom to be, too. Thirty. Maybe five-and-thirty. He looked familiar, or similar to someone she knew, but she couldn't immediately place just who that might be. Given the red light, she couldn't make out the color of his hair but thought it a dark shade. Dressed in the black greatcoat and wearing black breeches and boots, he might have been a coach driver or a highwayman. He even wore black gloves.

A shiver passed through Angelica, and not just because it was chilly in the domed building. For the first time that night, she considered what she had just done —left her house in nothing but her night clothes and confronted a man she didn't know.

On his property.

She didn't even have Muffin McDuff Paddlepaws with her.

Oh, what have I done?

CHAPTER 14

A CONCLAVE OF COUSINS

*M*eanwhile, at White's in St. James Street

Hoping he might be invited to join a card game or find a familiar face among those in attendance at White's, Gabe Wellingham entered the venerable men's club and allowed a butler to take his great coat, scarf, and hat.

He had barely stepped into the first room when he saw his oldest cousin, Thomas Grandby, waving to him. Across from him sat George Grandby, Viscount Hexham. "Ah, I wondered if you might have stayed in town for Christmas," Gabe said as he joined the two, directing his comment to Thomas.

"I had the chance to go to Cherrywood in Derbyshire with the rest of the family, but I have so much business to see to here in town, I begged off," Thomas replied as he motioned for Gabe to join them. "Have you met my cousin? George Grandby, Viscount

Hexham," he added, before Gabe could respond. "Gabe Wellingham is Trenton's oldest son."

Gabe gave George a huge grin. "Indeed. We know each other from school, of course, and met again in the park last month, I think it was. It's very good to see you again," he said with a nod. "I saw that you had returned to London this afternoon," he added as he shook George's hand and then Thomas'.

"We did indeed," George acknowledged. "Took the train down. A very civilized way to travel. I highly recommend it," he added.

"My parents and sister arrived early this afternoon. After being cooped up in a traveling coach for half the day, Father suggested a ride down Park Lane to get some air."

The viscount regarded Gabe for a moment. "Were you in a barouche, perhaps?"

Gabe nodded. "We were. Dashed cold ride, but it was invigorating" he replied. "We stopped to see our newest nephew, as well. Ugly little thing," he added as he screwed up his face in a grimace. "Good thing he's a boy."

George stared at Gabe, realizing Gabe had been the other man he had seen in the Trenton barouche, which meant that no one in the equipage was courting Lady Anne. "Is she... well?" he asked. "Lady Anne, that is? I haven't seen her since that day I first met you."

Angling his head to one side, Gabe gave a shrug. "I think so. Seventeen going on thirty, you might say, especially now that she has decided she wishes to be wed."

Having five sisters of his own, Thomas laughed. "They are like that when they are on the hunt for a husband."

Furrowing a brow, George wondered why Angelica had never seemed anxious to find a husband. She never spoke of having children or keeping a house of her own. It was almost as if she expected to be a spinster. He was reminded of her comment on the train, and was about to replay it in his head when Gabe allowed a huge grin in response to Thomas' comment.

"You hear stories of young ladies in want of a husband, but until earlier this afternoon, I didn't know my sister was one of them," Gabe remarked as he accepted a glass of brandy from a footman.

George straightened in his chair at hearing this bit of news. "You speak of Lady Anne?" he asked, realizing too late his overeager reaction would be noticed.

Thomas allowed a laugh. "*Now* I believe what you said about not following your father's lead when it comes to a late marriage," he said with a grin. "So Lady Anne has caught your eye, has she?"

Blinking, George allowed a shrug and decided not to protest too much. "How could she not? She's a beautiful young lady," he allowed. "My interest at the moment lies in her availability—and yours, of course—to join my sister and me for a dinner party we're hosting in a few days. I'm quite sure I can find seven or eight gentlemen to attend, but I think Angelica may find it difficult to line up an equal number of the fairer sex as our guests. I will be sure to let her know Lady Anne is in town."

As much as he wanted to blurt out his desire for Lady Anne, he knew he would be mercilessly teased. He was also worried word of his *tendre* might get back to the young lady by way of Gabe.

"I am quite sure Lady Anne would be honored to attend," Gabe replied, "As would I."

"It would depend on the night, of course," Thomas hedged. "I fear only one of my sisters stayed in Chiswick, but I know Emily would be delighted to attend," he continued. "And if it helps, the Norwick twins are in town." When he noted George's look of surprise, he added, "The earl opted to remain in London for the winter instead of heading down to Sussex. We have a common business interest that requires our attention here in London," he added, referring to the Earl of Norwick and an investment in a railway the two were considering.

"Splendid. I'll be sure to let Angelica know," George replied.

"Speaking of Cousin Angelica, you haven't mentioned if *she* is of a mind to marry," Thomas said as another round of brandies were delivered to them. "Now that she's come into her majority, I suppose she doesn't have to take a husband."

George angled is head. "From her comments on the train, I would say she is not, but... a possible match is one of the reasons we've returned to London before the start of the Season," he explained.

Thomas and Gabe exchanged curious glances. "Do tell," Thomas said as he offered a second brandy to Gabe.

"Father has been plotting, you might say, with Wadsworth. The earldom is in need of an heir and Wadsworth has only daughters. With a son rather unlikely at this point, it looks as if his brother, Benjamin, might have to do the honors."

"Sir Benjamin? The astronomer?" Gabe asked in surprise. "Why, he's a bit... long in the tooth, is he not?"

George nodded. "That was one of my first thoughts, too, but I have not yet met the man, which is another reason I wanted to host a dinner party," he replied. "We'll invite him, of course." He turned his attention on Gabe. "Have you met him?"

Gabe nodded. "Briefly. At Cambridge. He did a lecture there a couple of years ago. Clever man. Very learned, but not as... *proud* as one might expect of someone so educated," he said. "I think Lady Angelica would find him interesting. Diverting, even. I know Anne wasn't too bored when he spoke in Wolver-hampton last year."

Although he expected to feel jealousy at learning Lady Angelica would probably never marry him, Gabe had long ago given up thoughts of her as his wife. She had been merely a crush, for he knew better than to expect Angelica would ever marry a bastard—or any man without a title, for that matter.

"I'm relieved to hear it," George said. "She would not do well with a younger man, I think. Having a father as old as ours means she would not have the patience for displays of immaturity or the behavior of a typical young buck." He paused a moment. "I know you would tell us if you were courting, but do you have an idea of when you'll be in the market for a wife?" he asked, directing his query to Thomas.

His cousin allowed a guffaw. "It may not seem like it, but I am always on the lookout," he replied. "Truth be told, I happen to be related too closely to all the very best and finest young ladies in the *ton*," he claimed. "Including Lady Anne and Lady Angelica."

Gabe and George exchanged quick glances. "Good God, we're all cousins, aren't we?" George exclaimed.

"Indeed," Gabe agreed with a grin. "It's a good thing I will be allowed to marry a commoner."

"As am I," Thomas agreed with a broad grin.

George stared at them both, his brow furrowed. "If I am a cousin to you—" he pointed to Thomas—"and you are a cousin to him"—he pointed to Gabe—"am I cousin to you?" he asked of Gabe.

Thomas and Gabe both laughed. "No," Thomas finally replied, after he had sorted through the possible relations that might make him so. "But I'm quite sure if we went back far enough, we would find a common great-grandmother," he added. He pulled out a pocket watch and flipped it open. "Faith! Is it really half-past ten o'clock?" he asked in surprise. "I really must be going. I promised my uncle I would play a game of *vingt et tun* with him before he retires for the night."

Thomas said his farewells and took his leave while

George regarded Gabe. "May I... may I ask you something in confidence?"

Gabe allowed a shrug. "Of course."

"You mentioned Lady Anne is anxious to wed, but... is she being courted by anyone?"

His eyes darting to one side, Gabe leaned forward and said in a quiet voice, "May I tell you something with the understanding that you will not repeat it to her?"

George glanced around as if he expected someone might be eavesdropping on their conversation. "I promise I will not repeat what you say to anyone."

Inhaling slowly, Gabe hoped he had his sister's best interests in mind when he said, "Should you propose to Lady Anne, be assured that she would not only agree to wed you, but she would happily oversee your household and give you lots of babies."

George blinked, his heart racing at hearing how easy it would be to gain Lady Anne as his wife. "Just... just like that?"

Gabe nodded. "Well, except for the babies. You'd have to..." He cleared this throat. "Do your part, of course."

"Of course," George agreed, hoping his face didn't display the flush he felt washing over it. "I suppose I should... court her, though," he murmured.

"A ride in the park would be more than enough," Gabe suggested, realizing the second brandy was making it far too easy to speak. "Oh, and I suppose you might want to pay a call on Trenton. Just a formality.

He knows Anne is anxious to be a mother, and you'll one day be an earl, so I'm quite sure he will give his blessing. Along with a generous dowry, of course."

George blinked before a slight smile lifted one side of his face. "I see." He inhaled and let out the breath in a *whoosh*. He regarded his brandy for a moment before downing the rest of it in a single gulp. "Well, I think I have a battle plan worked out."

Chuckling, Gabe said, "You needn't treat courting my sister as such when there is no enemy. You'll find everyone is on your side."

Narrowing his eyes, George asked, "Including you?"

It was Gabe's turn to blink. "Including me," he replied with a grin, finishing off his brandy.

A few minutes later, the two shook hands and took their leave of White's, the effects of two brandies beginning to take their toll on Gabe.

CHAPTER 15

WHEN THE MOON HITS
YOUR EYE

*B*en Fulton regarded his intruder with a combination of shock and awe. Despite the lack of the small hat worn at a rakish angle and the golden blonde hair that was no longer piled atop her head, Lady Angelica was still recognizable. It wasn't until a half-moment later that Ben realized she was wearing bedclothes rather than the lovely blue carriage gown he had seen her in earlier. "I... I was *not* spying on you, my lady. Or anyone else for that matter," he stammered, once he had his wits about him.

Mental wits, at least. His body was just then catching up to the fact that a woman stood not five feet away, dressed only in a night rail and a dressing gown.

Angelica gave a huff. "*She looks amazing*," she challenged, repeating the words she had heard him saying just before she interrupted him. "*Golden beauty?*"

Ben stiffened and then rolled his eyes, finally understanding her meaning. "I was looking at Venus," he replied, doing his damnedest not to stare at Angelica. She was living up to her name given how she was dressed, her white bell-sleeved dressing gown barely covering a white night rail trimmed with row upon row of delicate lace. Her blonde hair was long and loose, the fine hairs that surrounded her face backlit by the lantern to form a sort of halo around her soft features. Even her fur slippers, the toes topped with white cottontails, made her feet appear angelic.

In the red glow of the observatory's only light and given her expression of anger, she was a beauty threatening to become a beast. Or a delectable devil.

Ben couldn't decide which.

"I'm not aware of anyone nearby with the name *Venus*," she countered, wondering if there might be yet another house in Park Lane that had changed occupants during her brief stay in Northumberland. She had only been gone from Worthington House for two months!

Blinking, Ben dared a glance behind him and then turned his attention back to Angelica, just then understanding her accusation. "Venus is the closest *planet* to earth," he clarified. And then, because he was positive she was Lady Angelica, he asked, "Might you be my neighbor?"

Angelica's attention went to the telescope. From this angle, she could tell it wasn't aimed at her window, but just to the right and beyond. "Venus?" she repeated.

He nodded before glancing around. *Where the hell was Peters?* Not that the servant would see to the introductions, but he was supposed to be bringing tea. At the moment, he really wanted tea. Or brandy. Brandy would be better. "Since there is no one to do the honors, allow me to introduce myself. I am Ben Fulton." He gave a deep bow.

"Lady Angelica," she replied with a curtsy, mentally working through relationships in an effort to remember if she had met the man. "My father is the Earl of Torrington, and yours...?"

"Is dead," he replied with a curt nod. He never liked admitting who his father was, and he wasn't about to start now.

Angelica blinked. "I'm so sorry."

"I am not." He gave his head a quick shake, realizing he was acting no better than his father ever did. "I apologize. I didn't mean it like that." He grimaced. "I did, but—"

"I understand," Angelica replied as she dipped her head. "I apologize for having barged in here like this. You must think me—"

"Brave," he interrupted. "I shouldn't want to ever anger you. Or dare look at you through my telescope, even if you would be more lovely to look at than Venus." He blinked suddenly, alarmed that he had actually said the words out loud.

Just then remembering she wore night clothes, Angelica grasped the edges of her dressing gown together and wrapped an arm in front of her body. "Why, thank you," she replied, her curt nod meant to convey she knew she had been right with her assertion that he *could* have been gazing at *her* through his telescope. Given his comment, she found she couldn't be too terribly angry with him. No other man had ever compared her to Venus.

Her brother had called her Medusa on a number of occasions, but it was usually when they'd been fighting and her coiffure had come undone in a dozen different directions.

Ben blinked and then did his damnedest to keep a straight face. "Would you like to look at her?" He waved a hand at the eyepiece he had been looking through when Angelica interrupted him.

Angelica inhaled softly. "May I? I've never had the opportunity to look through this type of telescope before."

"Of course," Ben replied, as he returned the chair to its upright position. "You've looked through a refracting scope before?" he guessed.

Not sure what type of telescope was set up in her father's study, she replied, "My father has one. He let me use it to look at a bird once." She decided not to add that she had surreptitiously spied on her brother and one of his friends when they were swimming one summer. It was her first and only look at a man's bare chest. Unimpressed, she hadn't repeated the endeavor.

"Here. Let me get it back into alignment," Ben murmured as he peered through a set of opera glasses. They had been secured to the steel tube with twine.

Ben moved a few dials. "Now, just, um..." He stepped out of the way and indicated she should sit where he had been perched.

Angelica took his place and then gazed up at him. "Are those opera glasses?" she whispered.

"They are," he acknowledged. "I have a finder scope on order—a smaller version of a telescope that assists with positioning the larger scope—but until it arrives, these do in a pinch." He leaned down so his cheek was nearly touching hers. "You'll want to look right here," he said as he pointed to a small lens.

"I never thought to look at the skies with opera glasses," she murmured, realizing she had only ever used a pair when attending the theatre.

She leaned forward and aimed her attention where he had just been pointing.

"Close your eye," Ben instructed. "Ah, the other one," he added when he saw she had closed the one that should have been looking through the lens. "Very good. Now, do you—?"

"Oh!" Angelica let out, the breathy exclamation in perfect harmony with how he imagined she might react if they had been somewhere else. Doing something else.

"You see her?"

"It's pale yellow, and a bit... blurry," she whispered. "It is supposed to look like citrine?" She lifted her head from the lens and added, "I certainly hope so, because I really don't want to have to wear spectacles at this point in my life—"

"She is supposed to be like that, yes," he reassured her, deciding he could allow a grin at hearing her concern about having to wear spectacles. They wouldn't lessen her beauty one whit. "She's a very cloudy planet, you see, so there's no way to see the actual ground beneath all those clouds." He reached over and turned another dial.

Angelica stared at him as he made the adjustment. At some point, or perhaps several, he had raked a hand through his dark hair, and some of it stood up from his head in short spikes. His brows, dark slashes made more so in the dim light, framed eyes the color of which she couldn't discern. She could make out his lips, though. Lips that at the moment were hiding the very finest work of the dental gods.

When he indicated she should take another look, she did so. The planet was more centered in the eyepiece, although the image had begun to waver. "Will you be doing this often?" she asked in a whisper, just before she stood up so he could have the chair.

Given the hour, she dared not speak in a normal voice. The domed building might not have been a Greek Orthodox church, but staring at the heavens seemed like a similar sort of worship.

"All the clear nights, I should think," he replied. He gave his head a shake when he saw how she seemed to slump. "I know. I realize there won't be that many, especially during the winter months, but I shall make do with what the weather gods provide."

Angelica nodded her understanding, and then remembered to pull the edges of her dressing gown together again.

"Oh, forgive me. You must be freezing," he said, just

before he doffed his coat and settled it over her shoulders.

About to put voice to a protest—she wasn't cold in the least—the warmth of him and his scent suddenly surrounded Angelica. She inhaled slowly before her eyes met his. "But you'll be cold," she whispered.

Ben didn't know why his guest insisted on whispering, but he found he preferred speaking in hushed tones. On a night such as this, with the clear skies overhead and the new moon just rising in the east, the domed room might have been a sanctuary, and the telescope a sort of altar.

"I have a blanket," he whispered, moving to the cot. He shook out the woolen square and quickly wrapped it around his shoulders before moving to sit behind the telescope. He dared a quick glance through the lens and knew the opportunity to view Venus had passed. The planet had slipped below the roof of the townhouse just beyond Worthington House.

"May I ask as to why you have an easel?" Angelica queried, one hand lifting so a finger could trace the designs in the intricate carvings at the top of it.

Leaning back in his chair, Ben regarded the blank paper that covered the easel. "I try to document what I see," he explained. "But I spent too much time gazing and—"

"And I interrupted you," Angelica said as she rolled her eyes. "I am so sorry. I should be—"

"I am not," he said with a shake of his head. "Truth be told, I rather like having the company."

"Still, it's late," Angelica murmured at the same moment the air seemed to swirl and the sound of a shutting door made its way to them.

"Ah, that will be Peters with the tea," Ben said, just before he allowed a look of concern. "I'll send him back to the house for another cup," he whispered.

Suddenly aware of her scandalous situation—she was dressed in nothing more than night clothes and no chaperone in sight—Angelica gave her head a shake. Her wide-eyed gaze went to the stairs, where the shuffle of quick feet could be heard on the stone steps. "I cannot be seen here," she whispered in alarm.

Ben blinked and glanced from the stairs to the cot. He waved her to it, and she quickly moved to take a seat. When she noted how her white dressing gown and night rail were stark against the dark canvas covering the cot, she pulled her knees to her chest and wrapped the great coat around them.

"Ah, there you are, Peters. I thought perhaps you had forgotten about me," Ben said as the butler topped the stairs and then placed the tea tray on the escritoire.

"Apologies for my late arrival. I thought to add a few more biscuits and a cake in the event your guest might want a snack." His head jerked in the direction of the cot, but his gaze didn't waver from his master.

"That was rather kind of you," Ben responded, noting there were two teacups on the tray as well as a sugar-pot and a creamer.

And he didn't take milk or sugar in his tea.

"You will, of course, say nothing of my guest to anyone else," Ben added, his manner firm.

Peters' expression took on a look of offense. "Of course not. I hold her ladyship in high regard, my lord," he replied as he arched a bushy eyebrow.

"You know her?" Ben asked in a whisper.

The butler did everything in his power not to roll his eyes. "She has been a resident of Worthington House since before my tenure began here," he whispered.

Ben made a mental note to ask the butler more of what he knew about her. "I'll escort her to her home, of course—"

"By way of the manner in which she arrived. Through the alley and the back door of Worthington House, of course," Peters stated, his other bushy eyebrow arching up.

The thought of both of Peters' eyebrows arching up at the same time had Ben thinking there would be enough hair there to cover the bald man's pate. "Noted," he replied. "You're dismissed for the day, then. Given the hour, I shouldn't expect you back at your post until well after ten."

Frowning, as if the suggestion he wouldn't be at his post bright and early in the morning was somehow an affront to his honor, Peters gave a shake of his head. "Very good, my lord. Do have a good night."

With that, Peters made his way back down the stairs, his steps fading to nothing before a slight breeze indicated the door had been opened and closed.

Well. That wasn't so bad, Ben thought as he regarded the tea tray and then turned his attention toward the cot. "Would you like some tea?" he whispered hoarsely. He gave a start when Angelica appeared at his elbow.

"How did Peters know I was here?" she asked in a whisper.

Ben considered the query for a moment before he said, "I've of a mind to tell you he simply knew because he is a butler and it's his business to know, but I rather imagine it's because he saw you enter the observatory when he was about to deliver the tea tray the first time."

Angelica allowed a long sigh. "Oh, dear."

"He assured me he won't tell a soul," he murmured. "Would you... do the honors?" he asked as he indicated the tea tray.

Angelica considered the circumstances. "Of course. It's the least I can do," she replied. She moved to the desk. "I take it you like sugar and milk in your tea?"

"No. Just tea," Ben replied as he regarded the dome and it's orientation. "Would you like to look at the moon?"

Angelica inhaled. "Now?" she asked as her eyes widened. She poured the tea, adding milk and sugar to her own.

Ben allowed a grin. "I just have to move the dome around so the opening is to the east." Both of his hands gripped a rod that protruded from one of the seams of the dome. He gave a push and leaned forward, obviously straining in his attempt to get the dome in motion. A slight groan sounded before the dome began to slowly rotate.

In the distance, a dog barked.

"Muffin McDuff Paddlepaws," Angelica said in surprise as she watched the dome move, its opening revealing different portions of the sky as it rotated.

"Muffin McDuff Paddlepaws?" Ben repeated, his breaths somewhat labored. "Is that some sort of... lady-like curse?" he queried.

Angelica had to suppress the urge to giggle. She had certainly said it enough when scolding Muffin. Frequently. "Our dog. He never barks, but he did during dinner this evening. And he just barked again."

When the sliver of moon appeared in the dome's opening, Ben ceased pushing and stood back to be sure the telescope and the moon were in alignment with the opening. "He probably took exception to the sound of the dome moving," he guessed. "I thought it would rotate more easily than this, but it is heavy, and it seems to stick a bit."

Angelica stood on tiptoe and studied the seam where the dome's bottom edge rested on the brick base. The dome seemed to ride inside a continuous metal guide on small wheels, much like the wheels of a train on its tracks. "Have you oiled the wheels?" she asked.

"They have been greased," Ben replied, impressed she would know of such things.

"Perhaps beeswax would work. Just inside the track, I mean."

Ben blinked. "Beeswax?" he repeated.

Color suffused Angelica's face. "I stick my sewing needles into it when they don't slide through fabric," she replied before pointing to the track. "But I also think the wheels are rubbing against the inside of these guides," she added, realizing he couldn't see them since his attention was on the opposite side of the dome. "Because of the curve."

He moved to join her, his gaze on where she pointed. "Why, I think you're right. The fit here is a bit tight," he agreed, moving to stand behind her so he could peer over her shoulder. "I'll have the man who constructed this take a look," he added, suddenly aware of how close he was standing to her. He could smell the lemon scent of her shampoo and the remnants of her floral perfume despite the odor of wool and his cologne on the greatcoat.

For a moment, he imagined what it would be like to have her visit the observatory every night he was working. Given the contents of the missive he had received from her father, he knew he already had the man's permission to spend time in her company.

He quickly shook off the thought. There was work to do, and she was merely a distraction. She had already cost him an opportunity to record what he had seen of Venus.

Ben moved back to the telescope.

"How long have you been doing this?" Angelica asked as she watched him change the orientation of the telescope as well as the direction it pointed.

"Just tonight is all." He fiddled with a couple of

knobs before he glanced up. "I mean to say, this is the first night with this particular telescope in place. I was using a smaller one for a few nights while I waited for this one to arrive." He pointed to a shadowed area where a long tube stood mounted on a tripod, and Angelica recognized a telescope similar to the one her father had in his study.

"Where did this one come from?"

"It was assembled up in northern Yorkshire and arrived on the train earlier today," he replied, tempted to add that she had been on the same train.

Angelica boggled. "You managed to get this one set up just... just today?"

Grinning at the surprise in her voice, he said, "I was prepared for it. I just had to mount the telescope once I finished unpacking it from its crate."

"It must have been awfully heavy," she remarked. She handed him a cup of tea.

"It's mostly hollow," he countered, "but the size of its crate made for a tricky trip up the stairs for my footmen."

Angelica's attention went to the stairs. Although they had been relatively easy to climb, she wouldn't have wanted to be carrying anything but her skirts. When she turned back, she watched as he took a long drink from his cup and then handed the teacup back to her.

Angelica's eyes widened when she saw that it was already empty. "Would you like more?"

"Indeed. A biscuit, too. I must warn you, after all these dark skies, the moon will be rather bright. Almost blinding," he said as he sat before the telescope and adjusted its position.

Seeing to pouring more tea and adding a biscuit to his saucer, she returned to stand next to his chair. She watched as he moved dials and turned knobs and made sounds of appreciation.

When he was satisfied, he stood up, took the cup and saucer from her, and waved to the chair with his free hand. "Take a seat. Have a look."

Angelica accepted the invitation without a word, lowering herself onto the chair and then carefully guiding her face until her eye was aligned with the eyepiece. She inhaled sharply as the brilliant white and gray landscape of the moon filled her vision.

"Are those mountains?" she breathed before she studied an adjacent area that appeared smooth and flat. "Or mole hills?" The harsh contrast of white against the black of space made the curved edge of the moon apparent, but without a sense of scale, she couldn't be sure of what she was seeing.

"The edges of a crater, I believe," Ben replied in a hoarse whisper, a grin appearing when he noted her excitement.

"Does it change? What we see, I mean?" she asked. The image made its way out of her field of view and she pulled away from the eyepiece in disappointment. "It's gone."

"We've moved is all," he said as Angelica gave up the chair to him. He adjusted the dials and soon the image was re-centered in the eyepiece. "There. It's back." He continued to look at the surface of the moon for a moment longer before he remembered her query. "As to what we see, it's always the same."

"So... the moon doesn't turn around? Like we do?"

He shook his head. "The moon doesn't seem to rotate, but rather keeps the same face to us at all times." He motioned for her to sit, but he didn't get up from the chair. "Just... sit on my knee and take a look at the other end."

Gingerly, Angelica lowered herself onto his thigh and gazed into the eyepiece. From this angle, she didn't have to struggle to reach the eyepiece. She could see exactly what he could see, and she inhaled in wonder. "It's so bright. And the shadows are so... harsh."

"There's no air to soften them," Ben murmured. He leaned forward to take a look when she straightened.

With his head so close to the side of her body, Angelica was tempted to wrap an arm around his neck to give him a better vantage. The thought that his head would then be pressed against her side—nay, against the side of one breast—had her resisting the urge, however. A pleasant shiver shot through her body just then, and she inhaled softly.

Ben sensed the shiver. "Are you cold?"

"I am quite comfortable, although I would hate to be the cause of your leg falling asleep." She was about to get up, but his left arm wrapped around her waist, as if to steady her.

"You're light as a feather," he murmured absently. He made an adjustment. "Take a look."

She did as she was told, marveling at seeing an entirely different landscape. He had moved the telescope so she was looking at what appeared to be the bottom of the crescent moon. "It's beautiful. But..." Angelica furrowed a blonde brow as she straightened. "If the moon doesn't rotate, then am I to believe we don't know what's on the other side?" she asked in alarm, the teacup gripped between her palms to provide warmth.

Ben angled his head and allowed a shrug. "We don't, actually," he confirmed. Then he noted how his breath blew out in a white cloud. His gaze went to Angelica's hands. She wore no gloves. "Forgive me, my lady. You're probably freezing."

"I'm fine, really," Angelica replied, but a wave of tiredness had settled over her.

"The air in here is definitely colder." As if to reinforce his claim, small snowflakes drifted into the observatory from the opening in the dome. "Damnation," he muttered under his breath. "Pardon me, my lady, but I have to get up."

Angelica quickly stood up and stepped to the side. She watched as he rushed to grab a long hook, similar to a shepherd's staff. He lifted it to a handle on the dome's door, hooked it, and then slid the door over the opening. Without the white glow from the moon, the room was once again bathed in red light.

"I should be going. I've kept you from your..." She pointed to the easel and its blank sheet of paper.

"I don't mind, truly," he said with a shake of his head. "I..." He stopped and dipped his head, about to ask if she might join him again sometime. "I'll escort you back to Worthington House, of course."

"You needn't," she argued, about to shed the greatcoat. She had already left the teacup on the tray.

"But I will," he insisted. "Keep the coat on, please, at least until you're in your house. And take another biscuit, and a cake. Peters brought them for you."

About to put voice to a protest, Angelica couldn't when he wrapped up the sweets in a napkin and added, "Just in case anyone asks why it is you're awake at this late hour."

Angelica grinned, realizing he might have at one time needed the excuse. "Thank you." She took the napkin and followed him down the spiral stairs. He carried the red lantern until he led them through the door, then turned to set it down on the ground. "We won't need it given the moonlight." Then, without warning, he lifted her into his arms.

Letting out a gasp of surprise, Angelica thought to insist he put her down, but a memory of how her father carried her to the nursery when she was a child came flooding back, as did the familiar scent of his cologne. She wrapped her arms around his neck. "You needn't do this," she whispered.

"Perhaps, but I shouldn't want your slippers to be ruined," he countered. The combination of light from the moon and the new-fallen white snow made it easy to see their way to the back gate.

Snow swirled about them as he hurried through the alley and then into the back yard of Worthington

House, the sound of his boots on the freezing pavers muffled by the falling snow.

Angelica opened the back door and slid down from his arms, amused by his determination to see to it her slippers didn't touch the ground. Once inside, she turned and unwrapped the greatcoat from around her body. After stuffing the napkin into a pocket in her dressing gown, she soon had the coat around his shoulders, replacing the blanket he had been wearing. A moment later, and she had the blanket folded and draped over one of his arms. "Thank you for a most interesting evening," she whispered.

"You're welcome," he whispered, reaching for her hand. He kissed the back of it, but didn't let go right away. "You're welcome to return, of course."

Angelica gave a curtsy. And then, not sure what possessed her to do so, she stood up on tiptoes and kissed him on the cheek. "Perhaps I shall."

Ben regarded her a moment before giving a nod. His gaze went up to just above her head, where a sprig of mistletoe had been hung from the door jamb. A servant's doing, no doubt.

Her gaze followed his, and her mouth parted with her inhalation of breath. Taking advantage, because he knew he would regret it for the rest of the night if he did not, he leaned over and took her lips with his own.

The kiss was quick. Nothing to cause scandal, surely. But he knew she was surprised by it. Hopefully not horrified. Mayhap gratified, for there was that brief moment when he was sure she returned the kiss.

Now he wished he had allowed his lips to linger. The temptation was so great, he nearly kissed her again. Propriety prevailed, though, and he stepped back and then bowed. "Goodnight, my lady." He turned and made his way back to the alley, disappearing behind the fence.

Closing the door as quietly as she could manage, Angelica stood with her back to it, her breath held in disbelief. The tips of her fingers moved to the edge of her lips, lightly brushing over the sensitive skin as she remembered how his lips had felt when pressed there. Firm and gentle, eager but not lustful.

Warmth spread through her entire body, and she found she couldn't suppress a smile.

Muffin's quiet 'woof' had her giving a start. "Shh," she said.

Once her eyes adjusted to the dark, she made her way up the back stairs and to her bedchamber, Muffin following close behind.

She was nearly to her door when her brother's voice came from down the hall. "And just where have you been?"

CHAPTER 16

CONTEMPLATING A CONSTRUCT

*M*eanwhile...

Ben stood at the back gate of Worthington House for almost an entire minute after Lady Angelica shut the door. The place on his cheek where her lips had touched was warm despite the plummeting temperature of the air that surrounded him. His lips were positively humming.

Had she truly kissed him? Or had he just imagined it?

He knew he had kissed her. Seeing the mistletoe had been the same as hearing an invitation.

Kiss me.

But the look of surprise on her face suggested she really didn't know it was hanging above her.

Ben walked the few steps down the alley to his gate as if in a daze, his way lit by the moon. "This is all your doing," he murmured, and then gave his head a shake.

What was he saying?

The moon was merely a celestial body that happened to have made an appearance at a rather fortuitous moment. He had barely realized he had his guest sitting atop his bent knee until the scent of her drifted past his nose.

He took in a deep breath, the cold air chilling his nostrils and smelling of coal smoke. Such a disappointment when he was imagining lemon and florals scents.

As he made his way in his garden, he realized this was only the second time he had ever passed through the wrought iron gate. He regarded the green-painted iron fencing that lined the alley, rather impressed the former owner had seen to having it installed over a simple wood or stone fence.

He glanced down at the remains of a flowerbed at its base, one that continued along the entire length of the back garden and around its sides. Dusted with white flakes, the dormant garden had him wondering what blooms there might be come spring.

Then he turned to gaze up at his observatory. From this vantage, the round brick structure appeared especially tall and almost like the turret of a castle. With a dome instead of crenellations, though, it reminded him of a Roman phallic symbol.

He could just imagine what the neighbors might be calling it.

Sir Benjamin's Last Erection.

The Cock of Bradford Hall.

Fulton's Tool.

Wadsworth's Staff.

Ben groaned. Perhaps he could have the gardener plant round bushes around the base to lessen the effect of its profile.

He blinked. Bushes would only make it worse.

Sir Benjamin's Cock and Balls.

Another groan escaped his throat before he dared a glance at the moon and then at the observatory. Bathed in the ethereal glow that peeked out between gray, snow-laden clouds, the observatory wasn't as bad as he first imagined. In the dark, though, without more than starlight, it was probably a rather frightening sight.

Then his thoughts returned to his visitor.

Lady Angelica hadn't been the least bit afraid to enter the gardens, find the door, and climb the steps to accuse him of being a Peeping Tom.

He could almost imagine her in her haste, her long blonde hair floating around her gorgeous face. Those ridiculous little slippers with their furry balls peeking out from beneath her hem with every determined step. Her white night rail and dressing gown flaring out around her, revealing the silhouette of her shapely body and long legs. All those qualities combined to make her appear as an angel in the dark.

My angel, come to scold me and then serve me tea.

A grin lit his face just then at remembering her ire. And then he nearly laughed. What would her father think if he discovered what she'd done on this night?

She can scold me whenever she wishes, as long as she serves me tea and keeps me warm while we stargaze.

Ben gave his head a shake.

Whatever in the world was wrong with him? One evening—nay, an hour or so—spent in the company of the young lady, and then an innocent kiss, and he was imagining a heavenly body. And not one he could admire through his telescope.

Well, he could, he supposed, if he actually aimed it at her bedchamber window.

He gave his head another shake, realizing there was another moniker his neighbors could associate with him.

The Peeping Tom of Mayfair.

Allowing a sigh that had a white cloud surrounding his chilled face, Ben retrieved the red lantern from next to the observatory's door and made his way into Bradford Hall.

He had some letters he wished to read again.

CHAPTER 17

A BISCUIT SAVES THE NIGHT

*M*eanwhile, back at Worthington House

"Just where have you been?" George repeated as he moved to join Angelica from the other end of the hall. Only one torch lit the hall near the top of the main stairs.

His twin sister held up the napkin. "The kitchens. I went down to get a biscuit and a cake," she replied, unwrapping the linen to show him. She hoped her slippers didn't appear wet, or that the hem of her dressing gown wasn't soiled from her traipsing through the neighbor's garden earlier that evening.

"For over half-an-hour?" he countered. He was still dressed, although he had removed his top coat, waistcoat, and cravat.

Angelica allowed a shrug. "I made a cup of tea." She broke the biscuit in half and offered both it and the cake to him.

He shook his head and then his eyes narrowed.

Although he had drunk too much brandy at White's, he was quite sure he could see clearly. "You have snowflakes in your hair."

Realizing she couldn't deny the obvious, Angelica gave a shrug. "That's because it's snowing," she replied happily. "I stood outside the back door a moment. The moon is lovely tonight. It makes the snowflakes look like falling glitter."

George blinked. "You'll catch your death!"

Assured he didn't suspect she had been doing anything scandalous—not that she had, if anyone had asked her—Angelica moved to open her bedchamber door. "I rather doubt it." After a pause, she asked, "What have you been doing this evening?"

He inhaled slowly before finally saying, "I was at White's with Cousin Thomas. He sends his regards."

"He didn't go to Derbyshire for Christmas?" she asked in surprise.

George shook his head. "He has business here in London, so he stayed. Emily did, too, by the way. He also said the Norwick twins are in town."

"Oh, good. I'll invite them to the dinner party," Angelica said, wishing they could end their conversation. She really wanted to get to the window in her bedchamber to discover if Mr. Fulton was still outside.

"Gabe Wellingham was there, too. He was a few years ahead of me at Eton."

"Oh?" Angelica's eyes darted to one side, pretending she wasn't familiar with the name. He would remember they had seen him in the park, though, so she gave up the ruse. "Oh! Lady Anne's oldest brother," she said with a brilliant smile. "I think he used to have a crush on me," she murmured before her eyes widened. "Is Lady Anne in town, too?"

He nodded, about to tell her what Gabe had said. But then he remembered his promise that he wouldn't repeat what Gabe had told him. Instead, he said, "I came up with what I think will be suitable verbiage for the invitations to the dinner party. I also made up a list of those I think should attend. Can you write them up on the morrow?"

"Of course. I'll see to it right after breakfast," she replied, anxious to get into her room so she could discover if Mr. Fulton was still about.

"I've been thinking about that building next door, and you're quite right. It is hideous," George stated. "I had a chance to look at it when I was on my way to White's tonight."

Angelica blinked and shook her head. "Oh, but it's not," she argued. At his look of disbelief, she added, "I was regarding it as I stood outside just now, and I think I rather like having an observatory right next door. I'm quite sure important work is being done in there."

His brows furrowing in confusion, George regarded her a moment before he asked, "Where is my sister, and what have you done with her?"

Angelica gave him a quelling glance. "Eat a biscuit and go to bed," she countered, once again offering him the broken biscuit.

George took the biscuit and eyed it with suspicion. "How many have *you* had?"

He didn't see the punch until it impacted his shoulder. The same shoulder she had punched earlier. "Ouch!" he breathed through gritted teeth. "Angel!"

"See you at breakfast," she said sweetly, just before she ducked into her bedchamber and closed the door, careful to be sure Muffin stayed on the other side of it.

George stuffed the biscuit into his mouth and mumbled his annoyance the entire way back to his bedchamber, Muffin on his heels.

Did I truly kiss him?

Once she managed to escape her brother's suspicious gaze, Angelica turned down the bedchamber's only lit lamp and made her way in the dark to the southwest corner of the room.

She contemplated her last moment with Ben Fulton as she stood peering through a small opening in the drapes that covered the south window. Munching on the half-biscuit, she spied on her evening's host.

He stood rooted in the center of what was left of the garden, apparently regarding the tall, barrel-shaped building as snow fell in large, fluffy flakes. *Probably just realized it looks like a phallic symbol*, she thought with a twinkle.

She had expected he would have already disappeared into his observatory, or perhaps into Bradford Hall, given how clouds now covered most of the sky and snowflakes drifted from above.

The light from the moon bathed him in a milky white glow, the clouds suspiciously parted in exactly the right spot for it to perform its magic. She could see that he was staring up, first at the observatory and then back to the moon.

She remembered the moment she had been perched on his knee, and he had leaned forward to stare through the telescope lens. Remembered the scent surrounding him.

Citrus and amber.

She inhaled deeply, imagining those scents surrounding her again.

She remembered his dark hair, and how close his head had been to the side of her body. How one of his hands had rested on the side of her waist, much like it would do if they had been dancing a waltz.

If she hadn't been holding her cup of tea, it would have been so easy to simply wrap her arms around his shoulders and neck, settle her head into the small of his shoulder, and close her eyes. Fall asleep in his warm arms. Kiss him when she awoke.

Frissons of delight skittered through her torso, sending warmth to her entire body.

Despite the inappropriate thoughts, she wasn't about to scold herself. She might be inclined to scold him again, though, the memory of his expression vivid in her mind's eye.

She allowed a grin and widened the opening of the

drapes, the subject of her recollection no longer where he had been a moment ago.

Her eyelids heavy, Angelica was barely awake when she realized Ben Fulton had disappeared from his garden.

Relieved he had finally taken shelter, she climbed onto her bed and promptly fell asleep.

CHAPTER 18

A PLAN IS REVEALED

*M*eanwhile, at Trenton House

Gabe stepped down from the hackney and made his way up to the front door of Trenton House. Given the late hour—it was past midnight—he was expecting to have to let himself in.

The front door opened, but instead of Barclay, his sister, Anne, stood in her night rail and dressing gown. "Do come in and make it quick. It's chilly out there," she said as she waved him into the vestibule.

"What are you doing up at this hour?" Gabe asked as he hurried inside, divesting himself of his great coat and scarf. Anne was quick to take the articles of clothing and hang them on hooks. She reached up and lifted his top hat, lightly dusted with snow, from his head. After wiping off the flakes with edge of her dressing gown, she placed it on a shelf.

"Reconnaissance, of course," she whispered.

Gabe stared at her. "How do you even know that

word? Let alone what it means?" he queried as he made his way into the hall. The pleasant buzz of inebriation had him feeling a bit lighter on his feet.

Or perhaps he just couldn't feel his knees.

"I am educated," Anne countered with a huff. "How is Cousin Thomas?"

Furrowing a brow, Gabe stepped into the front parlor, hoping the carpeted room would help deaden the sound of their conversation. "He is well. Seeing to business, as usual. And no, he is not courting anyone," he added, thinking that would be her next question.

"But what about Viscount Hexham?"

His eyes darting to one side, Gabe inhaled and then gave his head a shake, as if doing so might clear his muddled mind. "Were you...? Did you...?"

How did she know George Grandby was at White's?

"His first day back in London?" she asked rhetorically. "Of course he would go to his club," she reasoned. "And since he is a cousin to Cousin Thomas—"

"Yes, he was there, too. And yes, Hexham was with Cousin Thomas," Gabe said, and then, because the brandy still had him a bit tipsy, he added, "and yes, I mentioned you would marry him and give him lots of babies."

Her inhalation of breath could have been heard through the entire ground floor of the townhouse. "You didn't!" Anne's smiling face suddenly sobered, and she instantly paled.

Gabe regarded her a moment, rather amused at how mortified she looked just then. "Oh, you are correct. It wasn't quite like that. I said you would marry him, *oversee his household*, and give him lots of babies."

Anne sat down, hard, rather glad there was an upholstered chair right behind her knees. "Oh, well that makes all the difference," she replied sarcastically.

Thinking he might fall down if he didn't sit down, Gabe took the chair adjacent to hers, and not quite as gracefully. "He's going to speak with Father. Probably invite you for a ride in the park, and then propose marriage." He inhaled and then remembered how he had promised George he wouldn't say anything to anyone.

Damned brandy.

Soberly, he lifted a finger. "And here's what you're going to do," he stated firmly. "You're going to accept his offer of a ride in the park, and you're going to pretend we never spoke."

"Well, of course," she replied, her eyes darting left and right before she pushed his still-lifted finger from in front of her face. "Are you... *foxed*?"

He seemed oblivious to her query. "You will not speak of this conversation with Mother or Father."

"Of course not," she agreed, her heart pounding hard.

"And you're going to give me your pin money for a month to cover my matchmaking fee," he added.

"A month?" she countered. "I'll give you six months' worth!"

Gabe wasn't prepared for what she did next, for he was nearly bowled over when she launched herself from her chair, bent down, and hugged him harder than even their mother had done earlier that day. "I was joking about the matchmaking fee," he murmured, belatedly returning her awkward hug.

He finally pulled away and regarded her brilliant smile. "He's the very opposite of a rogue. Don't you dare do anything to... embarrass him. Or me," he warned. "And don't you dare say anything to Lady Angelica or to Mother."

"I won't," she promised.

"And while you're pretending you don't know anything of what I've told you under extreme duress and the influence of White's best brandy, do try to act a bit... *demure* in his presence, won't you?"

Anne's eyes instantly widened, taking on the appearance of the eyes of a doe he had nearly shot with an arrow the year before. Never mind that hers were cornflower blue and the doe's had been brown. "I am usually demure," she said in a quiet voice. "I excel at demureness."

A most unpleasant sound emanated from him just then. "Not when you're determined to marry," he argued.

Blinking a few times, Anne finally allowed a nod. "True," she murmured, remembering how she had been putting voice to her desire to marry far more often these days.

Gabe narrowed his eyes. "What's really going on here, Anne?" he asked in a quiet voice. "I could understand this kind of behavior if you had been out for a few

Seasons and you didn't have any marriage prospects, but... you haven't even made your come-out—"

"I don't wish to."

Despite how the room had started spinning, he straightened in the chair. "What?"

"I don't want to. To have a Season."

Blinking much like she had done, Gabe dropped his head onto a hand, rather glad his elbow had taken purchase on the arm of the chair to support it. "From my experience, and I do have just a few years of it, every young lady in London wants at least one Season. Most want two or three," he argued. "Even after they marry, women seem to live for the Season."

"But I do not," she replied quietly. "I don't want the petty jealousies over who has the finest gowns, or be the subject of endless gossip and ridiculous rumors, or to suffer the pretentiousness of chits who claim to be friends but then turn around and stab me in the back."

Gabe stared at her. "You're awfully critical of your sex." Then his brow furrowed and he inhaled sharply. "Is this because I am a bastard?"

Anne shook her head. "*What?* No. That isn't it at all," she replied, annoyance tingeing her voice. "You have Father's name. Our parents have been married since before you could walk," she reminded him. "You could have your pick of just about any young lady in the *ton*," she went on. "Including Lady Angelica."

He shook his head. "She's already spoken for," he countered, and then when he saw her look of shock, he rolled his eyes. "Damned brandy," he muttered. "You did not hear that from me."

"Did Hexham tell you that?"

Gabe's eyes darted to one side. "I'm not saying anything else," he said. "Except that I will not be marrying Lady Angelica. And I really don't wish to."

Anne settled onto the chair adjacent to his. "I was sure you felt affection for her," she whispered.

His head dipping—his supporting hand seemed to have disappeared—Gabe allowed a sigh. "At one time, I did," he admitted. "But... that was before I went to university. Before I had the opportunity to meet other people. Before I started my work at the museum. Before I learned there was a much larger world outside of the aristocracy," he explained. "Mother's world," he added in an exaggerated whisper.

He was definitely drunk.

Inhaling softly, Anne understood some of what he was saying, even though she had only been away from home for a year of finishing school. "So you can understand why it is I don't wish to have a Season."

Gabe allowed a chuckle. "I do," he murmured. He didn't, really, but thought he might after he had a night to sleep on it.

He doubted he would even remember this conversation come morning.

"I should probably tell Mother," she whispered. "Maybe over breakfast."

"You'll still have to go before the queen," he warned,

thinking that might be another reason why she didn't wish to have a Season.

"I will. Gladly. Especially since I'll be marrying a future earl," she said as she displayed a brilliant smile. "Thank you for what you did for me tonight."

Gabe frowned. "Don't thank me, Sister. It was all the fault of the brandy."

Anne stood up and gave him a quick curtsy, annoyed when he stayed slouched in the chair. "Oh, don't get up on my account. I'm only off to bed," she teased, just before she hurried out of the parlor.

Gabe heard her slippered feet padding up the marble stairs, and he contemplated heading to his own bedchamber. He was about to attempt it when he realized he wasn't alone.

"If she doesn't give you six months of pin money, then I certainly shall," Trenton said from where he was sitting in the dark, close to the parlor's only window.

"Father?" Gabe whispered, startled. He straightened in his chair and found the earl staring at him from over the top edge of a settee arranged so it faced the window. "How long—?"

"Since before you arrived," Trenton said on a sigh. He stood up from the settee and made his way to where Gabe sat, a glass of brandy in one hand and a book in the other. Although he wore a pair of dark breeches and a shirt, the shirt's button was undone, and he was barefoot. Gabe wasn't sure he had ever seen his father in such a disheveled state.

"Then you heard... everything," Gabe said, his mind

racing to replay the conversation with his sister in his head. Although racing wasn't quite right. His thoughts seemed to move at a turtle's pace.

"I did. A masterful plan you hatched."

"I didn't plan anything," Gabe replied. "It just sort of... happened." He gave his father an assessing glance. "Did something happen with mother?"

Trenton allowed a brilliant grin. "That, my son, is none of your business. Suffice it to say, she is sound asleep with a smile on her face, and I would be as well, but I think I napped too long in the coach this morning." He lifted his glass. "Thought a book and a brandy might help."

Gabe allowed a grin. "So... if Hexham pays a call—?"

"I will welcome him, ply him with my best brandy, and hand over a cheque for your sister's dowry," he replied with a chuckle. He sobered. "He would be an excellent match for Anne, although I have to admit I am surprised he would consider marriage at his age. He's younger than you, if only by a few months."

"I wondered the same," Gabe admitted, sobering a bit. "But he's determined not to follow in the same footsteps as his father."

Trenton nodded. "And you? Sounds as if you won't be seeking a wife at any of the balls this Season."

Gabe gave a shrug. "I think I shall wait for one to find me," he said with a grin. "Let her chase me 'til I catch her."

Trenton nodded his understanding, suppressing the

grin that touched his lips at hearing his son's comment. "Well, I'm off to bed. I've left your mother alone too long."

When Gabe's brows rose in surprise, Trenton chuckled. "I promised to keep the bed warm." And with that, he took his leave of the parlor, and made his way up the marble stairs.

Left alone, Gabe pondered the evening's events, and he, too, would have climbed the stairs to his bedchamber, but he was sound asleep before he could stand up from the chair.

CHAPTER 19
TWO LETTERS

M*eanwhile, at Bradford Hall*

Ben took a seat at the desk in his study and unfolded the two letters he had received nearly a week ago.

To say it had been a surprise to hear from his godfather, Milton, Earl of Torrington, would have been an understatement, except that he had opened and read one from his brother, Benedict, Earl of Wadsworth, just the moment before, and was therefore prepared for the older earl's letter.

Remembering how he had reacted then had him feeling rather embarrassed. He had cursed his godfather, yelled an obscenity in the direction of the ceiling, thrown a pen across the room, kicked his desk, and decided he wouldn't have anything to do with his brother for the rest of his life.

Now... now he understood.

He reread the letters and gave his head a shake,

deciding perhaps his brother wasn't a gap stopper.

Dear Ben (or Sir Benjamin, I should say),

I hope this letter finds you settled in your new home and happy with life in London. I know you will be once the telescope is installed and you're spending your nights stargazing again.

I hope your days might be spent in pursuit of what I have been unable to achieve.

I know this will come as no surprise to you, but I have given up hope of ever siring an heir. The issue has proven to be a point of contention with Sylvia, and I have lost her and her good graces, perhaps for the rest of our lives.

Therefore, my dear brother, it falls on you to carry on the Wadsworth title once I am in the grave.

Knowing you are unfamiliar with London and the Season and all that is expected of an aristocrat, I made sure the house I purchased on your behalf is next door to one in which a young lady of impeccable credentials lives with her twin brother. Their parents, the Earl and Countess of Torrington, are of an age when they no longer wish to pursue the entertainments of London but are satisfied with a life in the country. They do want their daughter married, however. And they would like her to remain close in proximity to her brother, at least until he has secured a wife.

I have been in contact with Lord Torrington on the matter, and he assures me he will write to you with an offer.

Do not groan, brother. Do not curse me (although I am quite sure I will hear it all the way here in Suffolk when you do read this), for I am doing you a Favour.

Marriage to Lady Angelica will provide you with a dowry on which you two—and your children—can live more than comfortably for the rest of your lives and still provide her with security for when you, too, are in the grave. My daughters' dowries, which I expect to have to begin doling out in a few years, will not allow me to support you in the manner you have come to expect, and you deserve to live a life beyond your new dome and modest income.

Having been introduced to the young lady, I can assure you she is a beautiful creature. Your children will be handsome, and they will suffer the attentions of two sets of doting grandparents.

I look forward to hearing your thoughts on the matter, but please do not put pen to paper until after you have had a chance to meet the young lady. You may decide she is a better companion than your beloved Venus.

Your brother,
Benedict

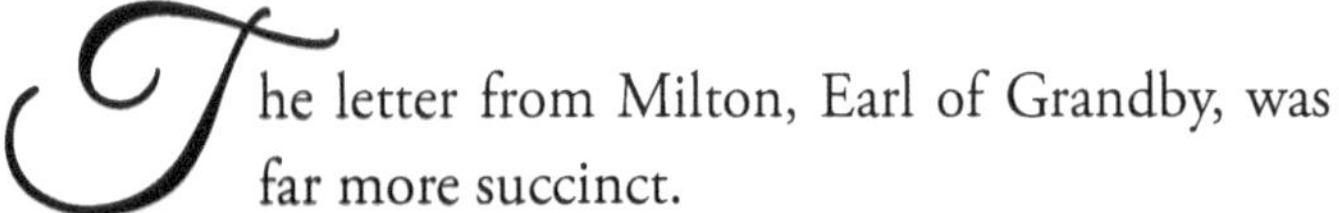

The letter from Milton, Earl of Grandby, was far more succinct.

Dear Sir Benjamin,

Congratulations on your recent knighthood. I should think your discovery of a new comet will eventually make you a Fellow in the Royal Society. Even though I am your godfather, I cannot take credit for having anything to do with your accomplishment; however, I do have bragging rights, do I not?

I understand from your brother (and another of my godsons) that you or your issue will be expected to take on the Wadsworth earldom upon his death.

May I suggest you do so with my daughter, Angelica, at your side? I do not make this offer lightly, for she is my pride and joy. Given my age at the time she was born, I never thought to see her married. In fact, I have spent the past three years denying permission to those who wished to court her.

I denied them not because they were lacking in excellent lineage or good fortune, but because they would not have been a good fit for a girl raised with a twin brother. Nor for a young woman who is both curious and educated. She requires a husband who is the same.

I believe that gentleman may be you. Even if you eschew your duties as an earl, Lady Angelica will make an excellent countess.

I look forward to your favourable reply,

Torrington

Post scriptum

I neglected to mention my daughter comes with a dowry. Should you wish to build another observatory or buy a larger telescope, be assured you will be able to do so. Angelica will no doubt wish to join you in your pursuit of your next discovery.

Ben settled back in his chair. No longer of a mind to curse, he could still feel a sting of annoyance at what had been arranged without his knowledge.

Without his permission.

Had Lady Angelica been apprised? Is that why she had paid him a call this evening? Wearing only her nightclothes, no less?

Her verbal lashing of him suggested otherwise.

Once more, a grin raised the corners of his lips. He decided he would do nothing more than wait and discover what he could of his future wife.

Future wife?

He rolled his eyes and wondered how *she* would react when she learned what had been arranged on her behalf—if she didn't already know.

Would she put voice to a curse? Throw a vase? Stomp her feet and clench her hands into fists? Punch someone?

Perhaps.

But he hoped not. He rather enjoyed her kiss.

CHAPTER 20

AN INVITATION TO RIDE

The following morning Angelica breezed into the breakfast parlor, surprised to find her brother already there. His nearly empty plate seemed forgotten, his attention not on that morning's edition of *The Times*, but on a sheet of stationery. The scratch of an ink pen on the fine paper was the only sound in the parlor.

"You're writing a letter during breakfast?" she asked as she helped herself to a plate and filled it with coddled eggs, toast, a slice of ham, and bread rolls.

George had frequently teased her about how much she ate in the mornings—their mother rarely ate more than toast and a single egg with her morning tea—claiming she would end up more than pleasantly plump. Despite years of large breakfasts and several biscuits at tea time, Angelica still displayed a fine figure and long limbs that had her standing taller than most women of her age.

George had stopped teasing her when he tired of being punched in the arm.

"An invitation to a young lady for a ride in the park," he murmured as he signed his name. He held out the sheet and reread it to himself, hoping it wouldn't seem presumptuous. "How does this sound?" He cleared his throat as Angelica quickly took her seat. A footman poured a cup of coffee for her and left the breakfast parlor.

"Dear Lady Anne,

"Just yesterday, I learned you have arrived back in town, as have I. Even though a parade is not expected in Rotten Row this afternoon due to the snow that fell last night, I wondered if you might join me for a ride, perhaps a bit earlier in the afternoon, in the hopes it would be warmer? My horse could use the exercise and I the fresh air. I could call upon you at three o'clock.

"I look forward to your reply,

"George Grandby, Viscount Hexham."

He looked up from the note to find his sister regarding him with a look of shock. "What is it? Too long? Too short?"

"You truly wish to court Lady Anne?" she asked, ignoring his other questions.

He straightened at the table. "Do you know something about her I should know?" he countered.

Angelica shook her head. "No. Other than she would make you a fine wife, and me a grateful sister," she replied, a brilliant smile replacing her look of shock. "Have you seen her since that day in the park?" she asked, her question sounding as if she was accusing him of hiding something from her.

"I have not," he replied defensively. "When would I have had the chance? We left for Torrington Park only a few days after that ride." He dipped his head. "That's not exactly true."

Her ham-filled fork stopped halfway to her mouth, Angelica stared at her brother. "Wot?"

He sighed. "I saw her. Yesterday. She was riding in a barouche that passed by the house when we first arrived," he explained.

"Did you... wave at her?"

George shook his head. "Should I have?"

Angelica rolled her eyes, and tucked into her breakfast. "It's too late now," she murmured, a teasing grin lifting the corners of her mouth. She enjoyed seeing her brother so bothered. He was too young to behave as a staid, stuffy aristocrat, as much as he wanted to put on airs that he was. She was determined to keep him humble. "If you have any hope of receiving a reply to your invitation before this afternoon, then I suggest you have a footman deliver that note right now," she added.

"You don't think it needs a bit of... of editing?"

"Probably, but it will do fine," she assured him. "When did you decide you wished to marry?"

George finished the last bit of toast on his plate and washed it down with a sip of tea. "Who says I have?"

She rolled her eyes. "You, if you're inviting a young lady for a ride in the park in the middle of winter. What's really going on here?" she asked.

Folding the note into the shape of a small envelope, George addressed it and then had the butler summon a footman. "Once you're married, I think I should like to be as well. Besides, I'll need a hostess," he reasoned.

As much as she liked the idea of Lady Anne as a sister-in-law, Angelica still wondered at her brother's motivation. "You're awfully young to be marrying," she argued.

"I'm not yet betrothed," he reminded her. "But I will not delay a match as long as our father did."

"A quarter of a century," she murmured.

"What?"

"That's the amount of time between your current age and that of Father's when he took Mother to wife," she said. "I suppose I would have expected you to marry at some age halfway in between." She seemed to do a calculation in her head. "Three-and thirty or so."

George made a sound of disbelief. "I think that is far too old to be starting a nursery," he argued.

Angelica's eyes widened. "And yet, Sir Benjamin is older even than that!"

Unable to argue with her reasoning, George allowed a huff. "I rue the day Father decided he wanted an educated daughter," he stated under his breath. He allowed a long sigh, wondering at her objection. "You should be happy for me. And glad that I am not of a mind to hire a mistress, or seek a woman's attentions at a brothel." He clamped his mouth shut, mortified that he had actually said the last out loud. "I apologize. I..." He sighed again.

Angling her head to one side, Angelica allowed a wan smile. "I *am* happy for you. I adore Lady Anne. I am merely worried that by marrying early, you will tire of your wife and then hire a mistress, or seek a woman's attentions at a brothel."

"Angel!" he scolded, shocked she would use his very words against him.

The footman happened to have arrived in the breakfast parlor the same moment she was making her point. George handed him the folded note, hoping the servant wouldn't mention his sister's comment to the other servants. "Take this to Trenton House in Curzon Street. I rather doubt you will be allowed to wait for a reply," he said.

Once the footman had bowed and took his leave, George turned his attention back on his sister. Before he could say anything, though, she said, "I apologize. You should marry Lady Anne. As soon as you can. Although she's just making her come-out this year, she is sure to have a half-dozen suitors and probably end up married before the end of it if you don't make your move first."

George allowed a chuckle. "I said the same thing about *you* a few years ago."

Angelica's face bloomed red with sudden anger, and George backed his chair from the table, mostly to protect his arm from being punched. "Remember, Father made sure none of your suitors at the time could have you," he reminded her quickly. "And since he is the one who has made the overtures regarding a potential match with Sir Benjamin, at least he won't object to him."

But Angelica wasn't remembering those other suitors.

She settled back into her chair and recalled her time with Mr. Fulton the night before. Recalled the brief kiss under the mistletoe. Recalled his final kiss and how warm it had made her feel.

She stood up and her brother quickly followed suit.

"What is it?" he asked in alarm.

She glanced at him and gave her head a shake. "Nothing. I will see to writing those invitations now," she murmured, and then she took her leave of the breakfast parlor and headed to her salon.

Would her father object to Ben Fulton if he decided to offer for her hand?

It was far too soon to be thinking of marriage to the astronomer, but wouldn't his nights be more interesting than an older knight's nights?

CHAPTER 21

AN INVITATION ARRIVES

Meanwhile, at Trenton House in Curzon Street

Having finished her breakfast and a cup of tea, Sarah, Countess of Trenton, was deciding between accepting another cup of tea or going to her salon to write letters.

The arrival of her daughter had her accepting the tea.

"You're up awfully late this morning," she commented as Anne stopped to kiss her on the cheek.

Anne moved to take her regular seat at the table and allowed a brilliant smile as a footman moved to fill a plate for her. "I was having the most amazing dream and decided I didn't wish for it to end," she said.

Sarah arched an elegant eyebrow. "Oh, my. Do you remember any of it?"

Grinning, Ann acknowledged the footman who poured her tea with a whispered "thank you" and said,

"I was on a ride in Hyde Park with Viscount Hexham. It must have snowed, for everything was white, and the snowed glittered in the sun."

"Hexham?" Sarah repeated. "You mean George Grandby, the heir to the Torrington earldom?"

Anne blushed. "I do. He would make a most excellent husband, do you not think?"

Sarah regarded her daughter with appreciation. "I suppose he would." She was about to say more, but Barclay appeared on the threshold. "Yes?"

The butler held a silver salver in one hand. "A footman just delivered this for Lady Anne."

Her eyes widening in surprise, Anne said, "Who even knows we are in London?" she asked as Sarah indicated she would take the note.

The countess' brows furrowed as she regarded the handwriting on the outside. Without opening it, she handed it over to her daughter. "There's no seal," she said as she turned her attention back to the butler. "Was the footman instructed to wait for a reply?"

Barclay gave a slight shake of his head. "He was told an immediate reply would be doubtful."

Sarah frowned at hearing this. "Did you recognize the livery?"

He nodded. "Torrington's, my lady," he said, at the very moment Anne let out an exclamation of excitement.

Barclay had to step aside when Trenton entered the breakfast parlor at the same moment as Anne's yelp.

"A note from Hexham?" he guessed.

"Indeed," Anne replied, her attention on the missive. She looked up in surprise, though. "How did you know?"

Her father bussed her mother on the cheek and then took his usual place at the table. Not about to admit he had heard her conversation with Gabe the night before, he merely shrugged. "I am your Father. I'm supposed to know these things," he replied, finding it difficult to keep a straight face. "Tell us what the future Earl of Torrington has written."

Anne read the letter aloud, knowing if she did not, her mother would merely take it from her and read it herself. "It's a dream come true!" she added as she held the note to her breast. "I can go, can I not?"

Sarah inhaled and looked to her husband, realizing he knew something she did not. "I'm sure your horse could use the exercise," she reasoned, her attention still on Trenton. "What say you, darling?"

Trenton gave a shrug as his plate was set before him. "I have no objections," he replied. "I suppose a groom should accompany you."

"At the very least," Sarah whispered.

Trenton gave her a knowing grin. "It snowed last night. Everything is white, and it's dashed cold. I rather doubt Hexham would try anything untoward." He lifted that morning's copy of *The Morning Chronicle* from the table and pretended to read.

Anne's smile was brilliant as she stood up and moved to kiss him on the cheek. "You are the very best father," she murmured, just before she attempted to take her leave of the breakfast parlor.

"Did you hear that?" Trenton asked as he regarded his countess. "I do not believe I have ever held that title before today." He turned his attention to the retreating back of his daughter. "Despite you're having dubbed me so, young lady, you will sit back down and eat your breakfast."

Anne gasped. "Might I send my answer with a footman first? I shouldn't like to keep the viscount waiting."

Trenton rolled his eyes as Sarah dimpled. "You may."

*B*efore Anne returned to the breakfast parlor and made her way back to her seat at the table, Sarah turned her attention on her husband. "You knew she was going to receive that invitation," she accused. "How did you know?"

He chuckled and returned his gaze to the newspaper. "I find I learn the most when no one knows I am in the room," he murmured. In a louder voice directed to Anne, he said, "You'll have plenty of time to decide on a riding habit after you've finished eating."

"Yes, Father," Anne replied, immediately tucking into her meal when she retook her seat.

As for the riding habit, she already knew which one she would wear. Her concern was making sure she was ready for conversation with the viscount.

Of course she had never danced with him at a ball. Never had an opportunity to speak with him other than those few minutes in the park the month before.

How could she learn more about him? Especially since her brother had already taken his leave of the house to go to the museum?

When she finished her meal, Anne took her leave of the breakfast parlor, nearly running in her haste to get to the library.

Surely there would be something there to help her.

CHAPTER 22

A KNIGHT CONSIDERS AN INVITATION

*L*ater that morning, at Bradford Hall

Peters regarded his master with a critical eye and stepped forward to adjust Ben's cravat. "That should do it, sir."

Ben nodded, not yet comfortable having Peters as his valet and butler. With such an empty household, though—just him and nine servants—it didn't seem necessary to employ a separate valet when Peters insisted he could fill the role. "I know I'm up a bit earlier than I expected, but could you see to a morning meal?"

"Breakfast is ready, sir, and your correspondence is on the table," Peters replied, his manner all business.

"Ah, very good." Ben paused a moment. "May I inquire as to how it is you knew I had a visitor last night?"

The butler angled his head, and seemed to think on the matter before he said, "I was about to deliver your tea when I saw her ladyship enter the observatory. She seemed... most *determined*." An eyebrow arched up, as if to emphasize the word 'determined.'

Ben cleared his throat. "There was a... a misunderstanding, is all. Tell me, do you know much about her family? Apart from the obvious, I mean."

Once again angling his head to one side, Peters seemed about to respond and then angled his head to the other side. "Her father is the Earl of Torrington, her mother is the sister of the Marquess of Devonfield, her brother has accepted a writ of acceleration and will attend Parliament come spring, and she has been out in Society some three years."

Furrowing his brows, Ben wondered at that last bit. One-and-twenty years old, and not married? Three seasons and no offers?

Then he remembered the letter from Torrington. He had dissuaded any potential suitors as unsuitable.

Could she be waiting for someone in particular?

The thought of 'me' had him rolling his eyes. She hadn't even known he existed until she was scolding him.

Despite how shocked he had been by her presence, he hadn't minded being scolded in the least.

"I cannot believe she is not betrothed," Ben murmured, even as he considered the contents of the letters he had reread the night before. If the Earl of Torrington's words were to be believed, Ben understood he already had the earl's permission to marry her.

"She is not," Peters intoned.

Did she intend to remain unmarried? Become a

spinster? Given the fortune she was probably due to inherit—or might already have—she could certainly afford to flaunt convention and spend her days doing whatever she wished to do.

Hire a companion and travel. Take up gambling and spend her blunt at a gaming hell. Buy up entire streets of townhouses and become a landlady. Start her own stables and raise racehorses. Build her own observatory and stargaze.

This last had Ben coming to his senses.

"Sir, if I might inquire as to your plans for the holiday?" Peters asked as they made their way down the stairs.

"Holiday?"

"Christmas, sir. Will you be here in town, or will you return to Suffolk?"

Ben entered the breakfast parlor and shook his head. "I do not wish to be at home in Suffolk," he replied, thinking he would prefer to be as far from his nieces and their mother as possible.

He wouldn't mind spending time with his brother, if only so he could punch Benedict in the jaw for the news contained in his letter. He knew it was unlikely they could escape the rest of the family, though. "I prefer to be here." He took a seat as a footman saw to filling a plate.

"Should the servants expect a Twelfth Night celebration?"

Familiar with the idea of serving a cake baked with a pea and a bean to the servants on the twelfth day of

Christmas—the two who received those slices would then be king and queen for the night—Ben thought the practice rather silly. "What if I simply gave them the day off? Christmas as well?"

Peters' eyes widened a fraction before he could get them under control. "That's very generous of you, sir. But... what will you do? And what about Boxing Day?"

Ben gave a shrug. "If the skies are clear on Christmas Eve, I shall spend the night in the observatory and then sleep Christmas Day. Do the same that night and on Boxing Day."

"But, what about meals?"

"I can raid the pantry, I suppose. I can boil water. Make my own tea. It's not as if I'll go hungry."

Peters seemed unsure before he finally gave a nod. "Very good, sir. I'll let the servants know during this evening's meal."

Ben gave a sideways glance at the footman who set a filled plate on the table. He was tempted to remind the butler he wouldn't need to—the footman would have the news relayed to everyone else in the household before they took their tea later that day.

After the butler departed, Ben read his correspondence. There was a short note from his brother congratulating him on the telescope, which meant Benedict had received the invoice. As he ate his coddled eggs, he noted his brother made no mention of the matter of his last letter.

Smart man. He had probably paid for the telescope as a bribe.

Next was an invitation to a special auction at Tattersall's, which promised a diverting afternoon admiring racehorses. Downing a rasher of bacon, he thought it unlikely he would ever have the funds to own a racehorse, let alone the stables and grooms required for such a sport.

The next letter was most welcome. That is, until he opened it.

An invitation to Somerset House for the next general meeting of the Royal Society, where twenty Fellows would be elected.

His name was not among those nominated.

Apparently, his discovery of a comet and subsequent knighting were not enough in the way of accomplishments in the eyes of those who chose the Fellow nominees.

Remembering Torrington's letter and the mention that Ben should get the honor, he ate another rasher of bacon. Having Torrington, his godfather, as his father-in-law was sounding better, but since the earl wasn't a member of the Society, he rather doubted the earl had much influence over the nomination committee.

Disheartened, Ben regarded the last two missives. They appeared identical, except in the manner in which they were addressed. One was made out to 'Mr. Fulton,' while the other was addressed to 'Sir Benjamin.' He opened both and laid them side by side.

Written in a feminine hand, the invitations gave off a familiar floral scent, and all thoughts of the Royal Society left his head.

Dear Mr. Fulton,

I am writing on behalf of my brother, George, Viscount Hexham, to respectfully request your company at a Dinner Party at Worthington House, Friday, December First, Eighteen-hundred and Thirty-eight, at Seven o'clock in the Evening. The Favour of a Reply is Requested.

Sincerely yours,
Lady Angelica
Post scriptum
The biscuit was indeed a good idea. And it was delicious. Thank you.

Ben blinked before a brilliant smile replaced his sour expression. His attention went to the second.

Sir Benjamin,

Milton, Earl of Torrington, requests the honor of your company at a dinner party to be held at Worthington House in Park Lane, Friday, December First, Eighteen-hundred-and-Thirty-eight at Seven o'clock in the evening. Although the earl will not be in attendance, his son, George, Viscount Hexham, will host in his stead. The favour of a reply is requested.

There was no signature, and given the two invitations, he realized two things at once.

Lady Angelica had no idea he was Sir Benjamin.

Lady Angelica had no desire to *meet* Sir Benjamin.

For a moment, he wondered how he would respond.

As Sir Benjamin?

Or Mr. Fulton?

Or both?

If he sent replies that he planned to attend on behalf of both names, there would be an extra, empty chair at the dining table. If he replied as Sir Benjamin, would he then send regrets as Mr. Fulton? Or vice versa?

He quickly finished his breakfast and hurried into his study to pen a response, deciding he rather liked how he was invited in the missive addressed to Mr. Fulton. Lady Angelica had obviously never met Sir Benjamin—he would know if she had—but then, neither had her brother.

He thought of the letters from Benedict and the Earl of Torrington, a mischievous grin forming. If he was to court Lady Angelica, he decided he would do so as a commoner. If she spurned him, then he would know it was better Sir Benjamin not consider her for matrimony.

The thought of her spurning him as Mr. Fulton had him almost changing his mind. A knight trumped a commoner, after all. But then he remembered her kiss, and he took pen to paper.

Dear Lady Angelica,

I hadn't thought to hear from you so soon after our last meeting. So glad the biscuit was of help, although I shudder to think of what might have happened to you should you have been without it. I do hope your brother did not scold you over much. Having an older brother myself, I understand what life with one is like.

Thank you for the dinner invitation. I shall be there in the hopes I am seated somewhere near to you. Until then,

Sincerely yours,

Ben Fulton

Post scriptum

Truly, I am not a Peeping Tom, but I do look forward to seeing you again.

He regarded the note for a moment, wondering if he was making a mistake in not signing it with the 'Sir' in front of his name. Doing so now would call attention to it, though, since it would be out of alignment with the rest of his carefully written lines. And he had decided to keep his knighthood a secret from her. At least, for now.

In a second note, this one signed with 'Sir Benjamin,' he sent his regrets with a note that he would not be in town.

Satisfied, he folded the notes, wrote *The Lady Angelica Grandby, Worthington House* on the outside, and applied a puddle of wax where the four corners were joined. About to stamp both with a seal made up of his initials, he instead opted for the one with a crescent moon and stars for his response as Mr. Fulton.

He wondered if she would even notice.

Summoning a footman, he instructed the tall man to deliver them at different times of the day.

Another moment, and he glanced over at the letters from the earls. Perhaps it best he send a letter of introduction to George Grandby. Otherwise, he might not be welcome to set foot in Worthington House.

Invited or not.

CHAPTER 23

A VISCOUNT SEEKS ADVICE

*L**ater that day, at Worthington House*

Angelica emerged from her salon with ink-stained fingers and a desire for a cup of tea and a biscuit. She had penned fifteen invitations for the dinner party following the sample her brother had provided, sealed them all with wax, and stamped them with her brother's Hexham seal.

She found George in his study, his head resting in one hand as he read a book. "A tragedy?" she guessed as she entered the wood-paneled room. The thick Aubusson carpeting not only cushioned her feet but seemed to absorb any extraneous sounds that might have come from the window behind the mahogany desk where her brother sat.

George regarded her with a grimace. "More like a comedy of errors," he replied. He leaned back in the chair and stared up at the coffered ceiling. "I may have… I may have made a mistake," he murmured.

Angelica inhaled sharply. "Surely not. What has happened?"

Rolling his eyes, George leaned forward and clasped his hands together. "As you know, I invited Lady Anne for a ride in the park," he replied. He ignored Angelica's feigned gasp—she had heard the invitation during breakfast that very morning—and added, "I know absolutely nothing about her. I've just spent the last hour reading about the Trentons in DeBrett's, and I still know nothing."

Allowing an impish grin, Angelica said, "What do you wish to know?"

George blinked. "Everything there is to know."

"Has she accepted the offer?"

Nodding, George said, "Yes. Which is why I find myself attempting to learn everything there is to know about her," he said again, looking as if he had stayed up entirely too late the night before. Well, he had returned from White's later than usual. "A footman delivered a verbal response about an hour ago. A happy yes, if I'm to understand the message after it had passed onto another footman and then to Winslow."

"I can only imagine," Angelica murmured. "I'm surprised I didn't hear her scream."

"What?"

"Nothing," Angelica said with a shake of her head.

"I probably would have had more notice if I had simply had our footman wait for a response."

"Probably," Angelica agreed.

"So tell me everything you know about her."

Leaning back in her chair, Angelica allowed a sigh. "Nearly eighteen, Lady Anne is the only daughter of the Earl and Countess of Trenton—"

"I know that."

"She had a governess from Wolverhampton whilst living in Trenton Manor and then was tutored at home for two years alongside her brother, William, heir to the earldom."

"Tutored?" George repeated. "Isn't that rather... unusual?"

Angelica allowed a shrug. "I sat in on your lessons," she replied.

Frowning, George said, "But I didn't know you were actually paying attention."

She gave him a quelling glance. "I had to pretend I wasn't, of course, but I was," she claimed, and then angled her head to one side. "Usually."

"So... she's educated," George reasoned.

"Her mother would have demanded it even if Trenton didn't wish it."

"The former manager of a coaching inn?" he countered. "There's an implication in one of these books that she was a... a serving wench."

"At one time she was. A barmaid. She understood the business of running a coaching inn, and she made the best of it by assuming the managerial duties when the owner's wife took ill," Sarah explained. "And despite marrying an earl, she continued to oversee the inn for several years until she could promote her protégé to the position."

"Another woman, I suppose?" George guessed.

"Indeed," Angelica answered, tamping down her ire at hearing the tone of his comment. "The Spread Eagle Inn, now an unentailed property of the Trenton earldom, is regarded as one of the best coaching inns in all of Staffordshire."

George sighed. "So now I know about her mother. What about Lady Anne?"

"She attended finishing school, one year of it here in London—"

"Warwick's," George murmured, remembering that was how Angelica and Anne had originally met.

"Yes," Angelica affirmed. "She finished last spring, and there was some thought she might go another year, but she argued that she wished to marry and start a family—"

"What about her Season?" George asked, his brows furrowing. All daughters of aristocrats wanted a Season. An opportunity to attend the entertainments. To see and to be seen.

Angelica angled her head to the other side. "She would gladly forgo it if she had an offer of marriage," she whispered. "And you did not hear that from me."

George's eyes widened. "How is it *you* know such a thing?"

His sister averted her eyes a moment. "She told me once, in confidence. I was at Warwick's to pay a call on another student, and she joined us for tea," she explained. "I had just finished my second Season that very month, and I remember I was bereft. I felt as if I had failed Father."

"You didn't fail Father," George said on a sigh.

"I didn't have a single offer of marriage," Angelica complained.

"Because Father wouldn't allow any of those twits to make an offer," he argued.

"Well, I know that *now*," she replied on a sigh. "I rather wish I had known it *then*." After a pause, she added, "You can speak of just about any topic with Lady Anne."

Dipping his head, he said, "Thank you. Is there just one that I would do the best with?"

Angelica dimpled. "Family. Marriage. Children."

"I was thinking that discussion might happen during our *second* meeting," he reasoned.

"Ask what she likes and doesn't like."

George straightened, obviously intrigued. "Such as?"

Rolling her eyes, Angelica just then remembered her brother had never courted anyone. "Her favorite flower. Then you'll know what to have delivered from one of the hothouses in Chiswick," she replied quickly. "Favorite color. Best holiday. Does she like horse races? Or the theatre? Favorite dance—"

"If she says the Scottish reel, then there is no hope for us," George stated as he leaned back in his chair.

Angelia gave him a quelling glance. "I'm so glad I won't be marrying *you*," she whispered. "Although every young woman's favorite dance is the waltz, and if you didn't know that, then it is entirely too early for you to be courting anyone."

"I like the waltz," George murmured.

"What time are you to take her for the ride?"

George sighed. "Three o'clock."

Angelica glanced at the clock that sat on the fireplace mantle and arched a brow. "Today?"

George followed her line of sight and then let out a curse. "I must change clothes right now," he said, and without another word, he took his leave of the study.

Grinning, Angelica sighed and briefly wondered if she might be able to spy on the couple. Given the weather and the layer of white that covered the park, she decided she would be noticed should she follow on horseback. Or even on foot.

Her gaze went to the telescope. If she could move it to the top story of the house and point it out one of the front windows, she just might be able to watch the couple as they made their way toward Rotten Row.

"Winston!" she called out.

The butler appeared almost immediately, which had her thinking he might have been eavesdropping on their conversation. "I need a footman to move the telescope to the top floor of the house. Is there an unused servant's quarters up there that looks out over the park?"

Winston's gaze settled on the instrument a moment. "Your lady's maid has vacated her quarters in favor of a room with her new husband," he replied. "That room's window faces Park Lane."

"That will do," she said happily. "I wish to bird watch."

His brows lifting to nearly his hairline, Winston asked, "Have you a particular kind of bird in mind?" Given the weather, he doubted she would see many.

Angelica allowed a brilliant smile. "Indeed. Turtle doves," she replied. "Two of them."

CHAPTER 24

FINALLY, A RIDE IN THE PARK

An hour later

"How do I look?" Anne asked, when her mother joined her in her bedchamber. She was wearing a sapphire riding habit with a pair of black boots and a rather sedate blue felt hat featuring several peacock feathers.

Standing in her black heeled riding boots, she stood as tall as her mother.

"Like a vision in blue," Sarah said with a sigh. Her daughter's blonde curls had been tamed into an elegant coiffure that added a few years to her apparent age. Given her cornflower blue eyes and ivory complexion, the sapphire riding habit was the perfect choice.

"The groom has brought your horse around to the front. Grimsby will be joining you—" Sarah ignored Anne's look of disappointment—"but he has strict instructions to remain at least ten feet behind you at all times."

Anne's eyes widened in delight. "Thank you."

"Oh, do not thank me," Sarah replied with a shake of her head. "Your father gave Grimsby those instructions."

Smiling, Anne wondered at the earl's permissiveness and was about to ask, but her mother said, "I think he likes the idea of you married to a... to a younger aristocrat."

Gasping, Anne said, "I am not even sure yet if Hexham is courting me."

Sarah nearly rolled her eyes. "Oh, he is courting you," she stated, her manner suggesting she had confirmed it with someone who knew.

Anne blinked. "Who... who told you?"

It was Sarah's turn to blink. "Who told *you*?" she countered. "And why didn't you tell me?"

Her eyes darting to one side, Anne wondered how to respond. She had an agreement with Gabe that she would say nothing. He had the same agreement with her, so if he hadn't said anything to their mother, then who...?

"Your father told me," Sarah admitted. "I can only suppose Hexham sent him a note before the invitation to ride arrived, or... or perhaps he asked his permission in person."

Anne let out the breath she'd been holding. "Well, then." She dipped her head. "I spent this morning in the library, trying to learn everything I could about the Torrington earldom," she said, her words hopeful. "I thought I could find something to help in my conversations with the viscount."

Impressed by her daughter's willingness to research a potential husband, Sarah regarded Anne with a wan grin. "And did you?"

Anne sighed. "Not very much," she admitted.

"So after he has asked a question and you have answered, then it will be your turn to ask one of him," Sarah said.

"Such as?"

Sarah shrugged. "What's his favorite color? Does he prefer the theatre or horse racing? Is he reading a particularly diverting book?" She paused. "What do you wish to know about him?"

Her eyes widening, Anne gave this last query a good deal of thought before she said, "How many children he would like. What time he prefers his dinner. Does he like to be kissed? If so, how often? Will he employ a mistress—?"

"I rather doubt you should ask him that last question," Sarah warned.

"I wasn't going to ask any of them," Anne countered. "Those are merely the things I would like to know about him."

Barclay cleared his throat, which had the two turning their attention to the butler. He stood on the threshold of the open door, apparently not wishing to interrupt their conversation. "Lord Hexham has paid a call and is asking if you are in residence, Lady Anne."

Nervousness gripped Anne. "Color, horse racing,

book, theatre," she recited as she regarded her mother. "It is not funny," she added when she noted how Sarah seemed to be suppressing a grin at her expense.

"It is not," Sarah agreed. "But it can be enjoyable. If you two are meant to suit, then you will."

Anne nodded and directed her gaze on Barclay "Yes, I am in residence, and I shall be right down." She, in fact, hurried past him and made her way down the two flights of marble stairs, her boots barely making any sound on the steps.

She was on the last landing down when she realized George Grandby was watching her from where he stood just beyond the vestibule.

"How do, Hexham?" she managed, slowing her descent in an effort to catch her breath. When she reached the bottom, she dipped a curtsy.

*G*eorge swallowed and then remembered to take her hand. She hadn't yet pulled on her gloves, but held them in her other hand. He bowed and kissed the back of her bare knuckles, aware his touch had set off something in her hand from the way it trembled.

Or perhaps those were his lips that trembled.

He couldn't remember ever having been this nervous before. Not even during exams at university.

"Lady Anne. It's so good to see you again," he murmured.

"And you as well," she replied, relieved to find he

didn't stand too much taller than she did. Dancing with him would be easy. Kissing wouldn't require she stand on tiptoe.

Blinking, she wondered from where that thought had come. Perhaps it was because he had kissed the back of her hand, and he still held onto it.

She thought to give it a slight tug so he would let go, but there was a pleasant sensation accompanying the warmth of his fingers. "Thank you for inviting me to ride with you today. Although we've only just returned to town yesterday, I am quite happy for the diversion."

His eyes widened. "Me as well," he said. He struggled with what to say next, and then remembered one of his sister's recommendations.

Favorite colors.

"I thought my favorite color was green, like the color of leaves and grass, but... now I do believe it is blue. Definitely blue," he murmured, his gaze going down her riding habit and then back to her eyes.

Anne allowed a grin. "I adore blue, too, although there are times when purple seems rather elegant."

"You would look positively glorious wearing purple," he murmured. "Or any color, really. Or nothing..."

His eyes squeezed shut at the same moment Anne blinked, and she could feel a blush staining her cheeks. "I'll remember that when I'm allowed to wear something other than white to a ball," she replied, well aware he still held onto her hand.

Apparently her father was as well, for Trenton

cleared his throat as he leaned against the doorjamb of his study. "You'll run out of questions for each other if you ask them all before you've even left the house," he teased.

George gave a start and turned to regard the earl with a nervous nod. Had the earl overheard his last remark?

Anne directed a quelling glance at her father and then remembered to do the introductions. "Hexham, have you met my father, Gabriel, Earl of Torrington?" She would have used her hand to wave in her father's direction, but George was still hanging onto it.

Trenton straightened and approached the couple. "We have met, of course," he said as he held out his right hand. "Hexham. I understand you'll be joining us in Parliament at the next session. Congratulations."

Forced to let go of Anne's hand to shake Trenton's, George just then realized how long he'd been holding onto it. "Thank you, sir. It's good to see you again." He paused a moment. "We won't stay out more than an hour or so, given the chill in the air."

"Ride for as long as you wish," Trenton replied. "But I trust you'll have her home before dark."

"Oh, of course," George agreed, heartened when Anne made a slight mewl of protest at hearing her father's edict. George offered his arm. "Shall we?"

Anne dipped her head and placed her arm on the viscount's, but she managed to give her father a scolding glance. "I'll see you at dinner, Father."

They made their way to where the groom held

onto the reins of two horses. The one on which George had ridden was Hermes, a bay stallion with black stockings and a white blaze between his eyes. The other, Anne's horse, was a small, gray Irish walker named Graydon.

The groom had brought a mounting block, and Anne made quick work of pulling on her leather gloves before climbing onto the side-saddle. She took a moment to ensure her riding habit splayed over the side of her horse before she accepted the riding crop from the groom.

"I do hope it's not too cold for you," George said as he mounted the bay. His greatcoat had swept over the back of his horse as he mounted, and with his short top hat, buff riding breeches, deep scarlet waistcoat, and pristine white cravat, he looked every inch the aristocrat.

"It's rather invigorating," Anne replied as she urged her mount into motion. George followed suit, and the two made their way up Park Lane to the next entrance into Hyde Park, Stanhope Gate.

Remembering more of his sister's recommendations, George said, "I couldn't help but notice the flowers in your hall. Very beautiful, and a surprise given the time of year. Hydrangeas, are they not?"

Anne realized his comments were to determine her favorite flower. "My father has a hothouse deliver them for my mother whenever we return to Mayfair," she said with a grin. "She adores them."

"And you?"

Anne gave him a brilliant smile. "I like whatever is blooming in the gardens," she said with a shrug.

"And when they are not? Like now?"

"Roses are my favorites," she finally acknowledged. "They are not bound by color restrictions and always give off the most pleasant scent."

She was about to ask him what his favorite flower was, but realized, as a man, he probably didn't have one. She remembered the invitation to the dinner party, though. "I received the most welcome correspondence earlier today."

"Oh?" George's response sounded strained, as if he wouldn't find it as welcome as she had.

"The invitation to your dinner party."

His manner changed instantly, and his response was quick. "Will you attend?"

Anne dimpled. "I would not miss it," she replied. "May I ask what special occasion has prompted such an entertainment?"

"Occasion?" he repeated.

She shrugged as the horses made their way along a crushed granite path that led to Rotten Row. Given the entrance they had taken into the park, they would be coming to the King's Private Road from the east and north. "A special event? A birthday, perhaps?"

"Ah, nothing but an opportunity to gather those of us who are spending Christmastide in town." But then he drew in a breath and said, "May I tell you something in confidence?"

Anne's eyes widened. "Of course, my lord."

George dipped his head before he said, "It's an opportunity to introduce my sister to the man she may very well marry."

Inhaling sharply, Anne regarded him with a look of shock. "She hasn't met the man she's going to marry?"

He shook his head. "Well, not this particular man. He is new to town, and my father is of the opinion he will make a suitable husband," he explained.

"Does *she* know this?"

He allowed a chuckle, although the humor left his face as quickly as it appeared. "She does now. I told her on the train yesterday."

Anne lifted her face to the sky and noted how gray clouds were once again filling in the blue, just as they had done the day before. "How did she take it?"

Sighing, George gave a self-deprecating grin and said, "If I hadn't made such a cake of explaining it to her, I think it would have gone far better," he replied.

"But she's willing to meet him?" she half-questioned.

He nodded. "She is. She sent invitations out this morning for the dinner party, and I expect we'll begin receiving responses on the morrow. I only hope the gentleman will agree to attend."

"Have *you* met your potential brother?"

George directed their horses to take the path heading south that would soon intersect with Rotten Row. A few trees and hedgerows and the east end of the Serpentine were the only hints that the King's Private Road lay just ahead. "I have not," he admitted.

"But you know his name?" she asked, just before she slowed and then halted her horse.

"Of course. He's Wadsworth's brother, Benjamin."

Anne pulled her attention from her horse's withers, her eyes wide with delight. "Sir Benjamin?"

"You know him?"

Anne dimpled again. "I only met him the one time, a few years ago," she replied. One of her blonde brows furrowed. "He wasn't a knight back then, but I remember he was quite a bit a older than us," she remarked, "but a fine gentleman."

"Where was this?" George asked, his gaze going to her horse. For some reason, she had pulled him to a halt.

"He was giving a lecture in Wolverhampton, and Father insisted we attend with him," she explained, looking as if she was going to dismount. "He thought it would be diverting, and it was. I could have listened to Sir Benjamin speak for far longer than the hour he was scheduled."

"What is wrong?" George asked, turning his mount around to face hers.

Anne slid the end of her crop down her mount's front leg until the walker lifted his hoof and then lowered it, gingerly, to the ground. "I think he's picked up a rock is all," she replied. She turned on the saddle, intending to get the groom's attention, but then realized that Grimsby wasn't behind them. A quick glance to her other side proved he wasn't riding to the side of them, either.

Had he even joined them on the ride at all?

George was down from his mount in an instant, hurrying over to examine the hoof. "Indeed he has," he agreed, once she repeated her means of making the horse lift his hoof. George made quick work of removing the stone with the edge of his thumb, but he hissed at seeing the indentation left behind. "That should do it, but he still might limp a bit."

"Oh, I can walk. I don't mind," she said.

"We'll just have your groom..." He glanced back the way they had come and then in the direction of Stanhope Gate. "Did... did he go a different way?"

Anne dimpled when she realized no one had instructed the groom to join her on the ride. "Back to the stables, no doubt," she said with a chuckle, just then remembering there hadn't been a third horse in front of the house.

George glanced up at her, concern etched on his face. "Do you wish to go back?"

She shook her head. "No. We can walk for a spell, if you don't mind."

"I don't mind," he said, as he made his way around her horse so he could lift her down. "You're quite sure you don't mind being seen with me? Without a chaperone?"

She turned her gaze on him and gave a brilliant smile. "Of course I don't mind. Besides, who would see us?"

A quick glance proved there were very few people about in the park.

His hands went to her waist while hers went to his shoulders, and for a moment, Anne felt as if she were floating on air. Although she could see her breath—translucent white clouds billowing in front of her—her attention was entirely on George. On his bright blue eyes and the bit of blond hair that appeared beneath the brim of his top hat. On his perfectly straight nose and the angular cheekbones that identified him as an aristocrat.

And on his lips. Lips that had opened slightly. Lips that touched hers at the same moment her feet touched the ground.

Although Anne had never been kissed before, she was fairly sure she knew what to do. She had seen her parents do it hundreds of times.

She moved a hand to behind his neck, just as she had seen her mother do, and then she angled her head slightly, reveling in how his lips seemed to lock into place over hers.

The scent of his cologne surrounded her in the warmth of citrus and bergamot. The taste of him hinted of mint. The air around her crackled with excitement. Her heart beat a tattoo she was sure he could hear, if not feel, through their coats as their bodies pressed against one another for support.

And they might have continued the kiss for another moment or two but for George's impatient horse.

The stallion nudged her arm, and when Anne ignored him, Hermes nudged her again. Harder.

Anne giggled as she was forced to pull away from

George. "Who needs a groom when a horse will act as a chaperone?" she asked in a light voice, her brilliant grin directed at his mount.

George had never felt such jealousy of an animal in his entire life.

Nor annoyance.

"My apologies. I...," George started to say, but Anne placed a gloved finger to his lips.

"Please don't. It was my first kiss, and I shouldn't wish to remember it as anything other than the most delectable treat it was," she murmured.

She didn't care if her blush covered her entire body. As chilly as it was, she rather doubted her embarrassment could be discerned from the rosiness already staining her cheeks.

"You thought it a delectable treat?"

Anne's eyes widened as she wondered if he might be teasing. "I did."

George's lips were on hers once more, his arms wrapping around her redingote to pull her closer. He kissed her thoroughly, his mouth open enough that he could slip his tongue past her lips to slide over her pearly teeth.

After a moment, hers did the same, although more tentatively. She might have attempted to do more, but once again, Hermes nudged her shoulder and then George's, far harder, nearly knocking both of them over.

Forced to separate, the two regarded one another, Anne displaying a grin of embarrassment while George turned his look of annoyance on the horse. "I've a mind to sell you at Tattersall's," he murmured.

A nicker was the bay stallion's only response.

Anne giggled again, the musical sound causing the horse to step closer to her. "Perhaps we should walk," she suggested, as she retrieved the reins of her mount and lifted them over his head.

"Indeed," George agreed, his gaze surveying the area around them. He had a sudden thought that they might have been seen. Hedgerows hid them from anyone to the north and somewhat to the south, and a few trees provided some privacy from the east. Given the cold, there was no one standing along the edge of the Serpentine.

Perhaps no one had spotted them while they embraced.

Relieved, he offered his arm and they continued on the path to the King's Private Road.

For a time, neither said anything until George asked, "Pray tell, was that really your first kiss?"

Anne dared a glance in his direction, surprised to find his eyes directed straight ahead. "Was it that obvious?" she asked, her voice sounding with disappointment. "It's not as if one can practice."

His head quickly turned and he regarded her with a look of surprise. "Your effort was not the least bit lacking," he assured her. "Which is why I asked."

Anne furrowed her blonde brows. "You've obviously had experience," she accused, although her words were light.

"If you can count a serving wench's attempt to kiss me in a public tavern in Oxford experience," he countered, and then he rolled his eyes. "I did not initiate it, of course," he hastened to add.

"But you did not stop it," she said, a brilliant smile appearing when he looked suitably chagrined.

"As you said, it's not as if we can practice," he murmured, his manner rather sober.

"Will you enjoy kissing your wife once you are wed?" Anne asked, remembering some of the topics of conversation she had discussed with her mother.

"I suppose it depends on who I am kissing," he replied, a grin finally replacing his somber expression.

"And your children? Will there be just a few? Or a brood?"

He dipped his head. "I suppose there will be as many as my wife will allow. I surely would like more than just two."

"And will you hire a...?" Anne clamped her mouth shut, stunned by her sudden boldness. Hexham was so easy to converse with, she hadn't thought to censor her questions.

"Hire a...?" he prompted. When Anne didn't offer a reply, he stopped on the path and turned to face her. "What?"

Anne's eyes darted to the side. "Forgive me. It's really none of my business. I don't know why I thought to bring it up—"

"A mistress?" he offered. "Is that what you were

about to say?" His expression displayed as much disbelief as it did disappointment.

She closed her eyes and nodded.

"I hadn't thought to," George whispered.

Anne's eyes opened, and she swallowed, sure he was angry with her. "My father used to employ them. Before he married my mother," she whispered. "Three of them, apparently."

"As did my father, and probably far more than three," he admitted in a quiet voice. "But not after he married my mother." He used a glove hand to lift her chin. "When I marry, it shall be for more than just duty. I have no intention of dishonoring my wife in such a manner," he murmured.

Anne eyes' widened, and she allowed a wan smile. "Then she will be a very happy wife, indeed."

George nodded. "I am glad to hear it," he said, a bemused expression replacing the harsh one he had displayed only the moment before. He once again surveyed the area around them.

"What is it?" Anne asked, her gaze taking in their surroundings.

"I... I have some questions."

Anne blinked. "For me?"

He nodded. "What's your favorite holiday?"

"Christmas."

"Do you like horse races?"

Anne inhaled. "I've never been to one, but they sound ever so exciting."

"Oh, they are," he assured her.

"Do you own a race horse?" she asked.

He shook his head. "I do not. But I might one day." He paused and took a deep breath. "Do you like the theatre?"

Anne seemed to consider the query for a time before she replied. "Usually. Sometimes the plays are tedious, but I like the operas and the naval reenactments, and I enjoy the experience of going to the theatre. And you?"

"The same, although I usually enjoy the dramas more than operas. I fear my understanding of Italian is a bit lacking," he admitted. "What's your favorite dance?"

Anne angled her head and seemed to struggle for a moment. "I've only ever danced with a dance master or... or one of my brothers," she replied, a reminder that she hadn't yet attended a formal *ton* ball. "But I think I like the waltz the best. Is that still scandalous to say?"

He shook his head and bestowed her with another kiss. A quick one. A kiss that surprised her as much as it did his horse, for Hermes reared his head and let out a whinny of protest before he had a chance to nudge either one of them.

"Do you have a favorite book?" she asked in a whisper, a bit concerned when she realized they had already discussed all the other questions she could remember to ask.

He furrowed a brow. "I so rarely read for pleasure," he murmured. "But there's one on breeding race horses that's especially interesting. Makes it very clear why it can take so many generations to create a contender for the Derby."

"I suppose it involves choosing the perfect dam and sire to create a fast colt," she mused.

"Or one with endurance," he countered.

"Or both," she suggested.

George regarded her a moment, his eyes glazed over as if he were lost in thought. "Have you thought of what your children will look like?"

Anne dimpled. "They will look just like yours."

"You're referring to the blond hair and blue eyes?"

Her grin broadened to a smile. "And the curls. They'll look just like little cherubs. And probably be just as mischievous."

"Will you do me the honor of becoming my wife?"

Anne stared at George, her lips still red from their kiss. "I will," she replied with a nod. Then she giggled. "I will."

George wrapped his arms around her shoulders and pulled her into a hug. And he would have continued to hold onto her but for the nose of a horse that was determined to separate them.

"That's it. He's going up for sale," George announced.

Anne giggled again before her expression sobered. "Perhaps it would be best if we didn't tell anyone of our betrothal just yet," she murmured.

His eyes widening with understanding, George nodded. "Agreed. With such a sudden announcement, people might think we've been carrying on a clandestine *affaire.*"

"Kissing behind hedgerows."

"Going for rides without a chaperone."

"Meeting in the park in broad daylight," she whispered.

"Like that day we met," George murmured.

"I was sure I felt something in the air."

"It positively crackled with energy," George agreed.

"Angels were singing."

"Thunder roared."

"And the rain poured down."

Anne blinked as a snowflake caught on the edge of an eyelash, and she looked up. Despite the bit of blue directly above them, the rest of the sky was gray, and the air smelled of snow.

"I thought of nothing but you that entire night," George whispered.

"And I, you," Anne said on a sigh. She angled her head up and kissed him once more as his arms surrounded her, and he held her close.

This time, it was Anne's mount that whinnied loudly.

George laughed as the snow fell in large flakes, dancing about their heads with every breath. "I should get you home," he said on sigh. "I shouldn't want you catching a cold on the day of my proposal," he added as he grabbed his mount's reins. "Or ever for that matter."

The four made their way back to Stanhope Gate the way they had come, and then, because Anne's walker no longer limped, George lifted his betrothed onto the side-saddle. They made their way back to Curzon Street and to Trenton House.

"I'll see you at the dinner party," Anne said, after George had escorted her to the front door.

"I do not believe I can wait that long to see you," he replied, kissing the back of her gloved hand.

"Then I look forward to seeing you tomorrow," she said with a grin.

Barclay opened the door, and Anne gave George one more glance before heading inside.

George merely gave the butler a nod and hurried back to his mount.

When the Trenton's groom appeared to retrieve Anne's mount, George was tempted to ask why he hadn't joined them on the ride. When he saw the groom give him a wink, though, George tipped his hat.

Despite the falling snow, George took his time getting back to Worthington House. For despite having sent a note to the Earl of Trenton asking if he might be allowed to take Lady Anne for a ride in the park, he hadn't exactly asked for permission to court the young lady.

Once he was back in his study, he would have to see to writing a letter. He had until then to sort just what he was going to include in the letter.

Just how much should a man admit to his future father-in-law?

A SPY KNOWS

The hour before, on the top floor of Worthington House

Angelica glanced out the window of the small servant's room in an effort to determine how much of the park she could see from her high vantage. Although there were trees scattered throughout the park, she could make out the Serpentine in the distance as well as the straight outlines of the crushed granite paths that led through the east end of the park.

A row of trees hid her view of most of Rotten Row, though, and she nearly gave up on her plan to spy on her brother and Lady Anne.

That is, until she spotted two people on horseback crossing Park Lane near the Stanhope Gate. The one wearing the blue riding habit had to be Lady Anne.

Angelica quickly aimed her father's telescope in the direction of the gate. Mounted on a tripod, the long instrument was at least easy to aim. However, given its height and the odd angle at which it was directed, it was awkward to bend her body and head so that she could look through the lens at the other end of the tube.

Mr. Fulton's telescope was far more comfortable to use, she thought as she made some adjustments with the knob that changed the focus.

A few scary moments had her lifting her head away from the lens and letting out a small shriek. One occurred when a bird in flight suddenly filled the field of vision, and the other was when she had the scope aimed at a dog in the act of doing his business at the park's east edge.

Just about the time she had the telescope focused and knew her brother was indeed one of those on horseback, he had moved out of the field of view.

She quickly readjusted the direction, pausing when she had Lady Anne—or rather, her blue hat with the peacock feathers—in view. A slight downward adjustment brought the two into view. From the way their heads moved, she was convinced the two were conversing.

Lady Anne looked happy, Angelica thought, even though it must have been cold. White clouds surrounded the nostrils of her mount and puffed out in front of her brother's face.

She could tell the two were headed for Rotten Row once they had negotiated the angled turn on the path. From her perspective, she could watch their retreating backs through the scope without having to move it very much.

Unable to hear the couple's conversation, Angelica found she was growing bored. What good was it to spy on them when their backs were to her? She couldn't see if they were speaking to one another, let alone guess what they might be saying.

And then Lady Anne's gray mount began limping. A few steps later, and he stopped. Hermes stopped. Her brother dismounted and hurried around to the gray walker's front, although from her vantage, Angelica couldn't tell what he was studying.

Had the horse gone lame?

Apparently so, for she watched as George helped Anne down from her mount. Down until her feet touched the ground and his lips touched hers.

Angelica blinked and pulled away from the telescope, redirecting her attention out the window. From this distance, she could barely see them, let alone see that they were...

Kissing.

They were definitely kissing.

And not just a brief kiss like the one she had bestowed on Mr. Fulton the night before, but a long and languorous kiss like the kiss Mr. Fulton had bestowed on her.

Angelica couldn't tear her gaze away from the lens.

She remembered Mr. Fulton's kiss from the night before, how it had warmed her, and how it had sent delicious sensations through her entire body. How it had left her happy but wanting more.

Sighing, she gave her head a shake in an effort to clear away the vision at the very moment the bay stallion seemed to have had enough of standing around doing nothing. He used his head to push against Lady Anne's shoulder, freeing her from George's hold.

Smart horse.

At least Lady Anne's expression displayed her amusement, but George looked as if he was making plans to sell the horse at auction.

Angelica let out a huff. The bay stallion that stood behind George wasn't even his horse. It was hers!

How dare he!

Then she realized George and Anne were no longer kissing but walking their horses on the southerly path to Rotten Row.

A moment later, and they disappeared from view, a combination of hedgerows and trees hiding them from the telescope's view.

Angelica sat down on the small bed.

Had George proposed already? If so, would he tell her over dinner that night? Or pretend nothing had happened with Trenton's only daughter?

Surely a chaperone would have prevented—

Angelica straightened on the bed.

She hadn't seen a chaperone following the couple. Not even a groom on horseback!

Perhaps she had simply missed him. Overlooked

him. Or perhaps he had been parked on the other side of the hedgerow in an effort to give the couple some privacy.

Which really wasn't the point of being a chaperone, unless her brother had given the man some blunt to look the other way for a time.

She had never thought George would take liberties with a young lady. Certainly not with Lady Anne. Her father was an earl. Should word get back to him that his daughter was seen kissing Hexham in the park, there might be hell to pay.

Or her brother would be forced to marry Lady Anne.

Which, now that she thought about it, might have been the reason her brother had kissed Lady Anne in the first place!

The devious devil!

She once again moved to the telescope, determined to discover what might have happened to the groom. Surveying the area around where she had last glimpsed the couple, she found only the couple. They had turned around and were now making their way back toward Park Lane, neither one of them on horseback.

And there was still no groom in sight.

The two were chatting amicably, though, and once they reached the gate, her brother lifted Lady Anne onto her horse and he mounted the bay. A moment later, and they disappeared from view, probably headed for Curzon Street.

Angelica couldn't decide if she was happy for her brother or not. She liked Lady Anne, though. She would be delighted to have her as a sister.

It would be far better if Anne was to be her sister because the two had agreed to wed without *having* to do so, though.

But did the poor girl have any idea what life with George would be like?

Angelica rolled her eyes. *George would be perfectly fine to live with*, she thought with a sigh. *I am the troublesome one.*

About to wallow in pity, she remembered the telescope. Her brother would no doubt notice its absence from the study and ask as to its whereabouts.

He wasn't a dull man. He would sort very quickly what Angelica had been doing with the instrument on the top floor of the house.

Unable to locate a footman, Angelica determined how to separate the telescope from the tripod. She managed to get the tripod down the three flights of stairs, back into the study, and into place with no problem.

After she had climbed the three flights back up and was in the servant's room, she lifted the telescope into her arms, much like she would a baby. She was down two flights of stairs and about to go down the last flight when she realized George was regarding her from the bottom of the same set of stairs.

"Whatever are you doing with Father's telescope?"

he asked as he handed his riding crop and top hat to Winslow.

"Bird watching," Angelica replied. "A raven frightened me to death, though, so I have given up." She continued down the stairs and was nearly past him when he cleared his throat.

"Bird watching?" he repeated.

"Yes. I was looking for one of those snow buntings that we sometimes see at Christmas at Torrington Park," she replied, sounding ever so reasonable.

But then she remembered the horse.

"And what do you think you are doing taking *my* horse for a ride in the park without asking?" she scolded.

George rolled his eyes and managed to look suitably chagrined. "Hermes needed the exercise," he countered, and then his brows furrowed. "How did you know I took your horse?"

"Because I saw you riding him right after the raven flew in front of the telescope," she replied. "Nearly frightened me to death," she added, just before she disappeared into the study.

Following her into the room, George halted as he watched her remount the scope to the tripod. She angled it just as it had been before it had been removed from the room, and then she turned to march past him.

George stepped into her path, and she nearly bowled into him. "You were spying on me," he accused.

Angelica's eyes widened in alarm. "I was not," she countered. When she noted how his expression indicated disbelief, she added, "You were simply in my line of sight when it came to the birds I was following." Her hands went to her hips. "You do realize that anyone could have seen you kissing Lady Anne," she said in a hoarse whisper, sure Winslow was standing just outside the door.

"Ah! So you *were* spying on me!"

"I was keeping watch over Lady Anne, since her chaperone seemed to have disappeared. Or got lost, or—"

"Never joined us," he finished for her. At her elegantly arched eyebrows, he knew he had stunned her into silence. "The man winked at me when I returned Lady Anne to Trenton House."

Angelica frowned. "So... how much did you have to pay him to stay behind?"

George let out a sound of disbelief. "I didn't," he replied quickly. "I truly thought he was following us until... until I realized he wasn't there. I offered to take Lady Anne back as soon as I discovered his absence, but she refused."

Rolling her eyes, Angelica said, "Of course, she refused. She must have known you were going to kiss her."

"I don't know how," he responded. "I didn't know until... until I was doing it. It was all just... just a happy accident."

Angelica angled her head to one side. "Your lips just *accidentally* collided with hers?"

George's eyes darted to one side. "Pretty much." He

watched as all the air seemed to go out of his sister. Along with the indignation. "You won't tell anyone, will you?"

She crossed her arms and allowed a sigh. "All that would do is force her into marriage with you, and I already know she's who you wish to wed, so what good would it do?" Her eyes widened, and then she inhaled softly. "Unless she doesn't wish to wed *you*," she whispered.

"Of course she does. Otherwise, why would she have agreed...?" He stopped, realizing to what he was about to admit.

"Agreed?" Angelica prompted.

George lifted his chin. "Why would she have agreed to go on a ride with me if she wasn't interested in marrying me?"

"Because that's what *courtship* is for. To determine if you want to marry the other person," she replied, as if she was explaining courtship to a young child.

"Since you haven't been courted by anyone, how would *you* know such a thing?"

Tears pricked the corners of Angelica's eyes, and George knew instantly he had made a mistake in teasing her. He stepped back before her fist could intersect his upper arm, and he stepped back again when he thought she might repeat her effort to punch him.

But Angelica merely hurried from the study and then up the stairs.

"Angel!" he called out, finally hurrying out of the

study in an effort to catch her before she disappeared. "I apologize," he called out.

But Angelica was already at the top of the stairs and making her way into the parlor.

The sound of the slamming door had George visibly wincing.

CHAPTER 26

A CONVERSATION IN
THE COLD

An hour later, in the garden behind Bradford Hall
Glancing up at the cloud-covered skies, Ben Fulton allowed a sigh of disappointment. After he had completed his correspondence that morning, he had spent the afternoon tweaking the settings on the telescope until everything was in perfect alignment.

He had sent a footman in search of beeswax, and upon the servant's arrival back at Bradford Hall, he had liberally applied the wax to the inside track of the dome. Rotating it slightly so he could apply the wax to the area where the wheels had been parked originally, he then performed a test to determine the ease of rotating the dome.

The entire time, he listened for the sound of a barking dog.

When none came, he allowed a grin of satisfaction and vowed to return to the observatory after the sun had set. Despite the low-hanging clouds, there were openings in the gray here and there.

Given the thick gray mass of clouds above him now, Ben wasn't even sure if the sun had set or not. He hadn't seen it since that afternoon, about the time the opening of the dome was aimed toward Hyde Park.

In need of light to see by while he waxed the track, he had opened the sliding door. While doing so, he had spotted a couple out on horseback.

His first thought was why anyone would wish to ride a horse when it was so chilly, but the couple seemed content. The horses were probably glad for the exercise.

Then he noticed a phenomenon that had him curious. Despite the snow-laden clouds that hung low over the park, there was an opening directly above the crushed granite path the two on horseback had taken into the park.

Indeed, a shaft of sunlight seemed to illuminate the couple as they made their way, and Ben felt a combination of awe and jealousy.

Young lovers? A married couple? Best friends out for a ride?

What kind of power did they possess that they could part the clouds and ride in relative brightness?

He wished he had such a divine power, for it was looking as if he wouldn't be able to use his telescope on this night.

About to turn around and head back into the house, Ben paused when he realized he was no longer alone.

"How do?" he said when he spotted Lady Angelica at his back gate.

"Good afternoon," she said, dipping her head in an effort to hide her sudden blush. "I apologize, but I saw you out here and thought to discover if you might be using the telescope tonight."

Ben moved to join her and lifted her gloved hand to his lips. Then he offered his arm. "You needn't apologize, my lady. I was out here surveying the skies in an effort to find just one opening in the clouds where I might direct my scope, but alas..." He shrugged. "I think it's going to snow again."

"So that bit of sky over there isn't enough then?" Angelica asked as she pointed to an opening in the clouds to the west. Given her vantage, she could see it from around the side of the observatory.

"What?" Ben responded as he led them around the cylindrical building. He stopped in his tracks when he saw the hole in the clouds she indicated with a gloved hand. "I fear that bit of sky will not be visible in an hour," he said with a sigh of disappointment, realizing it might have been left from earlier that afternoon. "Perhaps tomorrow will bring clearer skies." His gaze returned to her. "In which case, you are welcome to join me in the observatory."

Angelica allowed a brilliant smile. "I would like that very much, but I don't wish to intrude on your work." She sobered and dipped her head. "I used my father's telescope today, although it was not for a noble reason."

"Oh?" Ben regarded her with an upraised brow. "Birds are not a noble cause?"

"Oh, they are," she replied. "And I did see what I think was a raven. At least, I hope it was a raven, for it was quite frightening as it flew in front of the window." She was heartened to see his nod of agreement. "But I was watching my brother as he and Lady Anne went for a ride in the park."

Ben blinked. "That couple that was on horseback?"

Angelica nodded. "That was them."

"I saw them when I was working upstairs."

Angelica's eyes widened with worry. "Were you watching them through your telescope?"

He reacted as if he'd been slapped. "Of course not. Remember, I'm not able to aim my scope below the level of the dome," he said, just before he suddenly straightened. "Were *you* spying on them?" His words sounded neutral, but Angelica was quick to shake her head.

"Lady Anne is my friend, you see, and I knew my brother was escorting her this afternoon, and..." She sighed and turned to face Ben. "I *was* spying, I suppose. They had no chaperone, and I know my brother is quite smitten with Anne."

"Did you think Hexham would do something to... to ruin Lady Anne?" he asked in alarm. "In broad daylight?"

Angelica blinked and then angled her head. "Actually, I was afraid he would not." When she saw Ben's eyes widen, she quickly added, "I feared he would be tongue-tied and unable to converse with her. That he might not be able to make his intentions known with respect to marriage, and therefore would need to... to *show* his intentions."

"Show them?"

She nodded. "As opposed to... to telling her of them."

It was Ben's turn to blink. "You mean, you were hoping he would—?"

"Kiss her, yes," she said with a nod.

"And... did he?"

Angelica displayed a brilliant smile. "He did. Or she did. I'm not really sure which, but it doesn't really matter. I'm quite sure he's already proposed marriage."

Her countenance took on a glow of happiness that had Ben blinking again. He struggled to think of what to say, because if he didn't, he was quite sure he was going to join Hexham in the act of *showing*. "At his age? He seems... rather *young* to be taking a wife."

Angelica allowed a shrug. "I thought so, too, but he doesn't wish to wait as long as father did," she replied. "And I think he's afraid someone else will gain Lady Anne's hand if he doesn't marry her soon, much like what happened with Mother." When she noted Ben's expression of curiosity, she added, "My father knew he wanted to marry my mother when she was a child, but... he didn't tell her."

"And she ended up married to someone else," Ben guessed.

Angelica nodded. "Samuel Worthington. He had

made his fortune in steamships, and was apparently a very amiable man. But when he died, Father knew he had to court Mother or lose her for good."

"I suppose she had a number of suitors," Ben commented. The widow of a wealthy cit would have been popular for any man in need of blunt.

"She did, but my father prevailed. Thank the gods."

Ben remained silent for a time, his thoughts going back to Hexham and the girl he apparently intended to wed. "How many years has Lady Anne been out in Society?"

Angelica shook her head. "None. She's not to make her come-out until this Season," she explained, grinning when she saw his reaction. "I know it seems positively mad, but she will make a wonderful wife for him, and I will finally have a sister." She paused and added, "I'm quite sure she'll be at the dinner party. Did you... receive the invitation for my brother's dinner party?"

"I did, indeed," Ben replied. "I have already penned a response and had my butler see to its delivery," he added, realizing the notes he had written had probably been given to her brother to read before they would make their way into her hands.

"I am so glad to hear it. You may already know some of our other guests, but if you do not, it will be an opportunity to meet new friends."

"My thoughts, too," he agreed. "Being fairly new to London, my only opportunity to make acquaintances has been at the meetings of the Royal Society."

"You're a Fellow, no doubt," Angelica commented,

her attention having gone to a large, black bird that sat on the bare branch of a nearby tree. She had a thought that it was the same bird that had frightened her earlier that afternoon.

Ben dipped his head. "I am not. And apparently not in the near future, either. I received the latest correspondence from the Society only this morning. It contained the list of nominees we'll be voting on this spring."

"And your name was not included?" Angelica asked.

He shook his head. "Perhaps next year, after I've discovered a new planet or another moon of Jupiter," he commented. "Although I think I shall concentrate my work on asteroids."

"Asteroids?" Angelica furrowed a brow. "Are they what we call shooting stars?"

Ben shook his head. "Possibly the smallest ones that have fallen from their orbits," he replied. "Asteroids are generally found on a path between that of Mars and Jupiter. Chunks of... rock perhaps, that are simply very small planets. It's possible they were at one time an entire planet that broke apart."

"How interesting," she murmured, noticing how the clouds above had darkened with the impending nightfall. Their breaths hung in white clouds in front of their faces. "I should be going in," she said. "I've kept you out here in the cold—"

"Nonsense. I'm quite used to it," he replied. "I've spent many a cold night in an observatory in Cambridge, and I expect I shall spend many more here." Ben felt her arm shiver atop his, and he chastised himself. "I apologize that I'm unable to invite you into my home," he murmured. "Seeing as how there is no... lady of the house... or chaperone."

"Oh, it's quite all right. I need to be going in," she replied. It's time I dress for dinner."

Ben lifted her hand to his lips and kissed the back of it. "Perhaps I'll see you tomorrow?"

Angelica curtsied. "Perhaps," she replied with a grin.

She hurried to the front door of Worthington House, rather enjoying the look of confusion on Winslow's face.

He hadn't seen her take her leave of the house by way of the back door the hour before.

CHAPTER 27

PREPARATIONS FOR A PARTY

The following day
George regarded the silver salver on the round table in the great hall of Worthington House, stunned at the pile of white notes that littered it. A quick glance showed his sister's name on every one of them.

"Your correspondence is in your study, my lord," Winston said as he placed a vase of hot-house flowers in the center of the table. "And a footman from next door left a note for your attention."

"Starting her decorating a bit early, is she not?" George half-asked, noting the flowers were far more ornate than what his mother favored for everyday. Most of the blooms in this arrangement were red and white.

"If you are referring to Lady Angelica, she is efficient."

Efficient and confusing, George thought. He had half-expected his sister to take her dinner in the parlor after what had happened in the study the day before. Instead, she had shown up in the dining room only a moment after Winslow rang the bell, all smiles, as if she had completely forgotten his cutting comment about courtship.

"I take it she has already met with the housekeeper and the cook?" he asked, his gaze once again going to the pile of notes on the silver salver. He should probably read them all before she did—his father would have—but he didn't wish to intrude on her privacy. Remembering how he had felt upon learning she had spied on him only reinforced his decision.

"Indeed. And the gardener, too," Winslow replied.

George frowned, his gaze going to the front of the house. Although he couldn't see outside unless he looked through the front salon window, he knew there was at least two inches of snow on the ground. "Whatever for?"

The butler's eyes widened a bit before he gave a shake of his head. "I know not, sir, although I do believe he sees to a greenhouse from which these blooms arrived."

More flowers? George thought. Well, it couldn't be greenery. Following tradition, wreaths, garlands and a tree couldn't be brought into the house until Christmas Eve day. Which had him curious as to her plans.

When Angelica appeared at the top of the stairs, he glanced up and angled his head to one side. "Whatever is going on in that pretty little head of yours?"

George had learned long ago to combine his chiding with a compliment when it came to his sister.

Angelica grinned as she descended the stairs. "Dinner party planning, of course." When she saw the salver, she hurried over and began checking the seals on the backs of the missives. "It appears as if everyone has responded," she murmured, her gaze stopping on a seal of a crescent moon and stars. "Including our new neighbor."

George frowned and moved to join her at the table. "You invited our neighbor? The one with the observatory?"

Angelica nodded. "Of course. He lives alone—"

"But we've not been introduced."

"You haven't met Sir Benjamin, either, but you wanted me to invite *him*," she argued.

"*Father* wanted Sir Benjamin invited," he countered. He dipped his head then, deciding their argument would only result in a pouty sibling. "You did send *him* an invitation?"

"I did," she assured him. "I wasn't sure *where* to send it, though. But apparently the footman knew where to go." She held out a missive with the initials BBF in a bold font emblazoned in the red wax.

George cocked an eyebrow. "Very good. I'm off to read my correspondence. Then I have to pay a call on a member of the peerage this afternoon. Official matters. See you at dinner."

Angelica watched him go before she opened the note from Sir Benjamin. Although she felt only the slightest disappointment at learning he would not be in attendance, she decided it best she not tell her brother.

At least, not yet.

Opening the one from Mr. Fulton, she allowed a huge grin at reading his response. She knew from their conversation the night before that he would be there.

And he looked forward to seeing her again.

She thought of sneaking into his observatory that very night.

If she spied the red light from her bedchamber window, and if her brother was at his club, she decided she would.

CHAPTER 28

A MEETING OF LIKE-MINDED MEN

Later that day at Trenton House

"I appreciate you taking the time to see me this afternoon," George said as he took the seat Gabriel Wellingham offered him. "Especially on such short notice." Instead of the wooden chair in front of a large polished desk, Trenton had indicated an over-stuffed chair near the fireplace.

"I appreciate the excuse to have a glass of brandy and procrastinate," Trenton replied with a grin, moving to a sideboard where several crystal decanters were lined up. "Would you like one?"

George nodded. "Much obliged."

"My man of business is in Wolverhampton, so I aways have more correspondence to see to when I am here in London," the earl explained as he handed a glass to George. "My countess helps, of course, but she has her own letters to write for her business."

Surprised to hear this bit of news, George said, "Her business?"

Trenton nodded as he took the chair opposite. "The Spread Eagle Inn in Stretton. I bought it many years ago, but she's the one who knows the particulars of running a coaching inn," he explained. "It's where I first met her, in fact. Four-and-twenty years ago." He took a sip of brandy, a look of contentment settling on his features. "I suppose you're here about my daughter."

His eyes darting to one side, George thought the segue rather abrupt. "I am. I wish to marry her, sir, so I've come to ask for your permission—"

"You mean, you haven't already asked her?"

George's eyes widened. He was sure he and Lady Anne had an agreement that they wouldn't tell anyone of their betrothal. Before he could answer, though, Trenton allowed a chuckle.

"Forgive me. I've had such mixed thoughts on the subject, I have often wondered how I might respond to such a query."

"Mixed thoughts?" George repeated.

"Until a few nights ago, I wouldn't have thought to entertain queries such as yours for at least another three or four years," Trenton said. "But... I admit to having eavesdropped on a conversation that has since convinced me my daughter is ready to do her duty as someone's wife." He paused a moment. "I fear if I do not allow her to wed—and soon—she'll arrange to get herself with child just so she can have a baby of her own." When he noted George's look of alarm, he added, "She is desperate to be a mother."

"She did mention having thoughts of what her children would look like," George murmured.

"You mean blond-haired, blue-eyed, dimpled cherubs brimming with mischief?" Trenton asked with a huge grin.

George gave a shake of his head. "She didn't mention the dimples."

"Probably because she hadn't yet met you when she mentioned them to me," the earl said as he sobered. "A rather recent introduction, if I understand correctly?"

Nodding, George said, "We met for the first time in October. In the park. And I haven't been able to forget her since."

Trenton placed his glass of brandy on a side table, set his elbows on the arms of his chair, and steepled his fingers. "Dashed inconvenient at your age."

"Oh, but it's not," George argued. "That is to say... I don't wish to wait to marry. Especially given how long my father delayed his own marriage." He paused a moment. "And most especially because I fear if I do, Lady Anne will end up married to someone else."

Trenton's brows rose at hearing this last comment. "You feel affection for her." It wasn't a question.

George nodded, the memory of their kisses in the park fresh in his mind. Their conversation about their children had caused an odd sensation to form in his chest. "I do," he acknowledged. "I believe she holds me in similar—"

"Oh, she does. There is no doubt of that," Trenton affirmed. "Since you are expected in Parliament in March, is there a chance you would be amenable to a wedding before then? You'll want time for a wedding trip, of course."

A wedding trip?

George hadn't considered a wedding trip, but then he hadn't yet secured permission to marry Lady Anne, either. "Of course," he replied, wondering if two months might be enough time to take his wife to the Kingdom of the Two Sicilies. "Does Lady Anne speak Italian?"

Trenton's eyes widened and he allowed a nod. "She does. I take it you do not?"

George shook his head. "My command of Italian is sorely lacking," he admitted.

"She would be thrilled to go to Italy."

"Does that mean I can take her? As my wife?" George asked, his breath held in anticipation of hearing Trenton's response.

A smile displayed the earl's perfect teeth. "It does," he replied. "I'll see to her dowry, of course, and inform my wife."

Nodding, George said, "I'll see to a marriage license and a ring." He paused. "I admit, this has been far easier than I expected."

Trenton leaned forward in his chair. "Probably because I was informed of your regard for my daughter before you requested permission to take her for a ride in the park," he admitted. "It seems my oldest son cannot hold his tongue when it's come into contact with liquor."

His eyes darting sideways, George allowed a slow grin to appear. "Then it seems I shall have to thank him for that, sir."

The two men stood up and shook hands.

CHAPTER 29

A BROTHER TEASES A SISTER

*M*eanwhile...

"Ah, there you are," Gabe said as he joined his sister, Anne, in the front salon of Trenton House. "I've been looking for you."

Anne's eyes widened. "Whatever for?" she asked, immediately assuming he had discovered what had happened in the park the day before.

"Conversation," he replied as he took the upholstered chair across from where she lounged on a Greek sofa. An elaborate embroidery covered most of her lap, and her wicker sewing basket sat next to one of her feet. She held a needle mid-air, as if she might have to use it as a weapon. Having been stuck by one in the past—Gabe had teased her mercilessly about the tip of her pert nose—he leaned back in his chair.

Still on edge, Anne resumed her stitching. "You must really miss William if you are coming to me for conversation," she replied with a smirk.

"I do, but he'll be here soon enough. Father says he will be returning from university by the end of the week." When she didn't respond, he added, "It's about Hexham."

Anne stiffened, her needle now firmly embedded in the linen she was embroidering. Then she replayed his words in her head and her eyes widened. "Has something happened to him?" she asked in alarm as she straightened.

Gabe quickly shook his head. "Nothing that I know of," he replied. "But I was rather hoping... *you* would know the answer to that."

Although they had discussed Hexham the night before last, Gabe had been so foxed, Anne didn't know if he remembered any of the conversation. Suspecting a trap, she gave him a quelling glance. "I'm quite sure I don't know what you're talking about," she stated, lifting the embroidery hoop to resume her sewing.

"Your ride in the park with him. Father said you two went for a ride yesterday."

Anne's eyes darted to one side. "We did," she affirmed. "Although it was cold, it was quite pleasant until Graydon picked up a rock and started limping," she added. Actually, it was more pleasant *after* her horse had begun limping, but she wasn't about to tell him why.

"So your outing was cut short?"

Anne allowed a slight shrug. "Not really. We merely walked the horses to Rotten Row. But then it grew too cold to continue, and Graydon seemed to have recovered—Hexham had removed the rock from his hoof—" *and me from the horse, just before he kissed me*—"so we rode the rest of the way home."

A look of disappointment settled on Gabe's face. "Oh," he said on a sigh.

Noting the change in his disposition, Anne furrowed a brow. "What is it?"

Gabe rolled his eyes. "Did he have… trouble? Conversing with you, I mean?"

Anne blinked. "Not that I recall," she hedged. "Well, there were a few minutes in the hall when he first arrived. They were a bit… awkward—" *when he wouldn't let go of my hand*—"but Father appeared and seemed to set him at ease."

It was Gabe's turn to blink. The thought of their father putting a suitor at ease seemed almost unbelievable. "Huh," he said in response. He had a blurry memory of having discussed the situation with his father, but he couldn't remember if it had really happened or if it had merely been a dream.

When he didn't offer anything more, Anne's concern piqued. "Why are you so curious about Hexham?"

He shrugged. "I am not. About him anyway. I just thought…" He allowed a sigh. "After our conversation at White's a couple of nights ago, I was hoping for news that he would be…"

Anne angled her head to one side and then dared a glance in the direction of the door. "He would be…?" she prompted in a whisper.

Gabe cleared his throat. "My new brother."

Swallowing, Anne wondered how to respond. She had promised she wouldn't say anything of Hexham's proposal, but Gabe looked as if he was truly bereft. Since they had discussed Hexham's intent to propose two nights before, she thought she could at least set him at ease. "I believe he will be, although I cannot yet say when."

She and George hadn't discussed a possible wedding date. At the moment, she wished it could be soon, but knowing how involved arrangements could be for weddings—the reading of the banns, the ceremony, the breakfast, and the wedding trip—she doubted anything would happen before the spring.

"So... he did propose," Gabe said, not making it a question. "With Father's permission?"

Anne's eyes widened, and she suddenly felt fearful. "I'm not at liberty to say," she replied, returning her attention to her embroidery.

Gabe let out a sound of annoyance. "Not at *liberty*?"

"I made a promise, and I am keeping it," she stated.

"I can just ask Father," he countered.

"Then I suggest you do," she dared, managing to keep her doubt from showing as she lifted her chin.

Had Hexham even asked for permission to marry her? He had to have had permission to take her for the ride in the park—her father had been right there when he came for her.

But had he taken the next step?

And if or when he did, what would her father say?

"I *will* ask Father," Gabe stated. "Just as soon as Hexham leaves his study," he added, a brilliant smile replacing his look of suspicion.

As Anne's mouth dropped open, Gabe stood up, gave her a bow, and took his leave of the salon.

Left to wonder what her father was doing to the poor Viscount Hexham in his study, Anne set aside her embroidery and hurried out to the hall.

When she saw that the door to the study was closed, she took a seat in a nearby chair to wait.

Perhaps she could get to her father before Gabe did.

CHAPTER 30

A NIGHT WITH A KNIGHT

*L*ater *that night*
When Muffin McDuff Paddlepaws barked shortly after dinner, as Angelica expected he might, she dismissed her maid and parted the drapes in her bedchamber. The skies were remarkably clear, and a rectangular red light indicated the dome was open.

Donning a redingote over her warmest woolen gown, and pulling on two extra petticoats, gloves and half-boots, Angelica regarded her reflection in the cheval mirror. The extra layers made her bottom half appear almost rotund, but the evening was cold. Far colder than it had been the first night she had paid a call on the astronomer.

She made her way down the back steps, attempting to hold her skirts closer to her body lest she get stuck in the tight stairwell. She could just imagine getting wedged in and then having to wait for a servant to help dislodge her.

Getting through the back door was nearly as difficult, but once her coat was free, she quietly shut the door and hurried out to the back gate. The crisp air had her breaths billowing out in white clouds, reminding her of winters spent near Hexham, when her father would take the family on sleigh rides.

When she made it to the observatory, she slipped through the door, once again having to pull her redingote through the slim opening. When the door was shut, she moved to the base of the stairs and called out, "Mr. Fulton?"

Ben, bathed in the red light, appeared in the opening at the top of the stairs, a top hat and muffler joining his greatcoat and gloves for warmth. A smile split his face. "Ah, my lady," he said as he waved for her to join him. "I feared you wouldn't come, but I'm so glad you have. This cold is the best for viewing nebulae," he added.

When Angelica topped the stairs, she realized at once there might be a problem. With the additional petticoats, her skirts stuck out farther than normal. She seemed to take up all the available floor space. "Muffin barked, so I knew you were up here," she said, "But I fear I may be in your way far more than I was before," she added, as she dipped a curtsy. She turned and noticed how there was now a railing along the opening for the stairs. At least she wouldn't accidentally tumble down the curved stairs should she back up too far. "If you'd rather I not be here, please tell me. I will not take offense."

Ben shook his head and took her gloved hands to his lips. "Oh, but I do want you here," he countered. "I rather like the company. Your company," he stammered as he gave a bow.

Angelica's eyes widened a fraction. "If you're sure I'm not in your way—"

"Before the other night, I never had someone pay a call on me whilst I was stargazing," he said in a quiet voice. "Other than the butler, when he brings tea, of course, but he's never indicated an interest in even looking through the telescope." His brows suddenly furrowed. "Your dog barked?"

Angelica nodded. Glancing in the direction of the instrument, Angelica saw that it was aimed midway up in the sky to the south, right at Orion's Belt. "You mentioned nebulae," Angelica hinted. "Is there one in particular…?"

"Oh, yes. Here. Come look."

He moved to a different chair from the one that had been in front of the telescope before, this one with castors. The original was still there, and he quickly moved it so it was next to the one with wheels.

"It's all different," she murmured as she took a seat. The opera glasses were no longer strapped to the side of the telescope, and instead a small telescope was attached. *A finder scope*, she remembered him saying.

"Improved, yes," he said with a proud grin, taking the chair next to her.

Angelica stared through the eyepiece and inhaled softly. "What is this?"

"The Orion Nebula. I was just about to turn the dome and look for the Beehive Cluster when you arrived."

She allowed her gaze to linger on the strange sight, staring at the nebula and allowing a sound of appreciation until the pinkish-white flower shape left the field of vision.

Just as she was about to get up from the chair, she realized he had drawn the nebula on the easel-mounted paper. "Oh, you've captured it perfectly," she said in a whisper.

"I'll add a bit of color on the morrow," he replied as he stood up from the other chair. He took a hold of the dome-turning handle and gave a push. This time, the dome rotated easily. "Your suggestion works, by the way."

"Oh?" Angelica stood up and moved to the edge of the room, watching as the wheels turned in their track.

"Beeswax. Even when it's cold, it seems to do the trick for those wheels that were sticking."

Angelica gave a nod. "Except that Muffin McDuff Paddlepaws barked a bit ago. That's how I knew you were in here."

Ben paused in his adjustments and regarded her a moment. "I wondered at that when you mentioned it, but having given it some thought, I believe he heard me open the dome's door," he explained. "Unfortunately, I don't think there's anything that can be done for its track. At least not from down here." He turned his attention back to the telescope. "I'm looking forward to dinner on the morrow."

"As am I," she replied. "I was happy to receive your reply."

He made an adjustment and then said, "I know the invitation said it was from your brother, but, pray tell, how did he think to invite me? We've not even met."

Angelica blushed, hoping the red light wouldn't enhance her embarrassment. "I... I may have encouraged him in that regard," she lied. She hadn't told George she was going to invite their neighbor, but she had included his name on the list of those who had replied that they would attend. "Seeing as how you're our new neighbor and there are so few entertainments in London during the winter months."

He nodded his understanding and then indicated she should again look through the lens. She leaned forward and allowed a brilliant smile. "It looks like a swarm of bees!"

Ben grinned. "Hence the name, I suppose," he murmured, taking his turn at the eyepiece. "Pray tell, is this dinner in honor of a special occasion? Or a special guest?"

Straightening, Angelica allowed a sigh and watched as he continued to make adjustments using the small dials. "There was a guest my father wished us to invite. Apparently he thought it important we meet him." She decided not to mention why. "But he has sent his regrets," she added with a shrug.

"He must have been someone of great importance if

your father wanted you to meet him," Ben remarked, taking a turn at staring through the eyepiece.

"I suppose," she replied. When Ben lifted his head and regarded her with an arched brow, Angelica allowed a sigh. "He thinks the gentleman would make a suitable husband for me."

Ben furrowed a brow. "And you do not?" he half-asked, the telescope forgotten.

Angelica gave a shake of her head. "Oh, I've no idea. I've never met the man, and neither has my brother. Truth be told, we're both a bit curious, and so we were looking forward to at least meeting him." She gave a shrug. "Perhaps some other time."

Ben continued to regard her a moment. "You don't seem particularly... saddened by his having sent his regrets. Was he... perhaps not of suitable rank?"

Furrowing a brow, Angelica shook her head. "I..." She sighed again, her gaze lifting to meet his. "Whether or not he has a title matters not. At least, not to me."

Blinking, Ben stared at Angelica and allowed a sound of disbelief. "But... you're an earl's daughter. Certainly your father expects you to marry an aristocrat."

Angelica dipped her head. "Even if I decided to marry a commoner, my father has assured me he would give his blessing. That is, if the gentleman is sincere in his regard for me and not just after my dowry. Father wants nothing more than for me to be happy," she explained.

Ben regarded her for a time before he swallowed.

"So, if someone... someone such as me were to ask his permission to court you, he would have it?"

Angelica inhaled softly. "Of course," she breathed.

"And you would welcome my attentions?"

"Yes. Yes, of course," she whispered.

When his gaze darted up, her own followed to discover a sprig of mistletoe dangling from the very top of the dome. A moment later, and she was leaning over so her lips could meet his, her gloved hands resting on his shoulders as one of his hands moved to her waist.

Despite the layers of fabric, Angelica was sure she felt the heat of his hand warming her entire body. His lips were soft but firm as he angled his head to better capture hers. Their breaths mingled, warming the air around their faces. The soft moan that sounded after a moment might have been from her or from him or from both.

The swirl of cold air that drifted up from the stairs was most definitely Peters with the tea tray.

Ben was the first to pull away, but he did so slowly, leaving his forehead pressed against hers. "Thank you, my lady," he murmured. He straightened just before Peters appeared at the top of the stairs. "Ah, and our tea has arrived just in time for a look at the Beehive Cluster."

As before, Peters didn't seem the least bit surprised to see Lady Angelica. "My lady," he said, giving her a slight bow.

"Good evening, Peters. I can pour the tea," she offered, knowing she best stay seated until the butler had made his way downstairs. There simply wasn't room for all three of them at the escritoire.

"Very good. Shall I wait up for you, sir?"

Ben gave a shake of his head. "No need, Peters. See you in the morning."

Peters gave another bow in Angelica's direction and made his way down the stairs. His exit was accompanied by another swirl of cold air and the *thunk* of the door closing.

Angelica stood up and moved to pour the tea, remembering Ben's preference for no milk or sugar. And yet the tea tray included both a creamer and a sugar-pot. "How do you suppose he knew I was here this time?" she asked as she handed him a cup and saucer.

Ben allowed a grin. "I may have expressed my hope that you would join me."

Preparing a cup of tea for herself, Angelica felt a wash of warmth at the thought that he had been thinking of her as much as she had been thinking of him. "You could have sent a note."

"I thought I did," he countered.

Angelica regarded him with a look of surprise before she remembered he had written that she would be welcome again when he responded to the invitation to dinner. "You did," she agreed.

"Are you expecting a crowd for dinner?"

"There will be just twelve of us, I'm afraid," she said with a hint of disappointment. "So many of my friends are with their families in the country for Christmastide, while George's friends are all bachelors living here in town." She watched as he turned dials on the telescope, the instrument barely moving as he did so.

"Twelve is an excellent number for dinner. I remember my mother used to strive for twelve when she hosted dinner parties." He motioned for her to take a look through the lens. "Let me know what you think of this one."

"Oh, it's... it's beautiful. A bit fuzzy, or perhaps cloudy is a better word for it. I love how it gets brighter in the center," Angelica murmured. "Not at all like the Orion," she added as she settled back in her chair. "What is it?"

Ben took a quick look, a sigh of satisfaction sounding from where he leaned over to gaze through the eyepiece. "The Andromeda Galaxy," he said, "which means I now have everything calibrated correctly." He pointed to a ring surrounding the telescope and another along the side of it. "They are the measurements for longitude and latitude, and these..." he indicated a book. "Are star charts. I should now be able to easily locate anything in the northern hemisphere."

"Bravo," Angelica replied before sipping her tea. When she sobered, Ben furrowed a brow.

"What is it?" he asked, his gaze dropping to the main eyepiece. He replaced it with a different one and then turned his attention on the finder scope.

"I admit to a quandary as to how I should introduce you tomorrow evening," she replied.

He tore his attention from the finder scope and

regarded her a moment. "Well, as Ben Fulton, of course," he replied.

"But we're not supposed to know one another," she argued.

"Oh, I see what you mean." He motioned for her to take his place at the scope. "Now have a look," he said, finishing off his tea and moving to place the cup and saucer back on the tea tray.

Angelica bent down and peered through the lens, her breath held. The image was still of the Andromeda Galaxy, but now it appeared much larger. Closer. "Oh, Mr. Fulton. This is—"

"Amazing, is it not? And do call me Ben. I should hope there's no need for formality between us."

Angelica dipped her head. "Then you may call me Angel," she murmured. "If you wish."

He leaned down and kissed her. When he pulled away, it was to say, "I should take you home."

"Now?" she asked, obviously disappointed.

"If I do not take you home now, my darling Angel, you'll end up quite thoroughly ruined, and I'll be called out by your brother and forced to meet him in Wimbledon Common with pistols at dawn."

My darling Angel. She hadn't heard it said quite like that before, but she liked how it sounded. "George wouldn't dare challenge you," she argued. "He's a terrible shot, and he doesn't fence."

"Good, because I'm a terrible shot and not much better with a sword. Remember, I haven't yet written that particularly important letter."

Her eyes widening, Angelica knew immediately to whom the letter would be addressed. "Even without a sword, I see your point," she replied.

He allowed a smirk at hearing her pun and secretly wondered if she possessed a greater sense of humor than she had displayed so far. "Thank for paying a call this evening," he said as he offered his arm.

Ben escorted her back to Worthington House, once again by way of the back alley. He assisted with pushing her skirts through the back door opening, his grin threatening to erupt into laughter before she and her skirts were finally over the threshold.

"Sleep well," he murmured, before he settled a quick kiss on her lips. Then he made his way back to Bradford Hall knowing Angelica watched, a mix of elation and dread tempering his good mood.

CHAPTER 31

A FATHER-DAUGHTER TALK

*E**arlier that afternoon, outside Trenton's study in Trenton House*

The door to Trenton's study opened, and George Grandby turned to regard his host for a moment. "I do not mind if you would require me to court her longer," he said to the man who would one day be his father-in-law.

"I do not believe it will make much difference," Trenton replied. "You will still marry her."

"She could change her mind," George suggested. "Discover there are others who find her as perfect as I do," he added, frowning when he realized he shouldn't be providing reasons for the earl to change *his* mind.

"She won't find another as well suited as you," Trenton argued. "And she won't change her mind," he added with a shake of his head.

George inhaled. "If you're sure." He shook the earl's

hand again. "Now I suppose I need to devise the perfect proposal," he murmured.

"Keep it simple," Trenton said quietly. "Aren't you hosting a dinner party on the morrow?"

"I am."

"Perhaps you could ask her after the rest of your guests have taken their leave?"

George's eyes widened. "I could," he replied quietly. "Thank you, sir."

With that, George gave Trenton a slight bow and stepped out of the study. He made his way to the vestibule, never turning to see that the subject of their discussion sat only a few feet from the door to her father's study.

A swirl of chilled air passed by Anne as Viscount Hexham took his leave of Trenton House.

She was staring at the caryatid across the hall from where she sat, wondering at the vase that was perched on it. Usually empty, it now held at least a dozen roses of various colors.

"Ah, Lady Anne," Barclay said as he approached from the vestibule. He held out a pasteboard card. "The roses came for you while you were with your brother. I took the liberty of putting them in the vase with some water," he explained.

Anne blinked as she took the card from him.

Viscount Hexham's calling card.

On the back, he had written, *You were right. There are no restrictions when it comes to the colors of roses.*

The butler bowed and disappeared as Anne continued to stare at the roses, her heart rate increasing as the exciting words she had overheard just a moment ago replayed in her head. And she would have played them again except that a shadow fell over her, and then her view of the roses was replaced by the body of her father.

"Oh, how do, Father?" she asked as she looked up.

Gabriel Wellingham, Earl of Trenton, gazed down on his only daughter and then crossed his arms. "Pray tell, just how long have you been sitting here in the hall?"

Anne angled her head to one side. "No longer than a half-hour, I should think," she replied with a shrug.

"So.... long enough to hear every word Viscount Hexham just said before he left my study?" he half-asked.

A dreamy expression replaced her quizzical one. "Oh, indeed," she replied. She stood up and wrapped her arms around her Father's shoulders. "Thank you, Father," she whispered.

Startled, Trenton wrapped his arms around her waist and allowed a sigh. "You weren't meant to hear those words just yet," he said, one hand rubbing her back.

"Oh, but they were such welcome words," she replied, deciding not to tell him about her conversation with Hexham in the park. About the proposal Hexham had put voice to as snow danced around them.

The one she had already accepted.

"And you were right."

"I was right?" Trenton straightened in her hold. "I was right? We shall have to mark this date on the calendar as an auspicious occasion," he remarked. He dramatically moved a hand through the air. "Lord Trenton. Right about something," he added in a deeper voice, his tongue firmly in his cheek.

Anne giggled. "I will not change my mind."

"What if at this dinner party you happen to meet another man of your dreams?" her father asked in a quiet voice. "Someone else who would make an even more perfect husband than Hexham?"

Grinning, Anne shook her head. "Hexham is the only man I think about," she murmured.

Trenton inhaled. "What if something should happen to Hexham?"

"Happen?"

He shook his head. "Say... a horse steps on his face and he's forever disfigured."

"What an awful thing to say!" she replied as she stepped out of his hold.

"He'll no longer be *gorgeous*, I think is the way you described him," Trenton remarked. "What then?"

Furrowing a brow, Anne understood what he was trying to do. Her father probably thought she hadn't learned enough about the future earl to warrant marrying the man so soon.

She considered the question a moment before she said, "No matter how he looks, I will find beauty in the roses he gives me." She pointed to the vase of roses on the opposite side of the hall. "He will still be able to waltz, and escort me to the theatre. Our children will still be blond-haired, blue-eyed cherubs. And I will always remember what he looked like when he took me for that ride in the park."

Trenton nodded and then dipped his head. "Very well. You should know I have given him my permission to ask for your hand," he said, even though he was sure she already knew.

A bright smile appeared. "Now that I know he really wishes to marry me, I think I shall request we do so quickly. I should like to have a baby in the next year. Do you think Mother will be vexed if we married before Christmas?"

Trenton stared down at his daughter a moment, his expression turning to one of horror. Only moments ago, he had encouraged Hexham to consider a quick wedding so that there would be time for a wedding trip before Parliament resumed in March. But now the thought of his daughter getting married —definitely before Christmas—had him thinking twice about his decision. "Will you two be bound for Gretna Green?"

Anne allowed a giggle. "I think not," she replied. "Besides, I don't believe a train goes there just yet."

Trenton pretended immense relief, which wasn't difficult.

"Will Mother be upset if we marry soon?" she asked again.

"Possibly," he hedged. "Yes," he amended. "You barely have time for the reading of the banns, although I suppose Hexham can afford a special license."

She allowed a prim smile. "I know. I would dearly love a Christmas wedding." Her smile broadened. "Wouldn't it be wonderful?"

Furrowing his brows, Trenton gave a slight shake of his head. "You are your mother's only daughter. Do not deprive her of a proper wedding," he warned.

Sobering, Anne angled her head. "I will not," she said on a sigh. Remembering Gabe's intention to speak with their father about this very topic, she added, "Gabe thinks he knows something."

Trenton's brows arched. "Oh? I should hope he knows much, given he has completed his studies at university," he teased.

Anne rolled her eyes. "About *this*, I mean. About Hexham. About his intent to marry me."

Eyes darted sideways, Trenton remembered how he had unintentionally eavesdropped on their conversation a few nights ago. Of course, Gabe knew. Wasn't he the one who had told Hexham about Anne's interest in the viscount in the first place?

"I'd rather he not know about the wedding until *after* the dinner party," Anne said in a quiet voice. "I should hate word to get out before Hexham is ready to announce anything."

"I should hate that word gets out before Hexham

has an opportunity to even propose," Trenton countered.

Anne's eyes widened. "That, too."

Trenton allowed a chuckle. "I will fend off his inquiries," he promised. "And hope that he soon learns first-hand how confusing and delightful loving a woman can be."

"Loving?" she repeated in a whisper.

Her father angled his head to one side. "I would not allow Hexham your hand in marriage if he did not at least feel affection for you."

Anne remembered Hexham's kisses in the park, and she allowed a wan smile. She hoped Hexham wouldn't find her confusing.

Delightful, yes.

When Gabe appeared at the bottom of the stairs, he regarded his sister and father with a look of anticipation. "So... am I going to gain a brother very soon?"

Trenton lifted his head and pretended ignorance. "I thought perhaps you were going to tell us that I was gaining a daughter and she was gaining a sister," he replied.

Gabe's eyes widened. "But... but I'm not courting anyone," he responded, thoughts of his sister and Hexham evaporating.

"Perhaps you'll find someone at the museum," Anne murmured. "Someone exotic, like a mummy from Egypt," she teased. "Or that statue of Venus."

She managed to make it to the stairs before Gabe could form an appropriate response.

"Delightful, isn't she?" Trenton asked with a grin. "You'll have to pardon me. I need to go dress for dinner."

Gabe gave a sound of disbelief as he watched the earl head up the stairs.

He hated being left confused.

CHAPTER 32

A KNIGHT'S SECRET IS REVEALED

*F*riday, December 1, 1837, Worthington House

"Are you nervous?" George asked. He had appeared as if from nowhere as a reflection in the sideboard mirror, leaning against the dining room's door jamb.

Angelica turned to regard her brother, a blonde eyebrow arching when she noted he had finally changed for dinner. His black evening clothes and snowy white cravat did little for his fair complexion, but his waist-coat, a bright red tapestry with gold metallic embroi-dery, helped counter the stark effect.

Angelica had spent the afternoon being primped and poked by her lady's maid, the result of which was an elegant hairstyle with enough pins to keep every hair in place even if gale force winds swept through Worthington House.

The white silk gown she wore made her appear the epitome of her name. "Not for the reason you're thinking," she finally replied as she surveyed the place settings in the dining room.

With only ten guests and the two of them, she had opted to use the smaller Chippendale table and matching chairs for that night's dinner party. A few additional chairs lined one of the long walls in the event some chaperoning maids ended up with them as opposed to joining the other servants in their dining room.

"I thought to speak with you about one of our guests," George murmured as he unfolded the list that Angelica had given him the day before.

Stiffening, Angelica straightened from where she had set out place cards for Lady Anne, Ben Fulton, and Cousin Thomas. "Oh, dear. Has someone sent their regrets?"

"Nothing like that," he said with a shake of his head. He pointed to the name 'Ben Fulton'.

Before he had a chance to ask, Angelica said, "He's our new neighbor." She went about setting out additional place cards for the Ladies Dahlia and Diana Fitzwilliam, Cousin Emily, Alexander Tennison, Gabe Wellingham, David Bennett-Jones, and Mark Comber, all while attempting an attitude of nonchalance. "Lives in Bradford Hall."

George blinked. He folded the list and slid it into one pocket before extracting two notes from another pocket. "Have you met him?" he asked as he unfolded the missives and compared them side by side. He allowed the notes to refold of their own accord and replaced them in his topcoat pocket.

Angelica inhaled slowly, deciding it best she tell him the truth. "I have had the pleasure, yes," she said, a frisson passing through her entire body as she remembered Ben's kisses. Despite knowing her face displayed her sudden blush, she rather liked the momentary warmth it provided. The fire had just been set in the fireplace, and the dining room was still chilly. "In his observatory."

Nodding, George appeared about to take his leave of the dining room, but then he paused. "Did he show you his telescope?"

Had she something solid to throw at him—other than one of the crystal glasses on the table—she would have done so just then. Instead she took another slow breath and said, "Why, yes. Yes, he did. And he let me look through it. Showed me Venus, and the moon. The Orion Nebula, and the Beehive Cluster, and the Andromeda Galaxy."

George blinked again. "That must have been fascinating," he remarked.

"It was. They were beautiful. As is he."

Brows furrowed. "He is?"

"He is. And he's interesting and quite the gentleman. I kissed him."

"Really?" George's simple response gave no indication as to whether or not he was shocked by her revelation, which only emboldened her more.

"Several times. And he kissed me. There was mistle-toe, of course."

"Of course," George said, for lack of a better response.

"He's written to Father to ask if he can court me. If he asks for my hand in marriage, I will agree, of course."

"Of course."

"I don't care that he's a commoner."

The strangest expression appeared on George's face just then, but he quickly sobered when it was apparent guests were arriving. "Well, I suppose I should go meet my future brother," he said, and then ducked out of the dining room lest she throw anything at him.

Angelica stared after him, her mouth half-open in wonder.

Ben surrendered his top hat and greatcoat to a footman, greeting the other dinner guests that had arrived at the same time as he did. As the younger brother of an earl, he knew a few from their names but recognized only Alexander Tennison—he was a member of the Royal Society—and Thomas Grandby, because the two had attended Eton at the same time.

Not wanting to be first, he had watched the arrivals from one of the front windows in Bradford Hall and then taken his leave when several well-dressed young men departed a series of town coaches emblazoned with gold crests. By the time he was making his way up to the mansion's front door, the giggles of several young ladies joined the merriment.

There was a thought that the next few minutes might be the most awkward of his life. He had never met his host, and, therefore, he shouldn't have met his hostess.

Met her, or been in her company in the dark of the night, or kissed her quite thoroughly—mistletoe or not.

Following the butler, he emerged from the vestibule into the great hall and was immediately struck by the elegance of Worthington House. A round table, graced with a vase of red and white roses, suggested the lady of the house had already begun thinking of the upcoming holiday.

Christmas.

Ben imagined Angelica carrying a bouquet of those very flowers for their wedding. She would look stunning in a white silk gown, carrying red roses, her long hair caught up in an elegant chignon.

His hand went to his waistcoat pocket, sliding over the fabric in search of the gold band topped with sapphire and citrine gemstones he had purchased in Ludgate Hill earlier that day.

Satisfied it was still there, he allowed his gaze to settle on the woman who had just emerged from the dining room and was making her way to the ground floor parlor.

He was sure she blushed when she caught sight of him, and then he wondered how she could have known what he imagined she'd be wearing for their wedding.

He nearly cursed himself for not having paid a call on the Archbishop of Canterbury in Doctors' Commons to secure a special license. They could be married wherever and whenever they wished. His brother would complain bitterly about the cost, though.

Instead, he had purchased the simple marriage license from a clergyman at St. George's with the stipulation he use it within fifteen days.

He couldn't imagine what else might be involved. Well, a willing bride, but he was quite sure she would agree to be his wife, especially when she learned the truth about him.

Ben gave a shake of his head, not wanting to appear as if he was daydreaming. The butler stood aside when they reached the parlor doors, but Ben paused just beyond the threshold, turning to see that Angelica was making her way in his direction. A brilliant smile appeared at the very moment three young women suddenly stepped in front of her, and George Grandby stepped in front of him.

"Good evening. Would you be Sir Benjamin?" George asked in a quiet voice as he held out his right hand.

Ben stiffened, a thought that George's hand would soon form a fist and find its way to his jaw. "I am. How do you do? Hexham, is it not?" he replied, giving George's hand a firm shake.

"George Grandby," his host acknowledged. "Apologies for not having made your acquaintance sooner. My sister tells me you've taken over Bradford Hall." He motioned that they should move farther into the room, where one footman was serving coffee while another held out a plate of walnuts.

Relaxing a bit, Ben nodded. "My brother—Wadsworth— saw to buying up some of the baron's vowels, and as a result, he ended up with the house," he explained. "He had no need of it, and I was in the market for a home here in town, so I agreed to take it on."

George nodded his understanding. "So, you'll be keeping it?"

Ben angled his head to one side as he accepted a cup of coffee from a footman. "I will. Which is why I saw to having the observatory built. Astronomy is my avocation, you see."

"Congratulations on discovering that comet," George said as he took a cup of coffee.

Ben gave a start. "You know about that?"

"News does reach Northumberland," George replied with a grin. "My father insists on reading *The Times* every morning, even if the issue might be a week old."

"Thank you. The discovery made it possible for me to finally gain admission into the Royal Society," Ben explained.

Not having any knowledge of the scientific organization, George merely nodded. He leaned in and lowered his voice. "Are you in receipt of a letter from my father, Torrington, perhaps?"

Once again, Ben stiffened. "I am. So... you're aware of his... proposal?"

George nodded. "It seems your brother and my father have been plotting with one another, at your expense."

Furrowing a brow, Ben was about to counter the comment. "To say that I was surprised would be an understatement," he offered. "I had never thought to make a suitable match for reasons of inheritance." Then he frowned even more. "Why do you think it at my *expense?*"

George arched a brow. "Surely, at your age, you already had someone in mind to take to wife."

Ben dipped his head. "Truth be told, I had not thought of marriage until I received Torrington's letter."

George gave him a suspicious glance. "Why ever not?"

Not exactly sure he wanted to admit the reason for his continued bachelor status, Ben leaned in and said, "The Wadsworth earldom hasn't exactly been a boon when it comes to wealth, and apparently it would be unseemly for me to work. Without the means to support a wife, I hardly think I should consider marriage."

George nodded his understanding. "Then you will rely on Angelica's dowry to make your living."

Ben dipped his head again, not at all pleased with where the conversation was going. "If I am to marry her, then I'm afraid that is the case," he admitted.

"You would not be the first to rely on a wife's dowry to make your way in life," George said, *sotto voce*. He glanced around, finding Alexander, Mark, and Gabe joined in raucous conversation. "And given my father's position on the matter, I hardly think I need to interfere."

Hoping his embarrassment wasn't apparent, Ben said, "You would be within your rights to call me out. I admit to having kissed your sister, but I assure you, I have done nothing more."

George rolled his eyes. "A duel is out of the question. I'm a terrible shot, and worse with a sword," he said as laughter once again erupted from the group of three young men. "Pardon me. I need to greet my other guests."

"Of course," Ben replied, giving him a nod. He straightened, turning to discover Angelica standing directly behind him, speaking in quiet tones with one of the other young ladies.

"Good evening, ladies," he said, giving them a bow.

Angelica turned and gave him a curtsy, as did the other young lady. "Mr. Fulton," Angelica acknowledged him. "So glad you could join us this evening. She indicated her friend. "May I introduce Lady Anne? Mr. Fulton lives next door."

Anne Wellingham turned to regard the gentleman, her face splitting into a wide grin. "Why, don't you mean *Sir Benjamin?*" she asked as she held out her hand.

Ben cringed, just then recognizing the daughter of the Earl of Trenton. "Good evening, Lady Anne," he said as he lifted her hand to his lips. "So good to see you again."

Her eyes widening at hearing Lady Anne's comment, Angelica inhaled and stared at the knight for a moment. "Sir Benjamin?" she repeated softly.

"He's Wadsworth's brother," Anne said in a whisper.

"Oh, of course," Angelica replied, realizing almost immediately that she should have connected the family name Fulton to the Wadsworth earldom from the very start.

But why would she?

Ben had made no mention of his brother, and he had introduced himself as Ben Fulton that first night in the observatory. "I'm honored you could join us this evening after all, Sir Benjamin," she said, turning her attention back to him. Although she tried to school her features to hide her dismay—had the man intentionally made her look like a fool to her guests?—Angelica managed a slight smile. "I suppose this means Mr. Fulton won't be in attendance."

"Angel," he started to say, just as the butler appeared at the door and announced dinner was served. "May I have the honor of escorting you into dinner?"

Angelica regarded him a moment before her eyes darted about to take in the other guests. "Given the uneven numbers, perhaps it would be better if—"

"Lady Anne, may I escort you into dinner?" George asked of Anne as he stepped up, offering his arm.

Anne blushed and dipped her head. "Yes, of course, Hexham," she replied as she placed her hand on his arm.

"Oh, do call me George, won't you?" The two took

their leave of the parlor followed by several others who had paired up according to rank.

Ben offered his arm to Angelica. "Please, my lady. I can explain."

Angelica reluctantly took his arm, her gaze once again sweeping the parlor to be sure all the guests were making their way to the dining room. She turned her attention back to Ben. "I look forward to it," she stated, but her tone suggested she did not. "Although I do think I have heard quite enough."

Knowing almost immediately to what she referred, Ben stiffened. Dinner might not be the enjoyable affair he had looked forward to all day.

On what seemed like wooden legs, he escorted Angelica to her seat at the opposite end of the table from her brother. Then he found his own place— directly to her left—and knew he was in for a long night.

CHAPTER 33

A MOTHER SURPRISES

A half-hour earlier, at Trenton House

"There you are," Trenton remarked when he found his wife staring out the front parlor window.

Sarah turned and watched as he made his way to her side. "Why is it I have this feeling I have seen the last of my daughter before she is betrothed?"

Trenton inhaled slowly. "I meant to tell you last night."

"Tell me what?" Sarah's eyes were wide, and from the glimmer in them, Trenton was sure she was on the verge of tears.

"I gave Hexham permission to marry her," he admitted. "He was here yesterday—"

"He just showed—?"

"He sent a note, of course, but our talk was just a formality. I knew—we both knew—that when he asked her to go for the ride earlier this week, his intent was to court Anne."

Sarah dipped her head. "I am glad it is George," she said with a slight nod. "He is young, but mayhap old as well."

Trenton furrowed a brow. "He is far more mature than most his age," he agreed. "Probably more so than Gabe. He will make a fine husband. He feels affection for her. And she will want for nothing—"

"So nothing will change in that regard," Sarah managed with a wan grin. "Still, she is so *young*."

"And determined to be a mother—with or without a husband, I feared. I have a mind to blame that on my sister, but Lily has done nothing to encourage her in that regard."

"Nothing except to have babies Anne can dote on," Sarah reminded him. A tear fell from one of her eyes, and Trenton gathered her into his arms.

"Please don't cry," he begged as he placed a kiss on her forehead and then brushed the tear aside with his thumb. "Especially when she tells you she'd like a Christmas wedding."

Sarah's eyes rounded. "*This* Christmas?"

"She wants to have a baby next year, so the wedding had better be this Christmas," he countered.

"There's only a few weeks—"

"Plenty of time for you to plan a wedding breakfast with cook," he assured her.

"But what about a gown? Flowers? Arrangements for the church?"

Trenton shrugged. "You have accomplished far more than that whilst seeing to your business," he countered. "And in far less time. I have the utmost faith in you."

Sarah gave him a quelling glance before she allowed a long sigh. "I suppose it's doable," she murmured. Her eyes suddenly widened again. "Do you suppose Hexham will take her virtue on this night?"

His own eyes rounding in alarm, Trenton took a moment to consider how to respond.

Hexham was hosting a dinner party. Afterwards, the gentlemen in attendance would no doubt head to their clubs—George with them—so it was rather unlikely he would have time to bed Anne. He finally shook his head. "Not on this night." His brows furrowed, though. "Have you explained to her what happens in a marriage bed?"

Sarah angled her head back and forth. "Most of it. Just this afternoon, in fact."

Trenton thought the timing rather interesting, but asked, "Do you think she will know how to kiss?"

Rolling her eyes, Sarah said, "She grew up watching us," she reminded him, which had him suppressing a self-satisfied grin. "Besides, by now, they've probably already kissed. Perhaps several times."

The mixed feelings Trenton had experienced the day before returned, but he was determined not to second-guess his decision to allow George Grandby to marry his daughter. "Let us hope she doesn't have to teach *him* how to kiss," he murmured.

Sarah blinked, but then she allowed a brilliant smile. "*You* were a quick study, as I recall."

"That's because you were an excellent teacher," he replied happily. Before Sarah could respond, he pulled her into a hug and kissed her quite thoroughly. When he finally pulled away, he wondered at how she gazed at him. "What is it?"

"Why didn't you tell me last night that you had given away my daughter?" she asked, her voice tinged with reproach.

Trenton blinked. "Probably because you were having your way with me. You know I am without faculties for the rest of the night when you do that."

She tried hard to suppress a grin and could not. "Still, you need to make it up to me," Sarah stated.

Blinking again, Trenton's eyes darted to one side. "Gabe and Anne are both gone for at least several hours," he murmured. He glanced over at the Greek sofa and back at Sarah, his brows waggling.

Her eyes darted to the sofa and then widened in delight. "Gabriel! What about dinner?"

"Later," he said as he led them to the sofa.

She didn't scold him the rest of the night.

CHAPTER 34

A STUNNING
ANNOUNCEMENT

eanwhile, at Worthington House

As any good hostess should do, Angelica saw to it her guests were well fed and the wine glasses were kept full. Conversations varied around the table, from Mark bemoaning the lack of a good horse auction that month and Gabe listing the available entertainments in town during the winter months to the young ladies' discussion of the latest offering at the theatres. Laughter was frequent. Stories were entertaining. Lulls in conversation were few and far between.

And through it all, Ben surreptitiously watched Angelica as she presided over the dinner, her subtle gestures sending footmen off for the next course or refilling glasses with wine. When she seemed resigned to the fact that she would have to converse with him, she asked how he had acquired his title and from whom.

"I discovered a comet, and King William granted me a knighthood."

Angelica blinked. She wasn't sure why hearing the claim was such a surprise. "But... how did the king find out?" The monarch had just died the year before. Without a single legitimate heir, King William's niece, Victoria, had ascended to the throne and finally been coronated earlier that year.

"He didn't. At least, not until the Prime Minister informed him."

Angelica gave him a quelling glance, which reminded him of how she had looked that night she had scolded him for gazing at Venus. Without her having to say a word, he knew exactly how to continue.

"I wrote up my findings for a scientific journal. When word reached the Continent, some of the news sheets there covered the story, and *The Times* reprinted part of the article. Which is how the Prime Minister found out."

Angelica furrowed a brow. "Have you been searching for more comets?" she asked. As much as she wished to remain miffed at him—and she was miffed— she was still interested in his work.

"Not directly," he replied. "They tend to be something you find quite by accident." When she indicated he should continue, he had a thought she might yet forgive him for not having divulged his full identity. "You see, if you look at the same celestial body every night and record its appearance as well as the positions of the stars around it, you tend to notice when one of those stars has moved whilst the others around it have not."

One of the other gentlemen, David, asked, "How do you know it's a comet, though, and not one of those... asteroids, I believe they've been called?"

Ben turned to discover most of those at the table were listening to his explanation. "Well, you don't at first. It may be a planet or an asteroid, but if it's making its way toward the sun, it will get larger over the course of its travel through space. As it gets closer to the sun, it develops a tail. Starts to look like an angel." He glanced at Angelica and added, "That's when you know its a comet."

Angelica couldn't help but notice his reference to an angel and the fact that he was looking directly at her when he said it.

"Fascinating," Lady Anne whispered, her comment eliciting a series of murmurs around the table. Then the conversation turned to everyone's plans for Christmas as the dessert course was delivered.

Ben couldn't help but notice Angelica didn't offer her plans for Christmas. Then George addressed him from the other end of the table with the same query.

Having spent the entire day planning to get married, he blurted, "I plan to be married." When the guffaws and gasps ceased, he added, "I am just today in possession of a marriage license, so I was hoping I would be spending Christmas in the company of a wife, perhaps on a wedding trip to the Kingdom of the Two Sicilies."

George exchanged a meaningful glance with Anne

while a chorus of murmurs and best wishes circled the table.

From all those except Angelica, for although she had pasted a pleasant expression on her face, she was pale as she stared at her dessert.

"Have you apprised your future wife of your plans?" Alexander asked, obviously still amused.

Ben leaned forward and directed his reply to the Earl of Everly's son. "Not exactly."

Another round of laughter circled the table, and when Lady Diana Fitzwilliam seemed about to ask as to the identity of his intended, George made sure to change the subject.

Daring a glance in Angelica's direction, Ben felt his last bite of dessert turn into a rock as it made its way down. "This dinner was excellent, my lady."

Angelica allowed a prim grin. "Thank you, sir."

Bristling at her formality, Ben wondered what to do. What could he say to make her understand he meant no offense by withholding his title when he had introduced himself?

Once the post-dinner wine was drunk, Angelica pushed back her chair and announced that the ladies should join her in the parlor for tea. Ben realized he would have to speak with her later. He stood up, along with all the other gentlemen at the table, and watched as the ladies filed out.

He nearly drank all his port in one gulp.

CHAPTER 35

APOLOGIES AND A PROPOSAL

A few minutes later
"That was quite an announcement Sir Benjamin made during dinner," Lady Anne commented as the five women took seats near the fireplace. A maid hurried in with a tea tray and went about pouring cups for everyone.

"I half-expected my brother might join him with the same sort of announcement," Angelica remarked, a teasing eyebrow arched high. She thought to deflect attention lest anyone think Sir Benjamin's comment was directed to her.

Anne's face took on a pinkish cast. "I haven't been led to expect such an announcement," she fibbed, her eyes wide.

She had hoped for a proposal, of course. Had been hoping for one ever since the day she had returned to London, so George's proposal in the park had been most welcome.

The time she had spent with Hexham had been her first experience of being alone with a man who wasn't one of her brothers or her father, and yet she had felt just as safe with him. Even though he had kissed her, she was sure of his protection. Sure of his regard for her. Even more sure once they spoke of marriage. Of children.

She accepted a cup of tea and seemed to drink for fortification.

Angling her head to one side, Angelica said, "I would adore having you as my sister, and you would make a fine countess."

The other young ladies nodded in agreement before talk of fashion and Mayfair gossip prevailed, gossip that included a mention of the hideous building that had gone up behind Bradford Hall.

"I am quite sure we have a Peeping Tom in our midst," Lady Diana stated. As a daughter of the Earl of Norwick, she lived at Norwick House, only a few doors down in Park Lane.

Her twin sister, Dahlia, shook her head in dismay. "Now, Diana, astronomers are *not* Peeping Toms."

Angelica knew from having grown up with the young women that although they were twin sisters, they tended to take the opposite sides of any argument. She decided to defend the astronomer. "I thought the same the first night I arrived from Torrington Park, but Sir Benjamin was merely gazing at Venus."

Her cousin, Emily Grandby, straightened. "The

planet? Or do you have a neighbor by that name?" A few titters erupted at this query.

"The planet, of course," Angelica replied, not bothering to hide her grin. "He is an astronomer, first and foremost."

"One who intends to marry in a fortnight," Anne said softly. "And given the fact that Wadsworth doesn't yet have an heir, it's likely Sir Benjamin, or at least his heir, will be the next Earl of Wadsworth."

Angelica remembered the conversation she'd had on the train with her brother. He had said all this and more, but at no point had he said just whom it was he was talking about.

He hadn't mentioned any names, nor any titles.

And I didn't ask.

No wonder I've been caught by surprise.

"Is he an agreeable gentleman?" her cousin asked.

"Oh, very much," Angelica replied. "Very knowledgable, too. He's a member of the Royal Society."

"So... you were introduced before this evening?" Lady Dahlia asked.

Her eyes widening, Angelica nodded. "Of course. My father made mention of him to my brother. Asked that he make his acquaintance. I don't think any of us expected him to be living right next door. Would you like more tea?"

The drooping eyelids of her guests had Angelica glancing at the mantle clock. It was only half-past ten o'clock, but the gentlemen hadn't yet joined them.

Outside, snow had started falling again, the flakes following circuitous paths on their way to the ground.

Emily made her apologies. "Although I dearly love living in the country, the six miles to Woodscastle will take nearly an hour or more given this snow. I do apologize, but I really must be going."

Angelica angled her head, disappointment evident on her face. "You are more than welcome to spend the night," she offered.

Her eyebrows waggling, Emily leaned over and whispered, "Although it is tempting, I'd rather not be in the way of what is sure to be an interesting evening for *you*." She turned her attention on the other young women. "I shall see you all again the next time."

The others bid her farewell as Angelica walked Emily to the front door and Winston saw to summoning her coach. "Give my regards to my other cousins, won't you?" Angelica pleaded. "At least those who still live at Woodscastle."

Older than Angelica by three years, Emily gave a nod as she allowed Winston to help her with her redingote. "I will. And do consider his proposal. He's a very nice gentleman."

"Whose proposal?" Angelica asked in alarm.

Emily gave her a quelling glance, and she took her leave without saying another word.

Angelica turned around, intending to return to the parlor, but her way was stopped by Ben.

"Are you leaving already?" she asked, not sure why she felt disappointment just then.

Appearing a bit undecided, Ben shook his head. "I won't if I might be allowed some time with you after your guests have taken their leave."

Before she could give him an answer, the remaining ladies appeared from the parlor. A flurry of 'good nights' and 'good-byes' occurred as several gentlemen joined the exodus, although it was apparent they were heading for their men's club.

"I'm off to White's, sister. Wonderful dinner. Thank you for being my hostess," George said as he gave her an exaggerated bow. "I'll see you at breakfast," he added as he departed with the younger guests, Lady Anne one of them.

Angelica blinked when the vestibule was suddenly empty, and only Sir Benjamin and she were left in the great hall.

"I owe you an apology," Ben said, before she had a chance to suggest they move to the front salon. "I never once thought that omitting my honorific would cause you embarrassment," he added in a quiet voice. "You are, in fact, probably the first person to whom I've introduced myself since the knighting ceremony, and I quite... forgot." He swallowed. "I do rather prefer just being Benjamin Fulton," he added as he dipped his head.

"Your apology is accepted, of course," Angelica murmured. She allowed a long sigh. "I suppose you've received a letter from my father."

He nodded. "My godfather, yes. And one from my brother."

She gave her head a shake. "When my brother told me, we were on the train. I couldn't believe it. I... I never thought my father would do such a thing."

"Nor would I have expected it of my brother," Ben stated.

"Were you... angry?" she asked in a whisper.

Ben's eyes darted sideways. "I was," he admitted, wincing when he saw how Angelica seemed on the verge of tears. "And then this angel appeared one night in my observatory, and I found my mind changed on the matter quite completely."

Angelica's eyes widened. "An angel?" she asked in wonder.

He nodded and then took her into his arms. "Gave me a thorough tongue lashing. Accused me of being a Peeping Tom." He felt her stiffen in his hold, but he pulled her closer. "Imagine my surprise when I discovered I rather liked her."

"You do?"

"Oh, yes." He dropped his head until their foreheads met. "Especially when she kissed me." He felt more than heard her slight inhalation of breath. "Which had me wondering if she might be amenable to doing it every day for the rest of her life."

Angelica's eyes widened, her lashes nearly touching his cheek. "Kissing you?"

"That, and being my wife." His lips captured hers then, effectively cutting off any response she might have made.

Angelica was at a loss. She had spent the entire

dinner miffed with him. Besides having learned he was a knight, the minute before that, she had overheard him tell her brother he needed to marry for a dowry.

Her dowry.

She pulled her lips from his, and she stared at him. "Because of my dowry?"

Ben blinked, and blinked again. He allowed a long sigh when he realized she must have overheard more of his conversation with her brother than he thought. "Truth be told, I had never thought it possible for me to take a wife." At seeing her expression of concern, he added, "Because the Wadsworth earldom isn't exactly flush with funds, you see. So I never... I never looked for one." He sighed again. "Now I've been told if I marry you, we and our children can have a comfortable living, in a house right next door to your brother." He gave a shake of his head. "I cannot believe I did not welcome the news when I first read of it."

Angelica furrowed a brow. "So then... why didn't you?"

"Because I didn't know I would be gaining my very own delightful angel."

Knowing she had been anything but an angel on this night, Angelica allowed a wan grin. "My brother would take issue with you on that matter," she murmured. "I can be terribly disagreeable."

"More so than the night we first met?"

Angelica's eyes widened before she finally said, "Probably not."

"Then marry me. Be my countess, should I end up with the earldom, or at least be the mother of the next earl." He reached into his waistcoat pocket and pulled out the sapphire and citrine ring, not waiting for her response before he slid it onto her finger. "It's not large, I know, but—"

His words were cut off when Angelica took his lips with hers, one hand moving to the back of his neck. When she finally let go, her eyes glazed and her lips red, he asked, "Does that mean you will?"

She allowed a brilliant smile. "Yes," she replied with a nod. Then she sobered. "But with one condition."

Ben stiffened. "What might that be?" he asked, worry evident in his expression.

"That my parents be our witnesses at the wedding. They will come to London for Christmas if there is a reason."

"And you'll wear this gown?" he countered. He leaned over and plucked a rose from the arrangement on the table. "And carry red roses?"

Angelica blinked, glancing down the front of her dinner gown. "If you insist."

"Good." He straightened and took a deep breath. "I suppose you'll want to see the house. Make sure it's to your liking. If there's anything that needs to be changed, I'll see to it before we're wed."

A thousand thoughts seemed to collide in Angelica's head all at once. Thoughts of marriage. Her mother's comments about duty as a wife. Her duty to the

Wadsworth earldom. Her future as the Countess of Wadsworth. Heirs and spares, which meant giving birth to babies, which meant...

Making babies.

Ben was already in his mid-thirties. Some might think it was almost too late for him to be starting his nursery. The sooner they saw to the creation of an heir, the better.

Turning to discover no one else was in the great hall, Angelica said, "Then let's be off."

It was Ben's turn to blink. "Now?"

"My brother has gone to his club, or so he claims. He won't be home for hours," she replied, hurrying into the vestibule for her redingote. "The Wadsworth earldom needs an heir. We should get started just as soon as possible. There's really no time to waste."

Still on duty in the vestibule, Winston helped her with her coat as Ben pulled on his own coat and top hat. "I'm going for a tour of Bradford Hall," she told the butler. "Tell Banks I won't need her this evening. And there's no need for you to wait up for me."

"I'll see to it she's returned by way of the back door," Ben said in a quiet voice, ignoring the excitement he felt at what she had just said.

Did she really mean for them to... to make love?

Tonight?

Winston's brows did a perfect imitation of Peters' brows when he was surprised, and Ben had to resist the urge to smirk. He held out his arm, and Angelica placed hers on it.

They said not a word as they stepped out the door and slipped behind her brother, Lady Anne, and the other departing guests as they made their way to the front door of Bradford Hall.

CHAPTER 36

FAREWELLS AND A
PROPOSAL

eanwhile, in front of Worthington House
George bade his friends a farewell, claiming he would be joining them at White's once he had seen to it all his guests were safely on their way.

Gabe Wellingham, holding the Trenton town coach door open for his sister, waved to the other young bucks and made the same claim. "Are you coming?" he asked when he saw that Anne still stood with her hand on Hexham's arm.

Anne glanced up at George, about to give him her farewell when he answered Gabe's query on her behalf. "I will see to escorting your sister home."

Regarding Anne with a look of suspicion, Gabe finally allowed a nod. "All right, Hexham, but... one kiss. That's all," he warned, just before he climbed into the coach.

A moment later, and all the town coaches were headed up Park Lane.

George watched them go, and when they were out of sight, he turned to Anne. "Let's go back inside," he said, offering his arm again.

Her pulse increasing with every step they took, Anne remained quiet as he led her back into the hall and then up not one, but two flights of stairs.

"Where are we going?" she finally asked. After all the hubbub of that night's dinner party, the house was eerily quiet.

"I wish to show you something," he replied.

Anne blinked.

How terrible was she to think he might be referring to part of his anatomy? Although she was well aware of what a naked man could look like—she'd seen dozens of statues in the British Museum—her mother had just spent that afternoon describing what would happen to her on her wedding night.

Why her mother had chosen this particular day had been a mystery to Anne, but now she wondered how her mother could have known that this would be the night Hexham would propose.

Father would have told her, of course, although if he had, she might have expected her mother to shed some tears when she took her leave of the house.

So, did Hexham intend to ruin her this night?

Anne was almost sure he did when he stopped before a bedchamber door and opened it.

Inside, several candle lamps had been lit, bathing the peach and green fabrics and carpet in a golden glow. A large bed topped with a canopy of ruched peach silk took up most of the room, while a japanned screen, dressing table, and dresser filled the rest.

"Whose room is this?" she asked, thinking it was far too feminine to be his. "It's lovely."

"Yours, if you'll have me," he replied, and then quickly added, "You don't have to give me an answer right away, if you need some time to think on it."

"*Have* you?" she questioned, amused by his nervousness.

"Yes." He suddenly winced. "I guess I forgot the most important part," he whispered, mostly to himself.

Anne remembered Gabe's query about George having trouble speaking to her. "What might that be?"

Quickly pulling her into the bedchamber, George glanced around and finally moved them to stand in front of a window. Beyond the sheer drapes, he knew the Bradford Hall observatory couldn't be seen—this bedchamber was on the opposite side of the hall from Angelica's and faced the park. "Will you be my wife?"

A brilliant smile lit Anne's face, and she nodded. "Yes," she said quietly.

"You're sure?"

She allowed a giggle. "Quite sure." Before she could ask as to when they might marry, his lips had captured hers. When he pulled them away, slowly, he left his forehead pressed against hers. "I don't think I shall ever tire of kissing you," he whispered.

"And I shall never tire of being kissed," she replied with a smile.

He kissed her again, and then suddenly pulled away. "I forgot. I have a..." His hands moved to a waistcoat pocket, and after a moment, a gem-topped ring appeared between a thumb and forefinger. He held it up, the light blue stone catching the light from a nearby candle lamp. "A ring. To match your eyes." He lifted her hand and slid the gold band onto it, sighing with relief when it seemed to fit.

"It's lovely," she murmured, her gaze going from the ring to his eyes. "It's the same color as your eyes."

"Your eyes, you mean," he countered.

She dimpled and leaned up to kiss him. "Our children will have the same color eyes," she said in a whisper.

George dipped his head. "They'll look just like you."

"Oh, I do hope the boys take after you rather than me," she argued. "I would hate for them to have so many curls."

He chuckled at the thought of the blonde cherubs his sister had described when they'd been on the train. "How many should we have, do you suppose?"

She allowed a shrug. "How many would you like?"

His gaze darted to the side. "Four, perhaps?"

Anne grinned and nodded. "Agreed." Her gaze darted to the bed. "Did you intend to... to start tonight?"

George's eyes widened. "Oh, no," he replied as he shook his head. Seeing how her brows lifted, he allowed a sigh. "I suppose it would be my right, but... but I think it best we wait until... until closer to our wedding day," he stammered. "Or... or that night. When I can have you all to myself, and I'm not... I'm not expected anywhere else."

When he saw her look of disappointment, he nearly rolled his eyes. She was practically offering her virtue to him, and all he could do was stutter and stammer. "Your brother is expecting me at White's. If I don't join him and the others from tonight's dinner party, he will have to challenge me," he warned, a bit dramatically. He knew her brother had joined Angelo's Fencing Academy and had taken up the sport. "I'm a terrible shot."

"And not very good with a sword," she said with a twinkle.

His eyes darted to one side. "Well, not that kind, anyway."

A brilliant smile appeared. "Will we wed soon, then?"

"What... what were you thinking?"

"A Christmas wedding, perhaps? If that's too soon—"

"No. It's fine," he assured her. "It's perfect, really. Gives us time to take a wedding trip before Parliament convenes," he murmured.

"Oh, good. Because my father says I cannot deprive my mother of seeing to my wedding, but I don't wish to give her too much time to plan something elaborate."

He nodded his understanding, appreciating her desire for a simple affair. "As for the trip, where would you like to go?"

Anne remembered what Sir Benjamin had said during dinner. That he planned to take his bride to the Kingdom of the Two Sicilies. "Could we go to Italy?"

George adored how she gazed up at him. At how she asked in such a sweet manner when his sister would have insisted and then simply expected him to comply. "I believe that can be arranged."

Her brilliant smile had George pulling her hard against the front of his body. "Will you always be this easy to please?" he asked in a whisper.

Her eyes darted to one side. "Will you?"

Nodding, he gave her another kiss. He pulled away and suddenly sobered. "Oh, dear. I believe I have exceeded my limit when it comes to kissing you on this night."

Anne frowned. "Whatever are you talking about?"

"Your brother only gave me permission for one."

She allowed a giggle. "It's not as if I'm going to tell on you," she countered.

He chuckled and kissed her again. "Come. I should... I should get you home." At her pretend pout, he added, "Remember, if I don't make an appearance at White's tonight, Gabe will think I've had my way with you."

Loving how a pink blush bloomed on her face, George kissed her one more time.

Once they were in the town coach heading for Trenton House, he kissed her several more times, and then again at the front door of the townhouse.

"You'll kiss me every day?" she asked, just before Barclay opened the door.

"Every day," George replied. Given the butler was watching them, he merely kissed the back of her gloved hand and wished her a good night.

CHAPTER 37

DEVOTION TO DUTY

*M*eanwhile, *back at Bradford Hall*
Peters opened the door before Ben could lift the knocker.

About to step into the house, Ben paused and instead lifted a surprised Angelica into his arms.

"Peters, I am betrothed," Ben announced once he was in the vestibule. He lowered Angelica until her feet touched the floor.

"Best wishes, sir, my lady," the butler replied. "Will you be requiring my assistance this evening?"

Ben gave the butler a quelling glance, wondering if the query referred to something other than his duty as a valet. "I will not. Lady Angelica has requested a tour of the house, and I intend to be her guide." He helped with Angelica's coat and divested his own outer garments with Peters' help.

Angelica pretended to review the hall and the rooms

beyond as they made their way to the main stairs. "An excellent floor plan," she remarked.

"I hadn't noticed," Ben replied, glancing around as if he were seeing his home for the first time. "In fact, I don't believe I've even been in all the rooms." He seemed to struggle with the stairs, never before having to negotiate them with a hardened cock straining against his satin breeches.

Giving him a sideways glance, Angelica was about to tell him that her parents had made love in every single room of Worthington House save the servants' quarters. Instead, she said, "Are you a man of routine, then?"

"I suppose I have been," he replied, a brow furrowing. Did the woman have any idea of the agony he found himself in just then?

"If I should say or do something you find... annoying, you must tell me," she said as they made their way through the first story hall to the next set of stairs. She gave a cursory glance into the yellow and navy blue parlor and allowed a sound of appreciation.

"I cannot imagine what that might be," Ben replied, his body reacting in a manner it had not in a very long time. Desire had him feeling feverish. The scent of her perfume had his head feeling light.

"I intend to kiss you every morning at breakfast," Angelica informed him. "On the cheek, if a footman is present."

Ben blinked. "I will do the same. On the lips. I care not if a footman is present." Before tonight, he never would have thought to kiss a woman in front of a servant.

Angelica allowed a brilliant grin. "Unlike other ladies, I do not write my correspondence before breakfast, but rather afterwards. I find I'm too distracted by hunger otherwise. I would only write about food and dinner parties and the menus."

Ben grinned as they climbed the stairs to the second story. Before breakfast, he decided he would be thinking only of her, and what she might look like in the early morning light. He might have to rise with the sun on occasion just to find out. "I am terrible at writing letters, which reminds me that I must send one to your father and one to my brother on the morrow."

The thought of his future father-in-law had his cock behaving better, but not much.

"My father did give you his permission to marry me, did he not?"

Nodding, Ben replied, "He practically begged me to marry you. Which had me thinking you might be the spawn of the devil." His eyes widened in horror. "My sweet Angel, please pardon the curse."

"Oh, you're pardoned. There are times my brother thinks I am."

"Brothers are like that," he remarked, rather relieved she hadn't taken offense.

They made it to the third story and Ben paused. "Where would you like to start?"

A frisson had Angelica gasping. "Perhaps with our clothes. Removing them, I mean."

Ben blinked. "Oh, I meant, which room would you like to review first?" he asked, unable to hide a grin of amusement. He had realized it was too late to hide the silhouette of his turgid manhood.

"May I see your bedchamber? And then the mistress suite?"

Amazed at her enthusiasm, Ben led the way to the master suite. "I think I should warn you that one of my windows looks out at your window." When her eyes narrowed with suspicion, he added, "I saw you a couple of nights ago, after I escorted you to your back door."

"I watched you regard the observatory and then the moon," she admitted. "I wondered what you were thinking."

"I decided that when spring comes, I'll have the brick covered in stucco to match the house," he replied, hoping she would think it more appealing. Then he chuckled. "I was thinking it looked like a phallic symbol. The observatory, I mean."

Angelica angled her head to one side. "Oh, well I'm sure I wouldn't know of such things. At least, not yet," she murmured, hoping her blush wasn't apparent.

Ben stifled a grin as he opened his door, relieved that the bed was made and a lamp had been lit. A fire had been set in the fireplace, so the room was warm.

The deep navy velvet and gold fabrics that made up the counterpane, drapes, and upholstery on the chairs had been part of the house when he moved in, and he hadn't given a thought to changing anything.

"It's very masculine," Angelica remarked, a hand

sweeping over the counterpane and then up one of the posters.

Imagining that same hand sweeping over his torso had Ben eliciting a sound of frustration. "The mistress suite is just through there," he said, motioning to the dressing room door. "I spoke with the housekeeper this morning. She assured me the bed has fresh linens and that the room is dusted everyday. But I rather doubt any of the lamps are lit."

He watched as Angelica disappeared into the dressing room. When she didn't come out, he made his way in. No lamps were lit in the dressing room, of course, but in the dim light from his room, he could see that the door to the mistress suite was open.

"Angel?"

"Here," she replied in a whisper. She stood at one of the windows, the light from the crescent moon bathing her in an ethereal glow.

Ben thought she looked like an angel without wings.

He joined her, his fingertips trailing along the tops of her bare shoulder blades until she shivered and stepped into his hold. The bedchamber was chilly—the fireplace probably hadn't had a fire set in it since the baron had lived there. "If I told you I had no intention of returning you to Worthington House this evening—"

"I should hope not. I've no intention of getting dressed again after being ruined," she said in a whisper. "At least, not until the morning."

Ben blinked at hearing her response and then allowed a nod. "Very well." He gulped. "In here then?"

She glanced around the suite. Although she was unable to determine the colors of the furnishings or the carpets from the bit of moonlight through the window, she had the sense she would find the suite appealing in the light of day. In the near darkness, and even with the slight chill in the air, she thought it comforting. "You do not mind?"

He gave his head a shake. "At least let me see to a fire."

He moved to the fireplace, heartened to find some kindling and lumps of coal already in place. Striking a fuzee, he soon had the kindling lit, and a golden glow joined the moonlight.

Undressing one another as best they could—Ben had to see to his boots while Angelica turned down the bed—they were soon panting with anticipation.

Left wearing only her chemise, Angelica knew the transparent silk garment did nothing to hide her erect nipples nor her mons. Ben's gaze lingered on both, and she struggled to keep from wrapping her arms around her middle in an attempt at modesty.

"You really are an angel," he murmured, just before he took her lips with his, his hands sliding up her arms and then moving to the back of her waist.

Angelica thrilled at how his arms pulled her hard against the front of his body, how his warmth enveloped her.

Then he suddenly stepped back.

"Do you wish me to take the pins from your hair?"

Angelica considered how many Banks had used in the elaborate hairstyle and gave a shake of her head. "You'll be at it for over an hour."

He nodded. "Good. Because I wouldn't know where to start." He reached for her while she regarded him— all of him—with a sigh of relief. He was trim, with no sign of a belly, and his shoulders were broad and straight. As was his cock, which was clearly aimed in her direction.

"You're not frightened of me, I hope. Of *it*," he added as he waved at his bobbing member. "It's a bit... anxious is all."

Angelica tried hard to suppress a grin. "No. I feared you would be... old. All saggy and—"

"Old?" he repeated in mock alarm. "I'll have you know I am only five-and-thirty," he added, once again taking her into his arms and pulling her until her body was completely pressed against his. His cock settled against the silk of her chemise and pressed into her soft belly. Likewise, the mounds of her breasts pressed into his torso, and he groaned in satisfaction.

"You do not look like you are five-and-thirty," she whispered. She inhaled sharply when one of his hands covered one of her breasts and gently kneaded it through the silk. Her nipple, already puckered, hardened beneath his ministrations. Her thighs, which had begun to tremble, felt damp where they met at the top. An insistent throbbing had just begun there, demanding something be done.

"Nor do I feel like it," he whispered, his lips nipping the space between her neck and shoulder. His tongue trailed up to her earlobe, and his teeth nibbled the soft flesh. He thrilled at hearing her soft inhalation of breath. "I might have a week ago, though," he admitted.

He had been convinced she would change her mind about this. Insist they instead wait until their wedding day. But her devotion to duty seemed relentless.

"What happened a week ago?" she asked between soft inhalations of breath.

"Nothing. I hadn't yet met you," he managed to get out before his kisses dropped to the tops of her breasts.

"Oh. Oh!" She inhaled sharply when his lips settled over one of her silk-covered nipples. "I find I really need to lie down." She let out a squeak when she was suddenly lifted into his arms and then lowered onto the bed. He followed her down, his hands sliding up the sides of the soft chemise to expose her breasts and belly. A giggle erupted when his lips began trailing down the front of her body.

"Wait. What do I do?" she asked, between gasps for breath. Her hands found his shoulders, but soon they were beyond her grasp.

Ben allowed a chuckle as he slid a hand beneath one of her knees and lifted it. "Nothing, my sweet Angel." He did the same with her other knee. "But, please, whatever you do, don't stop me." And then his hands slipped beneath the globes of her bottom and his head dropped down between her legs.

Angelica inhaled sharply. *Stop him?* Why ever would

she do such a thing? His tongue had found the source of the insistent throbbing, and although whatever he was doing was only making it worse, she didn't mind. Not one bit. Especially when it flicked across that very spot at exactly the perfect angle. At exactly the right moment.

Her cry of relief and subsequent sob had Ben slowing his ministrations but moving one hand so his fingertips barely touched her belly as he stroked it. He could feel how her body jerked with each spasm of pleasure, feel the waves as they crested beneath her flesh.

His own cock, hardened and dripping with need, demanded surcease. Although he didn't wish to hurt her, he knew this one time might be painful. To bury his rod into her while she was still in the throes of her pleasure would surely be better than waiting any longer.

He didn't do it quickly, nor did he warn her. He simply impaled her slowly as he slid a hand beneath a thigh and lifted. About to lift the other, he found he didn't need to—she had already wrapped her legs around his back. Then she stripped the chemise from her body and moved her hands to his shoulders.

Pulling out just a bit, he held his breath before he thrust himself into her.

Surely this was heaven. There could be no other word to describe the sight of his satiated betrothed, her skin warm and rosy, her nipples taut. There could be no other word to describe the feel of her tight cocoon as his manhood filled it.

She met his second thrust, a move so surprising he

thought perhaps she had done this before. But her whispered, "Am I doing this right?" had him kissing her open mouth before he managed an, "Oh, yes, my love."

Her hands slipped down to his sides, and her fingers gripped his back. Her nails created half-moons in his flesh as he thrust into her again and again.

His release, intense and powerful and oh, so pleasurable, had him growling and ceasing his movements all at once. Angelica, unsure of what to do, tightened her hold on him as a wash of warmth filled her lower body. Then she watched as he slowly fell down onto her, as if his arms no longer had the strength to hold him up. His head ended up in the space between her shoulder and neck.

Angelica moved a hand to rest on the back of his head, her fingers stroking his silken hair as she felt his labored breaths against her neck. She allowed a sigh of contentment and then kissed him on the forehead.

"My Angel," he murmured, his eyes still closed.

Grinning, Angelica whispered, "My knight in shining moonlight." Indeed, his entire back was bathed in the glow of the moon through the window.

Sleep took them both. Cold woke them long enough to pull up the bedcovers. When they were once again snuggled up against one another, Angelica's head in the small of his shoulder and one leg resting between his, they whispered their plans for a quick wedding and finally returned to slumber.

. . .

he following day

As promised, Ben returned Angelica to Worthington House by way of the back door, early dawn not quite lighting the eastern sky.

Their parting kiss was interrupted by the scullery maid.

"Mornin', my lady," she said as she dipped a curtsy, her gaze going from them to the sprig of mistletoe hanging in the doorway.

"Good morning," Angelica replied with a smile. "We've been studying heavenly bodies all night. Sir Benjamin has the most amazing telescope in his observatory."

"Vera good, milady." The confused maid dipped another curtsy and quickly made her way to the kitchens as Ben struggled to maintain an impassive expression. "Are you always able to fib so easily?" he asked.

Angelica blinked. "But, everything I told her was true," she murmured.

Ben chuckled and kissed her again. "I have letters to write."

"As do I," she agreed. "But I must have breakfast first." She gave him another kiss before she said her farewell. "Perhaps we can look at the moon later?"

Angling his head so he could gaze at the sky above, he allowed a shrug. "If it's clear. And if it's not... well, I'm sure we can find a heavenly body to study."

A WINTER WEDDING OR TWO

A fortnight later, at St. George's
Milton, Earl of Torrington, and his countess, Adele, stood at the front of St. George's and watched as their daughter, Angelica, said her vows to Sir Benjamin.

Just to the right of them stood Gabriel, Earl of Trenton, and his countess, Sarah, who had already paid witness to their daughter, Lady Anne, exchanging vows and rings with George Grandby, Viscount Hexham, just a few minutes earlier.

Tears continued to stream from Sarah's eyes, even though her daughter had already been married for more than five minutes.

Lady Anne's brothers, Gabe and William, watched from a front pew. William, the heir to the Trenton earldom, had only just returned from university the week before and was stunned to discover Trenton House had been turned into a veritable war office.

Or at least, that's what all the wedding planning made it look like.

Having taken on the role of commander, his mother had reviewed stacks of drawings—of gowns and bouquets, cakes and frippery—and had given orders to modistes and drapers, florists and the cook, all in the name of creating the wedding she had always wanted for her daughter.

Or perhaps it was the wedding she had wanted for herself.

He couldn't help but notice that Anne didn't seem to have much say in the matter, but then his sister had always been easy to please. He decided his new brother was probably marrying her for that very reason.

Weddings were usually private affairs, but given the number of people in the pews, William realized invitations had been sent to everyone in the *ton* who had remained in London over the holiday.

He only wished the double ceremony would be over soon. His stomach was grumbling, and there was a wedding breakfast waiting at Worthington House.

"Sir Benjamin is a rather handsome man," Adele whispered to her husband. "Were you his godfather?"

"Were?" Milton replied with a smirk. "I still am. And he's the last."

"Last?" Adele repeated in confusion.

"The last godson to get married. I was beginning to

think he would never take a wife. Once I found out why, it was easy enough to offer a solution that worked for everyone involved."

Adele furrowed a brow. "So *you're* the reason our daughter is marrying a lowly knight?" she asked, obviously suspicious.

Milton's eyes darted to one side before he leaned sideways and said, "Not me. Her dowry. And the fact that their firstborn son will be an earl."

"You bounder!" his countess accused in a hoarse whisper. She took a deep breath in an attempt to keep the tears at bay, at least until after Angelica's vows were complete. She had already cried several when George had said his vows to his lovely new wife. "I suppose she might end up a countess," she added after a moment.

"That's the plan," Milton murmured, a brilliant smile appearing when the couple completed their vows.

*A*cross the aisle, Benedict, Earl of Wadsworth, offered his mother, Charity, Viscountess Lancaster, his handkerchief as tears streamed down her cheeks.

"I thought you'd be happy to gain another daughter," Benedict whispered. She had only the one, Hope, from her second marriage to Marcus Lancaster.

"Oh, I am. I just never imagined she would be an *angel,*" Charity replied, attempting to suppress a sob.

Angelica's gown, the white dinner gown Ben had insisted she wear for their wedding, had been altered to include a train. She carried a bouquet of red roses and mistletoe, a secret nod to their first kisses. A ring of red rose buds circled the pile of curls atop her head. When the light showed through the curls, it made them look like a halo.

Wearing a white muslin shirt, white silk cravat, and a black cutaway coat, Ben looked as if he might have already inherited the Wadsworth earldom. His red waistcoat, embroidered in what he later admitted were depictions of the constellations, was a gift from his brother.

"Did you see the ring?" Benedict asked in a hoarse whisper, once they had been exchanged in the ceremony.

"Rings," Charity corrected him. "Gold, and Angel had his engraved with their names and the date."

"As did he," Benedict said in defense of his brother. "I rather like the one he gave her upon their engagement, though."

Charity angled her head to one side. "Citrine and sapphire, although I cannot imagine why the citrine."

"Venus, Mother," Benedict replied. "His favorite planet, since that's the one that had them meeting for the first time."

His mother's eyes widened with understanding. "Oh, how romantic," Charity breathed, rather impressed with her younger son.

. . .

*W*hen the vows were complete, the priest made his announcement and then led the couple, the Trentons, and the Torringtons to the vestry to enter the marriage lines. Copies were then presented to Angelica and Anne, who promptly rolled them up and carried them with their flowers.

"*W*hen will they leave for Italy?" Adele asked when she and Milton were in the town coach and heading back to Worthington House for the wedding breakfast.

"A few days. Ben managed to get tickets on a sailing ship bound for Rome. They and their servants will be there in time for Christmas."

Adele sighed. "How romantic," she cooed.

"I'm glad you think so," he said with a nod. "I have tickets for the same ship."

Her eyes widening in surprise, Adele stared at her husband. "Milton!"

He merely grinned, not bothering to add that George had tickets as well.

EXCERPT

*Read on for an excerpt from Linda Rae Sande's Book 2 of
"The Heirs of the Aristocracy" Series*

The Puzzle of a Bastard

British Museum, December 1838

The wooden crate landed with a *thud* at Gabe
Wellingham's feet, and he winced. "Have a care!" he
cried out, incensed at the lack of regard the two barrel-
chested delivery men showed as they moved to lift
another crate from the back of a dray cart. "These are
priceless antiquities."

Clouds of white air appeared and disappeared in
front of his face, his exhalations of breath freezing due
to the chilly temperatures. With the large doors open to
accommodate the dray cart, the entire receiving area at
the back of the museum was cold.

From his vantage, Gabe marveled at what lay

beyond the doors. What was once called Long Fields and then Southampton Fields—the site of numerous duels and the Field of Forty Steps—was now covered in building materials for the museum's ongoing expansion. The ingredients for concrete as well as cast iron, stacks of stock brick, and blocks of Portland stone were neatly arranged and spread out as far as the eye could see. A pile of timber was diminishing with each passing day as carpenters built display cases.

From the largest building site in Europe had come the new East Wing, where the King's Library and some of the museum's senior staff were housed. One after the other, new exhibit halls were completed and quickly filled, and yet one of the workmen had said it would be more than a decade before Sir Robert Smirke's design for the grand neoclassical building would be complete. That would happen when the South Wing was built with its planned colonnaded portico.

Intended to make for a grand entrance on the side of the quadrangular structure facing Great Russell Street, its construction wouldn't start until the original Montagu House was demolished, and its demolition wouldn't begin for another few years.

Gabe wondered if he would still hold his position as an archivist of Greek antiquities when all of it was finished.

The last crate was set down atop the first one, its *thud* only slightly less loud than the first. Once again, Gabe winced and managed to catch the attention of a nearby carpenter.

"Sir?" the carpenter said as he approached. He carried a box of nails under one muscled arm and a hammer in the other. His dusty trousers, work shirt, and plain brown waistcoat were at odds with Gabe's light trousers, shawl-collared waistcoat, and long topcoat.

"How do, Barstow? I could use a strong arm," Gabe said as he indicated the two crates. "Our newest acquisitions from Greece," he added.

One of the benefits of the museum's ongoing construction meant there was always a carpenter nearby to help with prying the lids off the shipping crates.

Gabe hefted a pry bar and handed it to Barstow before helping himself to another. The two worked the sharp edges under the crate's lid, and soon the nails securing the wood gave way. Barstow helped to move the top crate off the one below it and they pried the lid off of it.

"Thank you," Gabe said as Barstow gave him the pry bar and went on his way.

Gabe took a deep breath and used his hands to move aside the excelsior that protected the first crate's treasure—an ancient Greek krater that featured a scene with the god Apollo. He lifted it from the bed of packing material, awestruck. The krater was intact. No obvious chips on the rims. There was a slight imperfection in the figure of Apollo, but he knew that could be repaired.

The museum employed an expert in pottery restoration. He hadn't yet met the man, but the evidence of his expertise could be seen by the trained eye in several of the artifacts already on display in the museum.

Setting the krater on a nearby table, Gabe turned his attention to the other crate. Pushing aside the lengths of wood strands, he frowned when he couldn't find what the packing list claimed was inside—a rhyton. The conical drinking cup wouldn't be especially large, but it should have been evident in the crate.

Gabe continued to push aside the packing material until his hand intersected something.

A shard.

He winced as he pulled out the dark brown curved piece of pottery. He pushed his hand back into the crate, reaching to the bottom to discover that the entire rhyton was in pieces.

Had it broken en route? Or had it been shipped this way?

He finally started scooping excelsior from the one crate into the other, moaning when he discovered the remaining pieces of the rhyton at the bottom. "Dammit," he murmured.

"Really, sir, it's not as bad as that," a voice said from his right.

A female voice.

One he was sure included a very slight Stoke accent.

Gabe straightened to regard the owner of the voice —a dark-haired woman who might have been his age. She was wearing a humongous apron and sporting a bun atop her head that was sprung so tight, he was sure her facial features were pulled out of their natural shape.

Her gloved hands were both fisted and resting atop her hips.

He gave a bow. "My lady?" he replied. "Isn't it... ruined?"

She rolled her green eyes. "It won't be after I'm finished with it," she said as she held out her right hand, intending to shake his. "Mrs. Longworth. I perform the restoration on pottery."

Gabe immediately bowed over her hand and brushed his lips over her knuckles, noting the gloves were not silk, but rather cotton, and slightly soiled from what might have been clay.

Frances Longworth gave a start, jerking her hand from his hold. When she realized she had overreacted, she stepped back and managed a curtsy. "Apologies. I... I just wasn't expecting... *that*," she stammered.

"Gabe Wellingham," he said, rather wishing there had been someone to do the introductions. "Archivist. I've recently been hired to catalogue the Ancient Greek antiquities."

The woman's gaze took in the cut of his clothes, the perfectly tied cravat, and the simple but expensive waistcoat that peeked above his fashionable black wool topcoat. One that was pinched in at the waist and then flared out in perfect pleats to the sides and back. "It's very good to finally meet you, sir," she said, as she moved to the side of the crate holding the shards that had at one time made up a brown rhyton.

"You, as well, my lady. How is it I haven't made your acquaintance before today?"

Lifting the front of her apron into a makeshift hammock, Frances carefully scooped the pieces into the apron and dipped a curtsy. "No need, I suppose. Good day." Cradling the pottery shards as if they were a baby, she turned to go.

"Wait," Gabe said as he moved to follow her. "Where...where are you taking them?"

Frances allowed an expression that suggested she thought him daft. "To my workroom, of course."

"But..."

"I'll have the finished piece delivered to you when it's reconstructed," she added, just before she left the receiving area.

Gabe watched her go, realizing two things at once.

Mrs. Longworth wasn't the man he had thought she was, which had him wondering if others in the museum's employ knew M. Frances Longworth was a woman.

And she would be positively lovely if her bun wasn't so damned tight.

ABOUT THE AUTHOR

A former technical writer and author of twenty-four historical romances, Linda Rae Sande enjoys researching the Regency era and ancient Greece.

A fan of action-adventure movies, she can frequently be found at the local cinema. Although she no longer has any tropical fish, she follows the San Jose Sharks and makes her home in Cody, Wyoming.

For more information:
www.lindaraesande.com
Sign up for Linda Rae's newsletter:
Regency Romance with a Twist
Follow Linda Rae's blog:
Regency Romance with a Twist